sins
of the
family

A Callie McFee Mystery

HY CONRAD

ISBN: 978-1-7355555-3-9 Paperback
ISBN: 978-1-7355555-4-6 Ebook

Library of Congress Control Number: xxxxxxx

Published by Mason Hill Inc.
Key West, Florida USA

HyConrad.com

For Jeanette Green, the best editor I've ever had the pleasure to work with.

ALSO BY HY CONRAD

The Fixer's Daughter
Toured to Death
Dearly Departed
Death on the Patagonian Express
Things Your Dog Doesn't Want You to Know
(with Jeff Johnson)
Mr. Monk Helps Himself
Mr. Monk is Open for Business
Mr. Monk Gets on Board
Mr. Monk and the New Lieutenant

PROLOGUE

It was obvious to Trevor that he was supposed to be impressed, and that irritated the hell out of him.

It was all there. The gnarled live oaks bending over a gravel drive. The sprawling mansion. The dark, polished wood of the study with the leather armchairs and the late afternoon sun slanting through the louvered shades. The powerful man in the dark, perfectly tailored suit, like a Texas Godfather, seated behind a burlwood desk, sipping something golden brown from a cut-crystal tumbler. Even the property's nickname, the Ranch, reeked of old-school privilege.

Trevor tried not to take it personally. This had not been arranged for him. The effects had been cultivated over many decades to impress the clients who'd come before, when this man and place had been the state's true center of power. Now it seemed little more than a monument to a bygone world. "A friend at work recommended you. He says you got him out of a DWI when he was eighteen. The record sealed. Probably ten years ago?"

Lawrence "Buddy" McFee looked puzzled, prompting the

third person in the room to speak. He was a short, thin Latino man in his forties, with close-cropped hair and a deferential attitude. A second-in-command, Trevor assumed, rather than a partner. "That was Joey Gibson," the man reminded his boss. "Senior prom night."

"I thought you might remember," Trevor said. "My friend's father is the Texas attorney general."

"Felix, yes. I put him in office. But what we have here is more serious than a prom night DWI." Buddy eased the tumbler onto a coaster and consulted a copy of the police report, resting in the expanse of his lap. "Intoxication assault. You were driving and you hit someone." He ran his finger along the printed page then let out a soft whistle. "That could've been a misdemeanor, but they chose to call it a third-degree felony. You got any idea why they are treating you so harshly, son?"

The smaller man cleared his throat. He too had a copy of the report. "There are extenuating circumstances, sir."

"Of course," the Godfather said.

"Okay, I saw her." Trevor Birdsong tried to keep his voice on an even keel. "I saw the old woman in the crosswalk." He hated having to explain himself. Why did he have to explain? "I couldn't brake in time. I did my best to swerve around. I tried. I would have made it, but she kept stumbling back and forth like a little Bambi in the headlights." He motioned with his head and hands, as if to make a joke of it. "There was no way I couldn't hit her."

Buddy McFee flipped to page two, cocked his head then looked up. "We'll forgo your speed and your level of intoxication. That seems well documented. The woman, Alice Santorini, a frail, seventy-eight-year-old grandmother of five…"

"What do her grandkids have to do with anything?" Trevor demanded.

"They just do," Buddy replied. "Mrs. Santorini suffered a broken leg, two broken ribs and a concussion. She was unconscious for several hours with her beloved family gathered round the hospital bed, praying for her."

"I stayed on the scene," Trevor protested. "I stopped."

"You veered off into a fire hydrant," Buddy reminded him, punctuating it with a chuckle. "You kinda had to stop."

Trevor scowled. "I could have driven away but I didn't. I called 9-1-1. That counts for something."

"You were the second person to call 9-1-1," the assistant pointed out. "Which tells me there was a witness. Despite the alcohol, you had the presence of mind to stay at the scene. That's good. Much more manageable than a hit-and-run in front of a witness."

"Kudos for not running," Buddy said.

Trevor had been tempted to run. Even after he noticed the man on the bus stop bench and knew that his license plate might be photographed or remembered, the temptation had been almost overwhelming. The damage to his Tesla's hood and left bumper had been serious, not severe, caused mainly by the fire hydrant. Nothing would have prevented him from driving off. But the glow from the streetlamp right above the bench made him think twice. At least twice. Back and forth several times. And now he was feeling noble, as though he'd always intended to do the right thing.

Buddy's McFee's assistant – Trevor didn't remember his name – looked up and seemed to be studying his boss's face.

He pursed his lips and turned to Trevor. "I'm sorry to waste your time, but Mr. McFee doesn't handle cases like this."

"My friend at work…" Trevor turned from the assistant to the lawyer. "He says you used to do this all the time."

"Only for friends," the assistant replied. "And the stupid children of friends."

"I suppose I can make an exception in this case," Buddy said magnanimously.

The assistant jumped in. "I'm afraid if this goes to trial, Buddy might not have the time, given his commitments."

Buddy snorted. "Course I'll have the time. Make the time. What are you talking about?"

"If it goes to trial? Litigating in a courtroom?" The words were spoken to Trevor but directed at Buddy.

"First of all, it's not going to trial," Buddy said. "I know most all the judges from way back. We get this reduced to a misdemeanor and it goes away. If it doesn't, then I welcome the chance to argue your case in a court of law. Nothing would please me more."

Trevor looked from one man to the other and back. "So, are you taking my case or not?"

"I am," the lawyer announced, pounding the arms of his leather chair. "My boy Gil doesn't know what he's saying."

The shorter man's smile was thin and insincere. "My mistake."

"Good," said Trevor. "So, that's it? Do you need anything more from me?"

"What more do we need?" The assistant sighed and rose to his feet. "We'll email you the paperwork. It should all be relatively quick and easy."

Buddy McFee remained behind his desk, his focus returning to the stapled pages in his lap. His brow wrinkled and his eyes narrowed. "Why isn't this a misdemeanor?" he asked, treating it as a brand-new thought. "You got any idea why they're treating you so harshly, my boy?"

Trevor was taken aback. Could it be the effects of the contents of the crystal tumbler? He had thought it odd for the Godfather to be nursing a drink during a business meeting, but this was old Austin. He had no idea what would be considered normal.

The assistant started off in the direction of the front hallway, effectively ending the meeting as he began to usher Trevor out. Their path led directly past the burlwood desk, where Buddy, still not bothering to get up, held out a hand. Trevor eased his hand into the soft, enveloping grip. With his other hand, purely out of curiosity, he picked up the cut-crystal tumbler and took a quick sip. It was the type of rude, unexpected thing that he often liked to do. The assistant turned just in time to see it.

Trevor smirked. Then he swallowed the mouthful of brown liquid and his smirk faded. He took one more, tiny sip, just to make sure. "It's water."

"Of course, it's water," the assistant confirmed. "Do you think he'd be drinking in the afternoon during a meeting?" Meanwhile, the Godfather said nothing.

"But…" Trevor was trying to process it. "It's brown. In a rocks glass. I saw him pour it from a bottle on the shelf."

The assistant raised and lowered a single shoulder. "It's an old habit. A tradition from when we were all young and virile and could indulge in a harmless few ounces without it affecting us for the rest of the afternoon."

"Yes, but you obviously wanted me to think… You wanted me to think he was drinking."

"It's called image," the other said without a hint of apology. "Even with a DWI case, we feel that projecting the old image is important. Is this a problem?"

"No," Trevor said, because that's what they wanted him to say. And through all of this, Buddy McFee stayed silent, his expression blank or perhaps mildly curious. The Latino assistant motioned him toward the door. Trevor walked himself out through the front hall to the gravel drive and the loaner that the Tesla dealership had given him for the next week or so.

This place doesn't feel like Austin, he thought as he drove slowly under the canopy of live oaks. All it needed was a little Spanish moss and it could pass for an old Disney version of the Deep South. Hardly Texas at all. Not that there was anything new or fake about the estate itself, except perhaps… Holy…

Trevor stared open-mouthed at the mini French chateau, complete with a mansard roof, off to the left of the stone pillars that framed the end of the driveway. He hadn't noticed it when he'd arrived, but… Okay, this definitely didn't fit, either with Austin or with the Deep South. But it wasn't new. The copper roofing had weathered into an antique green and had probably been like that for the last century.

A young woman with arrestingly red hair, stood by the front door, watching him as he watched her. A name came instantly to mind. Callie. Callie McFee.

His window was down and he offered her a little salute. A gesture of acknowledgement. She smiled and saluted back, which was all the encouragement he needed. He slowed even more, turned his wheels toward the mini-chateau and came to a stop. It would be a nice little flirtation, he told himself – with the Godfather's daughter, no less. He was secure enough in his own charm and attractiveness. He was certainly secure in his own position in the world. "Bonjour, mademoiselle," he said, leaning out of the window. "Tu ha une belle maison."

She glanced at the house, the maison in question. It took her a moment to understand his reference. Then she turned back, employing an impish grin and a little curtsy. "Merci, monsieur. Il a été construite par une des mes arrière-arrière grands-mères."

"Whoa." Trevor raised his hands from the wheel. "I give up. Your high school French beats my high school French."

"It was built by one of my great-great-grandmothers," she translated, while maintaining the impish grin. "Her husband gave her free rein to design a gatehouse where the groundskeeper's family could live. She found something like this in a book. Or so the family legend goes."

"I'd love to see the inside," Trevor said.

"It's a very ordinary inside," she countered. "My name is Callie."

"Trevor Birdsong." He placed the car in park, switched off the ignition and opened the driver-side door.

CHAPTER 1

THE PICTURE QUALITY is actually decent, Callie thought. The sound is decent, too. The footage had been taken – her mother had taken it – on an old RCA camcorder. At some point, Callie knew she had to transfer all of these to digital or risk losing them forever.

She had been five years old at the time, her brother about seven. Their young mother was behind the camcorder, saying a few soft words. But the focus of the footage, the focus of just about everything in their lives, was Buddy, her father, in his prime and larger than life.

The McFees had been at a carnival, benefitting some cancer foundation. Although the children were blissfully unaware, Anita McFee had already received her first diagnosis and was undergoing treatment. She would win this battle, without her children ever having a clue, but would lose the war just a few weeks after Callie's seventeenth birthday. But on the day of the carnival, young Callie hadn't thought twice about her father's sudden dedication to cancer research. He was just Daddy being Daddy, playing to the crowds and the cameras.

Buddy had dragged his picture-perfect family from stall to arcade game to event and, along the way, shamed the mayor into buying a full wheel of raffle tickets. Buddy had also taken over as auctioneer when the handmade quilts weren't going for a decent price. The final attraction that caught his eye that afternoon was the dunk tank.

In one of the dozen booths arrayed around the carnival sat a sad, nervous clown on a wooden platform, balanced over a water tank, holding onto the platform for dear life. Ten feet off to his side was a bullseye target on a pole, a smallish bullseye, just waiting for an oversized softball to hit it and send him tumbling into the tank of cold water.

The dunk tank was a carnival tradition, one that was already on its way to extinction for a variety of reasons, most of them perfectly valid. The clown perched above the tank was supposed to be hurling insults at the passersby, predominantly the male ones, commenting on their height or weight or dubious masculinity, in the hope of making them stop and get angry enough to buy a raft of softballs. But this clown, the man behind the white face, orange hair and red nose, was a foundation volunteer, a quiet, nervous man that you actually felt sorry for. And business was not good.

That's when Buddy McFee intervened. Within five seconds, he had appraised the situation and its potential. Within a minute, he was taking off his jacket and calling out the mayor and state representatives and anyone else with money to spare or a need for good publicity. The cameras were rolling, including the RCA camcorder, by the time he upped the price to one hundred dollars a throw, shooed the grateful clown away and took his place, still in his white shirt and expensive tie, perching himself over the water tank.

His insults were all G-rated, unlike the ones he employed during work hours, and they boomed out over the midway. Most of his jabs dealt with the fact that these bigwigs, most of whom he'd forced to show up, were too cheap or lily-livered to dare throw softballs at the current Speaker of the Texas House. Five minutes and several thousands of dollars later, Callie's father landed in the tank. The demand was so great that he did it three more times before Anita forced him into a few dry towels that someone had managed to track down.

As Callie watched, she compared this to her memory of that day. The color was brighter in her memory, and her father was funnier and more forceful. In her memory, he had caught her eye and winked and let her know that everything would be okay. She was surprised not to find it in the footage. Had she just imagined this moment of connection? How many of their moments together had she just imagined?

Their father/daughter relationship had always been complicated. In many ways, they were eerily similar; both impulsive, both problem-solvers willing to take a shortcut now and then, even if others might see it as marginally unethical. She had grown up idolizing him, admiring his skill and energy – and his happy capacity for alcohol.

Callie switched off the TV. "I know there's TV news footage of this," she told the young film student sitting next to her on the sofa. "But this is home movies. No one else has it. Plus, you can hear Mom and State and me all yelling at Dad. Pretty funny, no?" Was she sounding too desperate? She forced a casual laugh and turned to see her guest's reaction.

The film student, Melissa Miller, did not seem enthused. Callie had known her since childhood. Back then, the Millers, a solid, middle-class family, lived locally and celebrated most holidays and special events with their wealthy relatives, the Westermans, one of the more distinguished Austin clans. Callie wasn't quite sure of the relationship. Second cousins, she thought.

She used to feel sorry for Melissa – the long-ago Melissa, not this one. An only child, several years younger than Callie and her friends, Melissa went to a different school and wore cheaper, less stylish clothes. To add to her discomfort, she was big for her age and carried a few more pounds than the other, older girls. She'd always seemed lonely and too eager to fit in. Callie had tried her best to befriend her during all of those holidays and celebrations, putting a portion of her own popularity at risk. At some point, the Millers moved to El Paso and Callie didn't have to try anymore.

But Melissa was back. She was twenty-four now, tall and model beautiful, the extra pounds gone, with her straight, almost black hair cut short into a stylish bob. After taking a few gap years along the way, she enrolled as a film student at UT Austin and was once again inserting herself into Callie's life. The difference this time was that her project, her student film, a portrait of Lawrence "Buddy" McFee, was threatening to topple the world that Gil and Callie had so carefully built.

"If you want to use it in your documentary, you certainly can," Callie offered. "I have hours of tapes. We can sit down and go through them. I'd be glad to. Anytime."

"Actually, my focus is going to be on more recent stuff." Melissa stifled a yawn. "Everyone knows the old Buddy. I want my work to have some depth, to showcase his work over the past few years. His frame of mind." She pushed herself up off the sofa and spread her hands, like a filmmaker framing a shot. "What happens when a powerful man loses that power?" she asked no one. "How does he cope mentally? How does it change him? And how does that change the work he does?"

Under other circumstances, Callie might have made some snarky comment about the "real depth" of any student film. Instead, she felt a chill. She had no idea how perceptive the grown-up Melissa might have become. Exactly how smart and ambitious was she? Would the result be a tepid, clichéd saga of an aging powerbroker? Or would it be – God forbid – an exposé of Buddy McFee's current state? What might Melissa have discovered in her quest to get an A in "Creating the New Documentary" or whatever the hell her program might call itself?

"Fascinating," Callie forced herself to say. "I would love to see an early edit. Or at least an outline." She stood up now, facing her old friend across the length of the sofa. "I'm sorry if I seem a little protective. But I am. He's my father."

"Oh, Callie." Melissa's tone sounded overly sincere. "I would never do anything to embarrass or hurt him. Take my word." She placed a freshly manicured hand over her heart. "Plus, Aunt Diedre. If I did anything to blemish his name, I'd be drummed out of her will so fast…" She laughed, and Callie joined in.

"Well, if you need any more material or people to interview, I'll do whatever I can."

Melissa was already reaching for her jacket and looking around the floor for her bag. "I really appreciate all your family has done." Again, overly sincere. "All the interviews and letting me film around the house. But I think I have everything I need."

The two women walked out together and Callie watched as her guest, without even a goodbye wave, drove off, slipping between the pillars and making a left onto Hacienda Drive.

Callie stood by the door, enjoying the crisp fall air and thinking. Melissa had seemed so eager, so excited to learn everything. And then, like the flip of a switch, it was over. Callie had known student filmmakers from her own college days. They had always been ready to explore another dimension to their subject. But not Melissa. She had just stopped. When Callie found these home movies lying in an old file cabinet, she had to leave four messages and two texts in order to arrange today's little viewing.

The sound of tires on gravel caught Callie's ear and she looked up to see a lime green Tesla purring its way down from the house. She was always a bit nervous when people, clients or friends, visited her father these days. Through the car's open window, she noticed the driver. Her first impression was of thin, slight man, perhaps in his late twenties, with a carefully coiffed head of sandy brown hair combed back. The late afternoon light glinted perfectly off his subtle highlights. Too perfectly, she decided. Would he be offended if she asked him for the name of his colorist?

He saw her looking at him and acknowledged her gaze with a little salute. This was a very cocky man, Callie deduced, but she didn't mind. She saluted back then waited while the Tesla turned toward the gatehouse and came to a stop, its tires crunching softly on the gravel.

*

Gil was seated in the front living room when Callie walked into the main house. She didn't always show up for cocktail hour. Sometimes she actually pretended to have a life. For a few months, she had tried living on her own, in a bright, spacious one-bedroom on the Drag, right across from the UT campus. But, being a few crucial years older than the median population and not being a student, Callie had found it hard to make friends, harder than she'd thought.

There was also her father to deal with. Buddy's condition had deteriorated, something to be expected, but still unnerving. His good days and bad days were about even now, but it was getting harder to control and harder to hide his dementia from the world. She didn't think it right for Gil, not technically a part of the McFee family, to be burdened with all this. Luckily, she had rented the bright, spacious one-bedroom on a month-to-month basis.

Had this been in the back of her mind all along, she often wondered, to give herself an easy out? A yearly rental would have been cheaper. Had she always planned to abandon her lukewarm attempt at independence and retreat to the comfort of the Ranch? At least, she was living in the gatehouse now. It would be sad beyond imagining to move back into her old bedroom, with its memories and its French mauve wallpaper that she and her mother had picked out during one of her mother's own good days.

Gil glanced up from his longneck of Lone Star. "Thanks for joining me," he said. He used the bottle to motion her to the wet bar, discretely positioned in a far corner. "It's sad drinking alone, but not drinking at all is sadder."

Gil Morales had been Buddy's aide for nearly two decades.

Through various elections and triumphs, defeats and scandals, he had been at the big man's side. Gil and Callie had never liked each other. Gil was a political animal. He represented the work that had taken up most of her father's time – the secrets he couldn't share, the hours with the door to his study shut tight while the power elite plotted and argued and kept Texas being Texas. From Gil's point of view, Callie represented Buddy's divided attention and perhaps, if Callie had to play psychiatrist here, the family Gil had never allowed himself to have. Within the past year, since she'd come back to Austin, they had found common cause in protecting Buddy, in fixing things for the fixer, and their feelings toward each other had mellowed. It was a truce, she acknowledged, not a peace treaty.

A middle-aged Irish setter loped into the living room, heading straight for a tartan plaid dog bed under the piano. Angus had been brought in after the death of a previous Angus, a much-loved member of the family. Angus Two, a rescue, seemed to recognize his position as a replacement and had never made a full commitment to anyone in the house. He would come when called, especially around breakfast and dinner times, but he never wagged his tail ferociously, not like Angus One, who could knock over floor lamps in his excitement to see you.

"Is Daddy upstairs?" Callie crossed to the bar, aiming for the wine cooler and the few bottles of white that Sarah always kept chilled for her on the bottom shelves, just above the champagne.

"He is," Gil said and took another swig from his longneck. "We had a client. It wasn't horrible, but it took some of the spunk out of him."

"Was he in a mood?" she asked. *Mood* had become their code word for the worst of Buddy's condition.

"Just a little stubborn and forgetful. Will you be staying for dinner?"

"Why not?" Callie said as she found the Sauvignon Blanc then went in search of the corkscrew. "I have nothing else."

"Good. It'll cheer him up." Gil reached for his phone, swiped up and across and pressed the screen a few times. "Callie is staying for dinner," he said into the phone. "I hope that's no problem. Thank you, Sarah." Almost instantly, a response pinged. "No problem."

"I remember when you had to ring a little silver bell." They both smiled. "So, you have a new client. The guy in the Tesla, I assume."

"You know that," Gil said. "I saw him stop by the gatehouse. You brought him out some iced tea, if I'm not mistaken."

"You're not." She wasn't surprised or offended by Gil's act of surveillance. It was par for the course. "Trevor and I had a nice talk, long enough that I was forced to be a hostess and offer him something." She tried not to smile at the thought of the brash, quirky young man with the subtle highlights. "Is there some reason why I shouldn't have offered him an iced tea?"

"Nope," said Gil. "He came to us with a felony DWI, so iced tea was a perfect choice."

"Nice." A DWI. Callie felt relieved. "So, this is a straight-up law case? No influence peddling or fixing something a tad shady?" Ever since he'd reluctantly retired from politics, Buddy McFee had filled his days with peddling and fixing. The man was still a legend, and people still seemed to need his help.

Gil took a long, last swig. For a moment. their eyes locked over the rim of his bottle. "A straight-up law case. Your father still has his license. And frankly, this case seems pretty harmless. Buddy will have to work with the judge and the DA's office. But don't worry. It won't go to trial."

"If there's anything I can do to help…"

"Thanks. And what about your guest this afternoon? Our lovely Miss Miller?"

Callie paused to gather her thoughts and to pour herself a generous glass of the Sauvignon Blanc. "Would you like another beer?"

"That would be sweet. Now tell me about Melissa."

Callie retrieved the Lone Star from its own shelf in the wine cooler, opened it, delivered it and lowered herself into the wing chair across the coffee table from Gil's. "Why did you ever agree to it? A documentary, for God's sake. What were you thinking?"

"It was Diedre." Gil wasn't the type to shift the blame, but he was coming pretty close. "You know how sick she is."

About a year ago, Diedre Westerman, Melissa's second cousin – or perhaps something even more distant - had been diagnosed with stage four cancer. She was still in her forties but had no husband or children to comfort or to care for her. To add to Diedre's tragedy, her younger brother David and both their parents, Sean and Pegeen, were killed shortly after her diagnosis. The family had been on their way home to Austin, anxious to get back and help Diedre through her first round of chemotherapy, when their plane crashed in the Hill Country west of the city.

The accident left Diedre with no immediate family. She

had always been a private person, living at home her entire life, and this tragedy had just intensified her reclusive nature. It was just her and her doctors.

That was when Melissa Miller came to the rescue, transferring her classes from UT El Paso to UT Austin, and moving in with her depressed and ailing relation. Diedre was thrilled with the arrangement. And no one in Austin society could begrudge Melissa's sudden acquisition of new clothes and a Mercedes S-Class convertible. It wasn't taking advantage. It was family.

"How could Buddy say no?" Gil demanded. "Melissa asked Diedre, and Diedre asked Buddy. Hell, we thought it would be some sentimental, fifteen-minute bio. Hell, it still could be that."

"I don't know, Uncle Gil. I have a bad feeling." Callie took the tiniest of sips. "Mel was so enthusiastic. Dad and you gave her the run of the house."

"There's nothing incriminating in the house."

"Today I showed her some great home movies. She nearly fell asleep. She said she wants to showcase the new Buddy. Her actual words."

Gil shook his head. "Ironic, isn't it? You, this bloodthirsty journalist unearthing secrets left and right, all worried about another journalist unearthing our little secret."

"She's not a journalist. She's making a film. People find a film more believable."

As much as Gil was enjoying his beer at the end of a long day, he was also listening. "Okay. I'll have a few words with Diedre. Meanwhile, you stay close to Melissa."

"I'm not sure she'll return my calls."

"Well, do what you can. On the bright side, it's a student film. No one pays any heed. We should find out who her professor is. We might have some influence there."

Gil's phone pinged. He looked over to his side table and read. "Sarah says it's half an hour till dinner. Chicken-fried steak and potatoes. I swear, that woman's going to kill us with cholesterol."

CHAPTER 2

SHE LOVED THIS old courthouse. It was everything a courthouse should be. Built during the height of the Depression, it was designed to inspire judges, lawyers, the innocent and the guilty, with the power and seriousness of the law – the kind of building, Callie thought, that John Grisham had in mind every time he sat down to write a legal thriller. She had once looked it up online and found that the style was called PWA Moderne, the same used on the Hoover Dam and dozens of other courthouses and post offices. One of her great-grandfathers had been involved in its construction, perhaps more than one, making deals and greasing the proper wheels.

The interior was in keeping with the exterior but on a more modest scale, with limestone reserved for the courtrooms and Art Deco details gracing only the occasional doorway. Built-in wooden benches lined the wide corridors. That's where Callie found herself at the moment, sitting outside the chambers of Judge Letitia Brown. Cell phones and tablets were forbidden, even in the corridors, so she had brought along her Kindle and tried to get back into the lightweight novel that she'd abandoned sometime in July.

She'd arrived with her father and Gil, to act as moral support. Buddy had not been off the Ranch in over a month and, although today he seemed lucid and in good spirits, Gil had thought that having a familiar presence at Buddy's side as he stepped out into the world would help keep him calmer and more focused. At the moment, while Buddy and Gil were in the judge's chambers with their client and an Assistant DA, Callie took a break from chapter three of the frothy romantic thriller that had looked promising so many months ago in the Amazon ad.

As she squirmed on the bench, she wondered. Was this going to become a pattern? Would she spend the foreseeable future neglecting her own life in order to escort her father around, trying to keep him safe and out of trouble?

Callie eyed the door to the judge's chambers. They had not been happy with the assignment of Letitia Brown, a Black jurist who had come up through the ranks without any help from Buddy and the good ole boy network. Callie had met her for just a minute, as they all gathered in the corridor before the meeting went behind closed doors. The judge had been respectful to the ex-Attorney General, but there had also been a cool, no-nonsense attitude about her that Gil didn't seem to appreciate.

While preparing his case, Trevor Birdsong had made several visits to the McFee homestead. The visits weren't long. Gil saw to that. They would discuss a plea, review evidence from the scene, deal with the threat of a civil suit or update him with news from the DA's office – all things that could have been handled in a Zoom meeting. But each time, without fail, Trevor would come late in the day and stop by the French gatehouse on his way out. Callie flattered herself into thinking that she might have been part of the reason for the in-person conferences. That or her iced tea. She did make a mean iced tea.

She was just restarting the chapter – her third attempt to remember who all these characters were – when the approaching echo of footsteps on tile interrupted her. "Is this seat taken?" It was Oliver Chesney, her boss, spreading his arms over the expanse of empty benches and making a lame joke of it.

"What are you doing here?" she asked. It probably sounded ruder than she'd intended, so she skipped her follow-up question, which would have been, "Are you checking up on me?" It was a work day, after all.

"I could ask you the same," he replied. "Do you have some interest in Trevor Birdsong?"

He had caught her off-guard. "No. No." Why would he think she was interested in Trevor? Even if she were, it would be none of his business.

"He's in chambers with Judge Brown," Oliver said, pointing to the closed door. "That's what my sources tell me."

"No," she repeated. "I mean yes, he is. With my father. I'm waiting for my father."

"That's right. Buddy is representing him. I'd forgotten."

"Have you taken an interest in Trevor Birdsong?" she asked.

"As a matter of fact, yes." Oliver chose a spot farther down on the bench, so that they didn't have to crane their necks to look at each other. "When I saw you, I thought we might be working on the same idea. That's why I asked."

Oliver Chesney, publisher and editor of the *Austin Free Press*, had hired Callie when no one else would. He'd taken a chance and had been rewarded – they'd both been rewarded – with one of the biggest stories in recent memory.

Callie had mixed feelings about her boss. In many ways, he was what Buddy called a granola liberal, with a permanent three-day stubble, thin frame, checkered shirts and an office featuring four different recycling bins, plus one for compost. For Callie, this was either good and bad, depending on her mood and what she needed to get done. Oliver's one atypical trait was his accent, a panhandle twang straight from Amarillo. On some days, Callie would find this authentic and charming. On more cynical days, she would think of it as an affectation, designed to offset the rest of him and put people at ease. How could an educated man who'd lived in Austin for a decade maintain it, she wondered. Had he never noticed, for example, that the rest of the world did not say SEE-ment when they meant cement?

"So, what idea are you working on?" she asked. "Does the *Free Press* consider a plea bargain for a DWI as big news?"

"It might be. You know what Trevor does, right?"

Trevor had mentioned his job during one of their afternoon teas. He'd said it in a smug, irritating way, which only made Callie determined not to ask any more about it. "He's the branding manager for a company that makes dietary supplements," she said. "It's the one with a funny name. Kalaka."

"Ka'Kala," Oliver corrected her. "And it's not just supplements. It's expanded into this phenomenon based on natural healing. Herbs and oils from the most remote parts of the world. Plus the standard vitamins and supplements. All naturally sourced and done fair trade. Ka'Kala has managed to build trust in a generation that's become skeptical about all the hype."

"You sound like a convert."

His wide grin turned a little sheepish. "Maybe." He wiggled his right thumb. "I've had some carpal tunnel, ever since college. My doctor recommended their Wepapua ointment. That was their first product, from the heart of West Papua, Indonesia. Now I'm using their other stuff. They even have this app that tracks what your body needs and how it's affecting you. I'm surprised you're not into it yourself."

"Not unless they make a really nice, affordable white wine. Then I'll pay attention." Callie's smile faded. "What does a DWI have to do with Trevor's job? And why is that news?"

Oliver moved a little closer on the bench. He lowered his voice. "Rumor has it that Ka'Kala is going to be bought out. A couple of big firms are in pursuit. It occurred to me, when I heard about the arrest, that someone like Trevor, a pretty essential cog… If he goes to jail…"

Callie's head shook vigorously. "Trevor won't go to jail. Daddy will see to that. Not that he's doing anything shady," she quickly added. "It's a plea arrangement."

"I know your father," Oliver said. "I'm sure there's nothing shady."

There was something in Oliver's voice that made her want to argue. She lost her opportunity when the thick oak door opened and Judge Letitia Brown walked out, followed by the lawyers from both sides and the smaller, lighter presence of Trevor Birdsong. The Assistant DA and his assistant followed the judge as she headed farther into the bowels of the courthouse, while Buddy, Gil and Trevor lingered.

Callie got to her feet and examined her father's face. She couldn't tell what was behind his eyes right now, even though she'd spent a lifetime looking into them. Then she turned to Gil. His smile was subtle but it was there. "Everything's fine," he said. "It was a little hard-fought…"

"That woman doesn't like me," Buddy grumbled. "What did I ever do to her?"

"Not everyone has to like you," Callie said. Given the world's changing dynamics, fewer and fewer judges coming onto the bench would be admirers of Buddy McFee and his old Texas ways.

"True words," said Gil. "Like I said, it was hard-fought. For one thing, we were dealing with a previous DWI our client had neglected to tell us about. A little in-chambers surprise."

"Isn't that something you should have found out?" Trevor asked.

"We did ask you about any previous run-ins with the law. But you're right. We should have done our own checking." Gil clapped Trevor on the shoulder. "We got what we could."

Callie studied Trevor's face and noted a certain pallor blending in with his golden tan. "No jail time," she said.

"Course not," Buddy said. "But we did have to accept a compromise. That damned judge…"

"Not now," Gil said forcefully, his eyes fixed on Oliver Chesney, a man he knew, but not well enough to trust. "We can fill Callie in later, don't you think? Meanwhile, we still have a little business."

For the first time, Callie noticed the uniformed court officer standing in the doorway behind them, waiting, it seemed, to escort them somewhere.

"Trevor, hello." Oliver had somehow sidled past Callie and was reaching out to shake his hand. "I'm Oliver Chesney, from the *Austin Free Press*. I'm a big fan of Ka'Kala's. Your products. Your message. I would absolutely love to sit down with you sometime."

"*Austin Free Press*." Trevor extricated his hand. "That's Callie's paper."

"Yes, I'm one of her co-workers." Oliver very rarely said the word *boss*, only when he felt he had to.

Callie put on her sweetest smile. "Oliver came here to see if you're going to jail."

"No, no," Oliver protested. "Jeez, Callie."

"That's what you just told me."

"Not in those words." Oliver steepled his hands and pointed them at Trevor. "I came here to cover the news. What happened today was news. I'm so sorry for the way Callie made it sound. And I'm glad you're not going to jail."

"That's okay," Trevor said. "Does your paper want to interview me? I normally don't do interviews."

Oliver leaped at the idea. "An interview, yes. Even a cover piece. We can downplay the arrest. It will be about a local company reimagining the world of holistic healing. We can allow you a certain amount of feedback before we publish. Not approval, but feedback." He was displaying a blatant fanboy attitude and Callie felt embarrassed for him.

"Well, I think it might be better if your co-worker did the interview." Trevor turned to Callie. "What do you say? Are you up for interviewing me, Callie? Tonight? Over dinner?"

"Um, yes," she replied, making sure to avoid any eye contact with Oliver. "That sounds like a plan."

"It's actually my story," Oliver said. "I've done the research, as a loyal customer. If you want, Callie can join us."

"No, I think just Callie and me." Trevor evinced the smallest hint of a smile, the first since he'd stepped out into the corridor. His pallor was starting to fade. "I'll text you," he told Callie.

"You'll need my number for that."

Trevor was just pulling his phone out of his bag when the uniformed court officer reminded him, quite firmly, that there was no phone use in the courthouse. "I'll get your number from your father. Do you like French? In honor of your chateau?"

"Oui, je l'aime tellement."

"Bon. Then French it is."

The *Free Press* co-workers, sometimes known as boss and employee, continued to avoid eye contact, even as the officer ushered Trevor, Buddy and Gil down the long corridor, toward a bank of elevators.

"This isn't going to be an interview, is it?" Oliver asked.

"Not really."

"It's going to be a date."

"God, I hope so."

Callie didn't do the math. She didn't want to. But she probably hadn't been on a date in four months, not since she and Oliver went out to celebrate their last big story, although she wasn't quite sure if that qualified as a date. Is it a date if your boss picks up the check as a business expense?

Tonight's outing turned out not to be much of a date either, although it certainly wasn't the restaurant's fault. Camille's, a romantic and welcoming place, was touted as a secret gem in a trendy section of East Austin. Trevor, she was learning, was the sort of person who sought out "secret gems" in out-of-the-way but trendy parts of town. The reason behind the "dateless" vibe was that Trevor was preoccupied. He had been perfectly charming at the Ranch, over their iced teas, interested in her stories and willing to get to know her. But now there was just too much on his mind. She understood.

He was wearing a sports jacket, a light gray dress shirt and a red silk tie. "I like the tie," she said with a twisted grin. "No one under forty wears a tie."

His hand flew up to the knot. "Too formal? Sorry. I don't dress up often, just for special occasions. Important meetings. Dates. It's kind of a retro affectation."

"No, I like it." Callie usually dated larger men – taller than she and seemingly imbued with some authority and a lower timber to their voices. But Trevor had this boyish quality. Even his need to dress up showed a sensitivity that she liked.

"Today was quite the scene," he said, spearing a flat bean in his Classic Country Salad. "First in the judge's chambers, then the sentencing in the courtroom. I'm glad you didn't stay around for that. I mean, you see it in the movies. 'How do you plead?' 'Guilty, your honor.' I think that moment was the worst. I could barely stand up and get the words out."

"I can't imagine. It all happened so quickly."

"Yeah, I had a busy day. Your dad said it was the best way, before any reporters got wind of it and showed up with their cameras."

"Dad knows how to handle P.R." Callie reassured him. "He's done this a lot."

"I've never been processed before." Trevor let out an

unhappy chuckle. "Processed. Sounds like something from a meat-packing plant." He sighed. "I shouldn't make it so dramatic. Photos. Fingerprints. DNA swab. I guess I'm in the system now."

"What about your previous DWI? You weren't in the system?"

"Technically, that was a DUI, the underage version of a DWI. Young and stupid. There was no accident. No one was hurt and it was a misdemeanor. But this D.A. and this judge…" Trevor chomped through another bean. "They were against me from the second I walked it. Intoxication assault is a felony, they kept saying, although I don't know why it's an assault."

"Well, in this case a woman was seriously injured," Callie reminded him.

"It was an accident." He chewed then put down his fork. "Anyway, Buddy said that going to trial would be chancy and that this was the best I could do. A felony conviction with no jail time."

"No jail time. That's good."

"But now I'm a convicted felon. All because some old lady stumbled across the street."

Callie transferred her focus to her own salad as she tried to muster up some empathy. "Was the woman jaywalking?"

Trevor picked up his fork again. "No, she wasn't jaywalking. She was in the crosswalk and… and I ran a red light. Something I'm not proud of, okay?"

An uncomfortable silence fell over them. Yes, he was acting like a jerk, but Callie could only imagine his anxiety and distress. Being convicted and processed for a felony had to be unnerving. Looking around the dining room, she caught the waiter's eye and motioned to her empty wineglass. She had started the evening determined to only have one glass, maybe two. The main courses hadn't even arrived and she was already wondering if it might not have been smarter to order a bottle.

The silence lasted until the waiter returned, poured out a rather stingy measure of the Sauvignon Blanc and left. "Have you been here before?" she asked.

Her date glanced around the busy space, at the row of cozy tables for two along the window facing the street. "I have. I was seeing someone. Not very long. She introduced me to Camille's. It was her favorite spot. Now it's mine."

"Doesn't that get awkward, both of you coming here? Do you ever run into each other?"

"Not once." He rubbed his chin and shrugged, looking more helpless than she ever thought he could. "I keep expecting to. Maybe that's why I come."

Callie was not pleased. "So, you brought me here hoping you'd run into your old girlfriend. I'm flattered."

Trevor recoiled. "Oh, God, I'm sorry. It's not… You and I were joking about French and this was the only French restaurant I could think of. I wasn't going to tell you about Reggie."

"Reggie?"

"Short for Regina. We only dated a short while, before you and I met." He pointed to the window table in the corner, the one furthest from the action. "That was our spot."

"Only a short while?" Callie asked. "Sounds like you fell pretty hard."

"The worst part is that she ghosted me. I can't even find out what went wrong." He frowned. "Don't worry, I'm over her. It was just a shock."

Callie nodded and tried not to let her eyes dart around. Where the hell were their main courses?

"Not that you're a rebound, okay? Definitely not. If you'd dated me and dumped me before Reggie came along, then she would be the rebound date. It's all in the timing."

"Well, at least you put us in the same category," she said. But she was thinking; for God's sake, how long does it take to cook a rare steak, add a pepper sauce and throw on some fries?

Trevor took her hand, the one not holding the wineglass. "Look, I know we already changed the subject once, but can we change it again? I may have picked the wrong night and the wrong restaurant to try to be romantic. I just didn't want to be alone."

"I get it," Callie said. "You have a lot going on." And then her eyes lit up. "Oh, look. Food."

The waiter had arrived with their plates, a sincere apology for the delay and the offer of a free glass of wine. Or, if she didn't want another, he could just take a glass off the bill. Either way, he said. Callie went for the extra wine.

The meal, true to the ex-girlfriend's recommendation, was delicious, down to the recommended crème caramel for dessert. The subjects of love and felonies were dutifully avoided, giving way to the more reliable subject of movies. Trevor, it turned out, was a collector of low-budget horror movies. "My Dad and I used to watch them on late-night TV. If the movie's bad enough, the horror can be really funny. One of those 'so bad it's good' kind of things. You'd be surprised how many people collect them."

"You mean, like *Night of the Living Dead?*"

Trevor looked shocked. "Are you kidding me? No. That's a classic. One of the best."

"Um, okay." Callie thought back to her most cringe-worthy cinema experiences. She was not a fan. "*Texas Chainsaw Massacre*?"

"Another classic," he scolded. "At least the original. I only go for the really obscure. Things you've never heard of, like *Killer Klowns from Outer Space*."

She chuckled. "We'll have to watch one together sometime."

He nodded sagely. "You can learn a lot from a really bad horror flick. Believe me."

After dinner, Trevor escorted her into the misty night, walking her to her sliver Yukon, parked in a lot a block away. They wound up leaning side by side against the truck bed. During the walk, Callie had brought up Ka'Kala, which was only right, since the company had been the whole pretense for their date.

Almost instantly, Trevor was in his element. Seven years ago, he had come on as one of their first half-dozen employees and, according to his obviously well-rehearsed story, had almost singlehandedly crafted their image, turning the brand from the dream of a couple of adventure vloggers traveling the far reaches of civilization into a hipster sensation. Before the year was out, Ka'Kala would be acquired by some conglomerate. They would have to keep the name and keep intact the formulas and the ethos and the Third World sourcing of ingredients.

"I know people will say we're selling out. Your boss is probably one of them."

"Oliver can get…" She searched for the right word. "…enthusiastic about this sort of thing."

"Seems like our target demographic," Trevor said. "And we have no intention of letting them down. We'll still be working there. That's the plan. Only now, we'll all be driving Tesla Roadsters instead of regular Teslas."

"You're talking to someone with an aging truck," she said, patting the side of her old Yukon, "so I'm not going to be sympathetic."

Callie wasn't quite sure how to feel about him. Trevor seemed to operate with a strange combination of arrogance and vulnerability, toggling back and forth without warning, making his bouts of arrogance a little less offensive and his slides into vulnerability a little less heart-warming.

The date ended there in the parking lot. It had been a long day, especially for Trevor, and neither was in the mood to take things to anything beyond dinner. He leaned in and she accepted a friendly kiss but kept it purposely short. "I hope you and Regina get back together," she said, by way of explanation.

Trevor placed both hands to his chest and faked an expression of pain. "Touché. And I hope your co-worker doesn't get jealous."

She smirked, then imitated Trevor's heartfelt pose and pained expression. "Touché to you, too."

On her drive back to the French gatehouse, Callie made one more call to Melissa. Like her other calls, it went directly into voicemail. She'd been trying for days to engage her old friend, to casually ask about the documentary, to see if she could get any inkling about its focus. She'd even resorted to odd hours, early at morning or late at night, but with each unanswered call, she grew more nervous. Melissa was obviously avoiding her, and she had this sinking feeling that it wasn't going to end well.

CHAPTER 3

Callie had been working for months to get her drinking under control, although she didn't like to think of it in those terms. "Under control" implied that it had been out of control, which she didn't really feel was the case. She just wanted to be a little healthier, that was all, maybe lose a pound or two. Last night had constituted a tiny setback. She hadn't planned on a date that necessitated three glasses of wine. She comforted herself with the knowledge that Camille's had served almost criminally short pours.

Would she and Trevor ever arrange a second date? The smart answer would have been *no*. There was already enough trauma in her life. But she found herself thinking about him as she lay in bed that night and again the next the morning as she roused herself from her usual, fitful battle for sleep.

She was still thinking about him in the kitchen, over her first cup of coffee, when she checked her online newsfeed. She was surprised to see his name in one of the bold, sidebar headlines: *Ka'Kala Executive Convicted of Felony Assault.* The choice of words made it sound much worse than it was. But that's what headlines were made to do.

It was a little after eight when she faced the choice of driving into work or going for a run. The humidity, almost always higher in the morning, was fairly manageable at this hour and she felt that a run would help calm her nerves, or at least help tire her nerves out, which probably amounted to the same thing.

She had always loved the trails around the Ranch, especially the few that ran behind the main house and meandered off the McFee property, across neglected public roads and onto their neighbors' land. Today, after crossing the first dirt road, she took a left onto an inviting but unfamiliar path. Within five minutes, the terrain had grown a little rougher, the climbs and descents a little steeper. It was now a hiking trail rather than a running trail and she slowed herself down to an energetic walk. Her pace grew even more relaxed as she focused on the soft, comforting sound of leaves under her feet.

Autumn was her favorite time of year. The springs here were wet but colorful, the Texas fields festooned with wildflowers. The winters were clammy and dark. And the summers… Well, she preferred not to think about the summers. The late seasonal colors were not much to speak of, since the fall nights never got cold enough. This early fall weather was fine with her, with the first layer of leaves coating her path and crunching in her wake. The Spanish oaks would turn in a few weeks, along with the red of the sumacs, the yellow of the cedar elms and the brown of almost everything else. That would signal the beginning of the end and Callie wasn't yet ready for that.

As her pace slowed, she began to revel in being slightly

lost. There was something freeing about not knowing what was around the bend and not caring to know. There was no way she could be completely lost, not here in the woods that she had walked since childhood. The Murchison house was over there somewhere beyond that row of pecan trees. The Pattons had sold their place years ago, but the new owners maintained their trails and put in split-rail fences to mark their boundaries – not to keep anyone out, but just as a reminder.

Taking her time now, Callie made her way back across a creek and through to a familiar boulder, covered with moss. The faint noise of traffic made her change directions and led her to a dirt road where she crossed back onto McFee land. She was still in the woods when the stone of the main house peered out at her through a row of crape myrtles. A minute or so later, she reached the pond. Beyond that, the lawn, in need of a good mowing, sloped up to the flagstone veranda that ran the length of the house. This was where Buddy would sit out in the mornings, enjoying his coffee and muttering into his iPad. He used to mutter into actual newspapers, but change was inevitable. Even Buddy McFee couldn't hold it back.

She was halfway around the pond when she heard the shouts, echoing down the lawn. It was one voice shouting angrily, she realized, a male voice, and two other, more modulated male voices trying to calm him down. "Trevor?" she asked herself. It was definitely his voice, almost frightening in its intensity. For twenty years or more she had eavesdropped on enraged politicians and tycoons and had rarely heard any of them so upset. She approached quietly, not wanting to hide herself, but not wanting to draw attention either.

"How could you be so incompetent?" he roared. She could

see him now. "I should sue. I'm going to sue. You bastards should have warned me." Callie froze in the deep shadow of the gazebo.

"Being fired is always a possibility with a felony conviction." It was Gil, facing Trevor under the veranda roof. Between them, slumped in his rattan, was her father. "I apologize if we didn't make that clear."

"You did not make that clear. I would have gone to trial if I'd known. I would have done anything."

"Is it laid out in your employment contract?" Buddy asked softly.

Trevor shouted at him. "It's laid out. Any felony conviction will result in instant termination. The sanctimonious H.R. asshole who called this morning pointed that out over and over. Not even a meeting. These shitty, holier-than-thou, P.C. companies… He looked over to Gil. "Did you even ask to see my employment contract?"

"You didn't know this was in your contract?" Gil asked.

Trevor bristled. "It's a thirty-page contract I signed years ago. It was your job to think of this possibility and read the fine print. That's why I hired you."

"We felt it was more important for you not to serve time," Buddy protested, but Callie could see, even from a distance, that his heart wasn't in it. "If we'd taken this case to a jury trial…"

"I would have risked it," Trevor shouted. He was pacing now. His volume had not diminished. "If you'd bothered to inform me, I would have taken my chance in court."

"Aren't you being extreme?" Gil asked, his voice smooth with reason. "You're a talented young man with plenty of jobs in your future. If you want, Buddy and I can use our pull…"

"You don't get it. My God." Trevor stopped pacing and pounded his fist on a small wrought iron table. It tipped over, sending a crystal vase crashing to the flagstones. Callie remembered the vase as one that her mother had bought during a trip to Rome, her favorite city in the world.

Trevor barely reacted. The other two men winced, but that was all. "If you'd bothered to read…" He took a breath, lowered his voice and explained, as he might explain to a child. "I have stock in Ka'Kala. Now that I'm fired, I have to sell my stock for the price I bought it. Maybe a few hundred thou. After all those years. After all I contributed."

"You should have told us." Gil's mumble was barely audible.

"In a few weeks, Ka'Kala will be sold. That's a given. My shares will be worth twenty million at least. That's what you cost me with your stupidity. Maybe thirty. Thirty million."

Buddy opened his mouth and closed it several times, like a fish trying to breathe air. "It's my opinion," he finally said, "that a jury would have convicted you. A second drunk driving offense? An elderly, sympathetic victim? Highly probable. In that case, you would have gone to prison and still been fired."

"And that should have been my choice. My risk."

Buddy nodded, his head lifting off his chest and slowly returning. "You have a point. It should have been your call."

"Can I go back and reject the deal?"

Gil and Buddy exchanged glances. "No," they both said, almost in unison.

Gil continued. "You accepted. The judge convicted you. You're already convicted."

"Then I'm going after you." Trevor was pacing again, each

turn bringing him closer to the French doors leading into the sunroom. "Malpractice. Negligence. These things can be reversed if your lawyer doesn't represent you."

"You can certainly pursue that angle," Buddy said, his voice gaining in confidence. "I can make a list of lawyers. There are a few who aren't friends or fans of mine. I'll put asterisks by their names. But they're not necessarily the best."

"Is that supposed to scare me?" Trevor's laugh had an edge to it. "Friends and fans? I saw the way the judge treated you, you senile, old piece of shit."

At the word *senile*, Callie's heart went cold.

"I should have known." Trevor slapped himself on the side of the head. "Stupid, stupid. I'm a goddamn marketer. As soon as I saw your fake plantation and your fake whisky, I should have run the other way."

Gil followed the young executive as he stormed through the French doors and the sunroom and the rest of the house, heading for the front hall.

As soon as they were gone, Callie stepped out from the shadows and crossed the rest of the lawn. She knelt by her father's chair, being careful to first brush away the thick shards of crystal. He looked up from his lap and focused on her face. "Callie, honey?" he whispered. "This is not good."

"I know Trevor a bit," she said. "I can talk to him."

"I should have checked his contract." He reached up a shaky hand and wiped his forehead. "What the hell's happening to me? Callie, darling, it scares me."

"Everything will be fine." She tried to make it sound convincing. "Uncle Gil and I will take care of it."

Gil returned a minute later, walking slowly, the blood

having drained from his face. He was only slightly surprised to see Callie kneeling on the flagstones. "How much did you hear?"

"Enough," she said, getting up and crossing away from her father. Gil followed her into a corner. "Why did you push him into a plea bargain? A felony conviction is a big deal."

Gil looked her straight in the eyes. "You obviously have an opinion on this."

She did have an opinion. It wasn't a nice opinion, and she wasn't quite sure how to phrase it. "If this had gone to trial, then Buddy would have wanted to be in court, to defend Trevor, right? I know my father. The answer is yes. He's a grandstander who hasn't been in front of a crowd in years."

"Okay." Gil maintained his eye contact. "What's your point?"

"Is that why you pushed for a plea? You, meaning Gil Morales. The last thing you want is for Buddy McFee to stand in front of a judge and jury. You're not a lawyer, so you couldn't do your magic and protect him. Is that why you pushed for a plea? To protect my father?"

"I'm not even going to dignify that with a response," Gil said then changed his mind. "The boy was going to be convicted, and this was as good a deal as we could get. Our mistake was not reading his employment contract."

"Is there anything we can do?"

Gil ended the staring contest and slowly scratched his cheek. "I'll put feelers out. If Trevor connects with another lawyer, we'll know. This may mean bringing someone else into the loop. That can be managed. The McFees have built up a lot of good will."

"I'm not sure good will can help us. Does Trevor have a case?"

Buddy's assistant eyed his boss, who was still staring down, barely moving. Then Gil took Callie by the elbow and drew her into the sunroom and away from the doors. "Trevor wants the court to set aside his deal and go to trial, based on our failure to inform him of all the ramifications."

"So, he has a case."

"Yes." Gil spoke quickly and clearly. "In the long run, it may not make any difference. Even if the judge overturns the deal and Trevor goes to trial and somehow doesn't get convicted, he's already been legally fired. That twenty to thirty mill doesn't disappear. Someone gets it, probably his bosses. They will not want to rehire him and give it back."

"So, it doesn't matter if he sues or not."

A soft moan came from deep in Gil's throat, not a typical reaction from a man who was always so perfectly in control. "To us it matters. First, your daddy's name will be dragged through the mud. There'll be questions about his condition, questions asked in an open court where we can't lie. And he'll be liable to a civil suit. Trevor can claim damages."

"How much damages?"

"Depends on how the felony court case goes." Gil took a deep breath. "We have to keep a dialogue going with Mr. Birdsong. I notice he's been stopping by the gatehouse." Of course he noticed. "Have you been seeing him off the property? Be honest."

Callie shot him daggers. "Are you asking if we had a date? Yes. Are you asking if we had sex? No."

Gil shrugged. "Well, that's better than nothing. Get in

touch with him. Find out what he's thinking. Be sympathetic. Tell him you're on his side. Don't try to talk him out of anything."

She nodded then glanced back out to the veranda. "Is Daddy going to be all right?"

Gil nodded back. "Luckily, we have a doctor in the loop. I'll get Oppenheimer to come over. Meanwhile, you should get to work."

"I could call in sick."

"No. Your Daddy and I need to talk and plan – if he's up to it. This doesn't involve you."

"Plan what?" She never quite trusted their plans. "What are you planning?"

"I'm not sure yet. Some way to shut this down."

"Uncle Gil?" She tried to look him in the eyes. "You're not going to do anything stupid?"

He met her gaze. "We've already done stupid. Now, get on your way. We don't want you getting fired, too."

CHAPTER 4

CALLIE PARKED IN the side lot and left her jacket and bag in the passenger seat, taking only her phone. She entered the converted warehouse through a side door and took the stairs, which deposited her near one of the unisex restrooms.

At the *Austin Free Press*, there was no strict policy on work hours. Many reporters worked on stories from home or had meetings off-site. But Callie liked to minimize her absences, saving them up for occasions when she couldn't so easily fake showing up on time and being diligent.

Today's workload was larger than usual, including a rewrite of Jennie Larson's latest, a backward glance at this year's South by Southwest and a forward glance at the promise of next spring's festival. Jennie, she noted, was slowly becoming a decent writer, despite a lack of natural ability that was almost shocking.

The work was a welcome distraction, but not quite distracting enough. Every hour or so, she would leave Trevor a voice message or a text. She would have emailed him as well, except she didn't have his email. She tried to keep her tone, in the messages and texts, concerned and empathetic, without letting any panic creep in. As far as Trevor knew, she had not been a witness to his threats at the Ranch. "I heard about your job. So terrible. Is there anything I can do? Please call me." She sent multiple variations of these sentiments. "I'm worried about you. Please let me know you're okay. Do you need company?"

Callie treated herself to a late lunch of two vegan granola bars from the company's health-conscious vending machine then returned to the shelter of her cubicle. It was well after five. Others were leaving. But she was not looking forward to her drive home and the sullen, somber dinner she would be expected to share with Buddy and Gil. She felt guilty about feeling this way and helpless that her dozen or so pleas to Trevor hadn't resulted in a single response.

When her phone finally rang, she almost leaped for it. "Trevor?" Of course, it didn't have to be Trevor. It could be Gil or her father or Oliver… She hadn't even checked her screen.

"Who's Trevor?"

Callie checked now. It was Melissa. Under normal circumstances, she would have been thrilled to have Melissa finally return one of her calls. "Trevor is a friend."

Melissa's laugh was lilting and untroubled and annoying. "Sounds like more than a friend, the way you answered. Look, I'm sorry I haven't been back to you. My bad. Do you want to get together? How about drinks?"

"Sure." Callie put her on speaker and fiddled with her phone's calendar. "What's a good day?"

"Right now," Melissa said. "Do you have time? Are you at the office?"

"I am, but…"

"Oh, great." She seemed genuinely pleased.

"But I'm not sure about tonight." Callie did have time, yes, but she was not in any mood to deal with her friend and her documentary. One crisis at a time.

"Come on," Melissa said in a coaxing, pleading voice. "I'll tell you all about the film. I know I've been putting you off."

"How about tomorrow?"

"No," she replied emphatically. "Tomorrow I'm submitting an outline to my professor. I was hoping to run it by you before showing it to her. See what you think?"

It was exactly what Callie wanted, but why did it have to be now? "Okay."

"Great. You're in the Warehouse District, right?" Melissa had been to the *Free Press* offices once, back when she'd been so eager to learn about Buddy's legendary career. "How about Rainey Street? There's this new wine bar. Corkers. I've been wanting to try it. Meet you there?" And before Callie could object, she hung up.

Rainey Street was a part of town south of the Warehouse District, a few blocks off the river, anchored by Rainey Street itself, where cute, little bungalows had been transformed into restaurants and bars, with a peppering of food trucks thrown in-between. Callie's GPS found Corkers without a problem and a few minutes later, she was stunned to find a parking space almost directly across from it.

An outdoor table for two opened up just as she was crossing Rainey Street and she raced to grab it, barely beating out a middle-aged couple who'd been dawdling by a chalkboard that listed today's by-the-glass specials. Callie wasn't in the mood to be nice. She watched as the couple glared at her and then walked off, perhaps in search of a wine bar with an even more winsome name.

She sat down and inspected the crowd, outside and in, straining to see if Melissa was already here. No, not yet. When her phone dinged with a text, she sighed. She had raced out of the office for this last-minute thing. Melissa had practically begged her. And now… Callie was totally unprepared for the name that appeared on her screen. She nearly dropped the phone.

"**Trevor Birdsong:** Maybe we should talk. Can you come over? I don't feel like leaving the house."

"Absolutely," she answered, watching the words pop up as she spoke them. "Where do you live?" He texted her back, giving her an address on Davis Street. She consulted her phone. It was only a few blocks away.

"Fantastic. I'm in the neighborhood." She was tempted to blow off Melissa and go right now, but she didn't want to upset her friend, who might be just as big a problem as Trevor in the long run. One potential calamity at a time. And all in the name of her daddy. "I can be there in an hour. Are you okay?"

He said he was calmer now, more at peace with what had happened. Callie was glad but also a little unsettled. She asked what he meant by *at peace* and he said that what happened was primarily his fault and that he needed to face the consequences. "I can't change the past. But I can't see a future, either."

"Of course, there's a future," she assured him. "We'll talk about it."

"That damned company was my life. I don't know what to do."

Again, she toyed with the idea of going. He needed someone and had chosen the casual friend who'd been pestering him all day. But a second later, Melissa came into view, waving cheerily as she hurried down the street. Callie sent off one final text, promising Trevor she would be there as soon as she could, then put her phone face down on the table and got to her feet. "Mel."

"Callie!" Melissa bounded past the chalkboard and up to the table, greeting her with a quick hug. "Sorry I'm late." There was an energy to her that Callie hadn't seen in quite a while. "What you must think."

"No, no. I'm just thrilled that you're letting me be part of the process. I can't imagine how personal it must feel, making a film."

"It's also personal to you and Buddy. I can't forget that." Melissa sat down and settled in. Then she opened the bag on her lap and rummaged through. "Just want to check my car keys. Yes, they're here. So…" She looked up, took a deep breath and delivered a warm smile. "How are you?"

"Um, fine." Callie chuckled. "A little distracted." She glanced at her face-down phone just as it pinged. Her heart jumped. "I'm sorry. I have to check this. A friend…" She flipped it over and read.

"**Trevor Birdsong:** I should have been stronger. Please forgive me."

Callie just stared. It took her several seconds of staring, as if the words had no meaning. And then suddenly they meant everything. "Oh, my God."

"What is it?" Melissa asked.

Callie was already on her feet, her phone in one hand, her bag in the other. "I have to go."

"Why? What happened?"

"I think my friend's in trouble."

"What kind of trouble?"

Callie hemmed. "I don't want to say. Can we reschedule? Maybe tomorrow?"

Melissa was getting to her feet as well. "No problem. Can I help?"

"No. No thanks." She checked her phone again, scrolling up the thread of texts. "Davis Street."

"Is that where your friend lives?"

Callie didn't answer. She was already stepping out onto Rainey Street, touching the address in Trevor's earlier text and waiting for Google Maps to appear and do its job. A map came up and a red dot glistened, informing her that it would be a four-minute walk. She turned in all directions, eyes on the screen, trying to get her bearings.

"Are you driving?" Melissa was at her side, looking concerned.

"No. Walking."

"Then I'm coming with you."

Callie didn't have the presence of mind to say no. If she'd had the time and the focus, she might have thought it best to keep Melissa and Trevor far away from each other. The woman with the documentary and the man with the grudge. Instead, she turned left, sidestepping the strolling couples and groups of college students, only vaguely aware that Melissa was right on her heels. The next left brought her to Davis Street. According-ing to Google, it was just another block and a half.

The quaint bungalows of Rainey Street didn't extend their charms onto the side streets, which were filled mostly with apartment buildings and parking lots. As she crossed at the next corner and drew closer, she could see that only one old bungalow remained on Davis, a well-maintained, single-family outlier that matched exactly the red, glistening dot. She picked up her pace, almost running now, and flew down the walkway leading up to the porch.

Callie saw the doorbell, but decided that would be too subtle, too easily ignored. "Trevor?" she shouted then began pounding on the old oak door. "Trevor!"

"What's wrong?" Melissa asked. She'd come up on the porch, too, and was staring through a curtained window. "I can't see anyone."

"Trevor!" Callie stopped pounding and tried the doorknob. Locked. She jiggled it. Still locked. She pounded again. Meanwhile, Melissa, at the curtained window, was trying to push it up, smacking the frame where layers of old paint held everything in place. "We should call the police."

The window wouldn't budge and Melissa gave up. "Is your friend sick? Is this an emergency?"

"Yes," Callie said then reconsidered. "I don't know."

"Are you up for breaking a window?" Melissa pointed to pineapple-shaped doorstop at the top of the steps.

"What? No." It seemed so extreme. But then Trevor's last message had been extreme. 'Please forgive me.' The expense and trouble of a broken window wouldn't be a big deal. It was the implication that stopped her. What if Trevor was inside, just taking a nap or wearing earphones? What if he had gone out for a walk and came back to see this – a crazy girl; two crazy girls – breaking into his house because they thought he might be suicidal? Would he be flattered? Would he be offended? Or would this act on Callie's part just intensify his feelings of hopelessness?

And what if it wasn't his house? He could have accidentally transposed a number in the address. Wouldn't that be embarrassing? And illegal. Breaking and entering a stranger's home. Callie looked over to the driveway and was reassured to see a lime green Tesla plugged into a recharging port on the side of the house. That was a good sign.

A crash of glass interrupted her muddled, inner debate. "What the hell?"

Melissa stood by the right sidelight, one of the glass panels that framed the door, holding the iron doorstop in both hands and displaying a wild grin. She'd used the pineapple tip to stab through the glass, not far above the mechanism. It had left a hole the size of a golf ball, with cracks radiating the length of the window. "Sorry." She said it in a very un-sorry tone.

Callie was relieved. Her friend had done what needed to be done and – best part – Callie couldn't be blamed. She wrenched the doorstop from Melissa and took over, cracking more glass and poking away the shards. Melissa untied the scarf from around her neck and handed it over. They'd both seen enough movies to know the correct, safest way to reach through a broken window. Callie wrapped the scarf around her hand, reached through the frame and felt around for the lock. For a second, she was concerned that the lock might work with an interior key, but no. It was a simple thumb-turn. Callie flipped the knob, retrieved her hand, opened the door and stepped inside.

No lights were on in the living room. That fact, combined with the small, curtained windows and the room's dark wainscoting, made it hard to see. "Trevor?" Her eyes slowly adjusted to the shadows. When there was no response, she made her way to the next room, the kitchen. "Trevor? Sorry about break-in." Melissa had entered as well and was only a few feet behind her. Callie kept her tone light. What was done was done, she reasoned. They would explain themselves as best they could.

And then she saw Trevor. He was by the back door, half on his knees, half on his side, his body leaning forward, his head suspended in mid-air, held in place by the red necktie around his throat.

CHAPTER 5

It had turned into a breezy evening. Callie sat on the bench on Trevor's porch, holding her arms tightly around her, listening to the police tape as it crackled across the open doorway. On the porch's top step sat Melissa in deep conversation with Callie's older brother, State McFee, homicide detective. His full name, rarely used, was States Rights McFee, a display of commitment their father had made twenty-nine years ago during a legendary standoff between Texas and the federal government, a commitment that his son now had to live with.

State stood at the bottom of the steps. Like Callie, he had fair skin and blue eyes, inherited from their mother, and thick, Irish-red curls, inherited from their father. State had always kept his hair short, almost military, but over the past few months had started to let it grow. In a certain light, State resembled the Buddy McFee of her RCA camcorder memories. But there was also a softness to him, as if he hadn't been baked as long or as hard as the rest of the McFees. He would never, for example, even think of taking the clown's place in the dunk tank.

State's notepad was open and he wrote in pencil as Melissa spoke. He was the only person Callie knew who regularly used a pencil and one of the few who regularly used a notepad.

Trevor's body had been removed and the only two people left behind the crackling tape were a police photographer and an evidence officer, who was busy bagging and labeling a few last items: Trevor's phone and keys and, of course, the necktie. Callie's couldn't help thinking that her prints would be found on that tie, if a soft, silk fabric like that could retain prints. She didn't know. There were so many things she didn't know about police work, but she was learning.

Callie had been frozen by the sight; a young man, not much older than she, bent sideways on his knees, dangling forward from a doorknob, a stylish red tie pulled tight against the front of his throat. Her first impulse had been to try to save him. She rushed in and pushed his body back toward the door. With that push, Trevor slumped completely onto the kitchen floor, loosening the necktie enough to let her work it free from the flesh of his still-warm neck.

She had a vague recollection of Melissa, who'd been less prepared than she, walking in and screaming hysterically. It was Melissa who called 9-1-1. A minute later, well before the paramedics and the police cruiser arrived, Callie made her own call to Gil, and it was Gil who arranged for State to become the detective of record.

Melissa pushed herself up from the steps, looking exhausted. She made eye contact with Callie, offered a small, sympathetic smile then made the universal gesture of "I'll call you" as she headed down the walkway and out through the gate.

State flipped his notepad shut and slid the stubby pencil behind his ear. "You okay?" he asked. Callie decided to ignore both the question and its staggering stupidity. She made room for him on the bench. He took a seat beside her, just as he had hundreds of times in various church pews and rear car seats. "So, that's Mel, huh?" he said, nodding toward the tall, striking woman disappearing down Davis Street. "The sad little girl who tagged after you at all those garden parties? How times change."

"I could have saved him," she said, barely loud enough to be heard. "Just a matter of seconds. He was still warm."

"Well..." State did his best to look comforting. "Bodies don't lose heat all that quickly, about one and a half degrees per hour, something like that."

"Yes. But if I'd come over when he asked... If I'd bailed on Mel before he sent me that last text..."

"No, darlin'." State could sound just like their father when he wanted, which she found comforting right now. "I've been on call for a lot of suicides. Part of the job. And I've seen a lot of people blame themselves. Okay, I get it when it's kids or teens. Then people maybe should blame themselves or feel responsible. This guy was a functioning adult, making his own decision."

"But I was right there, a couple blocks away. He needed me and I chose to be at a wine bar."

"You had no way of knowing. Then you did what you could."

"Which was exactly nothing. I didn't even know you could kill yourself that way. From a doorknob?"

"It's not uncommon. I've seen maybe three or four. The throat's a fairly delicate thing."

"I know. I've been strangled, remember? You lose air pretty quickly." When her brother didn't respond, Callie glanced over and saw that he was checking his phone. "Am I interrupting?"

"Sorry. It's just…" State held up his phone. "This was date night with Yolanda. Twice a month."

"Twice. Aren't you the romantic duo!"

"There aren't that many sitters willing to take on the twins. We were just leaving the house when Gil called. You should have seen the sitter when we walked back in. I wound up paying a full four hours, just to keep her from quitting."

Callie shook her head. "Doesn't it ever bother you, being at Dad's beck and call, bending the rules for him?"

State took her question seriously. "It doesn't happen often. And those bent rules are the reason I made homicide detective, so it's a bargain I'm okay with. Most of the time." He stuffed his notepad back into his jacket pocket. "So, why is Dad interested in this? Is it you? Did you drive this guy to suicide and Dad wants to keep it on the hush? You don't seem the type to drive your boyfriends to suicide."

"Thanks for the compliment. No, I'm not the reason Dad and Gil are on this. Trevor was fired today and Dad…" She hesitated. "I'm not sure how much I can say."

"I'm a cop. I think you have to say."

Callie was just mulling this over when her brother's phone dinged. "Yolanda?" she asked.

He studied the incoming text. "It's Gil."

"Good, he can explain."

Looking up from his phone, State sighed. "We have to go

out to the Ranch. Both of us. Now. It's part of our bargain with the devil."

It wasn't as late as Callie had thought, not even nine, and a drive out to the Ranch was hardly an imposition, considering that she lived in the gatehouse. It was a different matter for State. He stepped off the porch and onto the grass for his call to his wife, but it didn't take a lip-reader to realize that Yolanda Adamos McFee was not thrilled.

When they arrived at the main house, the front door was open and the lights were on in the study. Buddy and Gil were waiting. It was a room long dedicated to business, not to family get-togethers, and as much as the retired politician smiled and hugged his children and asked heartfelt questions about his grandsons – how were they doing in school? What did they want for their birthday? Did they ever ask about their old granddad? – it was clear that this was a business meeting.

The children took their places in the brown leather chairs while Buddy sat at his desk. He seemed as lucid and alert as she'd seen him in some time. That, at least, was reassuring. Small blessings. "How did you get mixed up in this?" he asked.

Callie explained, directly and succinctly, of her attempts to get in touch with Trevor, of his sudden invitation to come over and of the final, desperate text that sent her running to his bungalow on Davis Street. "I was having drinks with Melissa Miller. She insisted on coming with me and trying to help."

Gil stood behind Buddy's chair, ramrod straight, like a vigilant bodyguard. "Melissa?" he said, shaking his head. "This gets better and better."

"Should I have taken an extra few minutes and tried to

get rid of her?" Callie's voice oozed sarcasm. "Would that have been better?"

"I apologize," Gil stated without inflection. "Speed was of the essence, you're right. Does Melissa know of your father's connection?"

"She didn't at the time, but as soon as this hits the news…"

"Of course," Buddy said. "And which one of you broke into his house?"

"It was a joint effort," Callie answered. "Technically, me. But she was right there. She saw everything."

Buddy nodded then turned to his older child. "Tell me about the physical evidence."

"Physical evidence?" State asked. "It was suicide."

"Don't play dumb," Gil chided. "What made you determine suicide?"

State didn't take offense. Instead, he opened his notepad. "Well, first, chronologically, we have his frame of mind. He'd just lost his job, and sent Callie several texts, the last of which stated…" And he read. "'I should have been stronger. Please forgive me.'"

"And the physical evidence?" Buddy asked for a second time. "At the scene?"

State flipped a few pages, taking a moment to gather his thoughts. "The front door was locked, according to Callie and Melissa. The back door, where the body was hanging, was locked with a key and a slide bolt, untouched by either of the initial entrants. The windows were locked throughout the house, including the two front ones which appeared to be painted shut."

Buddy shifted in his chair. "Any neighborhood witnesses?"

"The house has no adjacent neighbors. We'll send a uniform tomorrow, door to door."

"I asked you to take prints," Buddy said. "Did you take prints?"

"We did. Phone, keys, doors, windows, all the surfaces in the kitchen. We took elimination prints from Callie and Melissa. His tie is in forensics, although I don't know what that will show us."

"You should have a tox screen done," Buddy said. "To see if he was impaired."

"Got it." State flipped to the last page of his notepad, pulled the pencil from behind his ear and wrote down the instructions. "Dad?" he asked as he wrote. "How exactly are you involved?"

Buddy seemed prepared for the question. "Trevor Birdsong was a client. DWI. I advised him to take a plea, which he did. It was the right thing. But the consequence was that he lost his job and a fair amount of money. He wanted to reverse the deal but he couldn't, so he blamed me. He said he was going to sue me for malpractice." He turned to his daughter. "Did I get everything, sweetie?"

"Pretty much," Callie said. He had left out the part about the world possibly discovering his dementia, opening the door to other, similar lawsuits and forcing his retirement from any kind of useful life.

State slipped his pencil behind his ear. "So, Mr. Birdsong commits suicide. And you're afraid the public will blame you."

"I'm not afraid," Buddy said, raising his voice. "But one might argue… An ass, for example, might argue that following my legal advice contributed to the young man's tragic choice."

"There could be some contributing factors that we're not aware of," Gil interjected. "Personal issues. Family. A history of depression, perhaps. Or it could be something else entirely."

Callie clenched her jaw. This kind of spin, absolving your actions by blaming the victim, was par for the course in her father's world.

"I get the psychological thing," State said. "But that's not my job. You drag me away from home, and that's fine. But then you ask all sorts of questions."

"I'm sorry to have disturbed you. Truly." Buddy reached a hand across the desk, an unfamiliar gesture of connection. "Gil told me about your date night. And those boys. What a handful." He chuckled then grew serious. "It can't be easy, being my son."

"It's wonderful being your son," State protested. "That's not my point."

"I know." Buddy retracted his hand. "You're wondering why I got you involved in a suicide. Well, that should be fairly obvious."

Callie inhaled, an involuntary gasp. "You want it to be murder."

Buddy looked offended. "It's not what I want, sweetie. I'm just bringing up the very real possibility." He grunted and pushed himself to his feet. Callie recognized this move for what it was, part of her father's theater of persuasion. He paced the Persian carpet, a gift from some former Shah of Iran to some former McFee, gesticulating as he paced. "Right now, with the news just coming out, is a delicate time. People are shocked by any young death. They want to know the cause. If the detective in charge says 'undetermined'... well, that buys us time. It could well have been murder. There was money involved. Feelings of anger and betrayal."

Gil joined in. "We're just saying that you need to give the case some time. Investigate."

"Indeed," Buddy agreed. "I've known many an apparent suicide that turned out to be homicide. Just last week there was a drug dealer in prison found hanging from his bars. Same sort of situation."

"It wasn't murder." Callie was outraged by the thought. She was on her feet now, too, interrupting Buddy's theater with a heartfelt performance of her own. "The doors were locked. The windows were locked. He texted me. It's the most clear-cut suicide… You want to twist the truth to your own convenience. You want to make it someone else's fault. That is pathetic, Dad, it really is."

"Don't talk to me that way," Buddy shouted back, a drop of spittle flying onto the carpet. "If I'm anything, I'm a judge of character. I've stared down governors and presidents, locked eyes with them, read them like books. I'm telling you, this Birdsong wasn't a man to take his own life."

"Dad." State seemed to need to say something, but the words weren't coming. "Dad."

"State will prove it for us, won't you, son? Keep an open investigation. Do some legwork. Take a week or two. I can work with that."

"Dad, this is too much. Too much." State was finally finding the words, his hands trembling on the arms of his chair.

"Now just hear me out." Buddy raised his hands, palms forward. "As an officer, it's your duty to explore every angle."

"I did explore them. But you're asking me to hint at a

murder that didn't happen. What about the man's family? What about them?"

"What about your own family?" Buddy demanded.

"You want these people to think their son was murdered? If I don't close this out, you know that's what they'll think."

"And which is worse?" Buddy asked. "Personally, I think they'd prefer a murdered son to a suicide. They would welcome that possibility."

"And what happens when they discover the truth? You can't play with people."

"State, my boy." It was Gil, still ramrod straight, still behind Buddy's desk. "This whole thing may blow over. If we luck out and Birdsong didn't hire a lawyer and didn't confide in anyone about his unhappiness, we'll be fine."

"That we can handle," Buddy added.

"But if he did… Then Buddy will be the lawyer who made his client kill himself. The facts won't matter. It won't matter that Trevor would have been convicted anyway. It won't matter if someday you stumble across his killer and reopen the case. The damage will be done."

Buddy held a hand out toward Gil, as it to push back his intensity. Then he dialed back his own.

"Your partner just had a baby, right? Detective Pasquale? I think we sent her something nice. That leaves you flying solo. No one else needs to get involved." He seemed genuinely perplexed by his son's rebellion. "It's nothing you haven't done before."

"God help me, I know," said State. "From the beginning, it was always, 'Boy, I need information. Downplay this. Up-play that. Get me the M.E.'s report.' I'm nothing but the family cop, one more part of a system you can manipulate." He rose to his feet. All four were standing and suddenly the room felt too small.

"I never wanted you to be a cop." Buddy pointed a finger, his hand shaking. "I wanted you to follow in my footsteps. Another generation of McFee men at the heart of Texas politics. What I wanted was a dynasty. But it wasn't to be. Sorry to be harsh, but you didn't have it in you."

"Dad!" Callie had never heard her father even hint at this, even though they all knew it to be a fact.

State saw his sister's reaction. "That's all right," he reassured her. "I didn't want the dynasty."

Buddy snorted. "Oh, I know what you wanted. You wanted a black and white world with no wiggle room, no room for bargaining or nuance. Well, guess what? That world doesn't exist."

Callie held her breath as State turned and headed for the door. She didn't want her brother to leave, not with their father getting in the last, hurtful word.

State stopped in the doorway. "It's my world, and it exists."

"You think so," Buddy said, his voice growing calmer, almost gentle. "And I admire that, son. It's a noble attribute, seeing right and wrong as polar opposites. You're a good cop. I shouldn't belittle that."

"There is black and white," State argued. "Either he committed suicide or he didn't."

"And I say he didn't. If you keep the case open, that stays viable. The truth, as I see it, stays viable. What does that cost the department? Next to nothing. But if you close it and I'm right, his killer gets away. Is that what you want?"

"I'm sorry. I'm sorry I was such a disappointment."

"You're not a disappointment. You're a McFee." Buddy clasped his hands, as if in prayer. "And I'm betting that counts enough for you to delay your report about the suicide. Alleged suicide. Am I right?"

Now, Callie thought. Now was the time for State to walk out. To cease to engage. To drive home to Yolanda and his twins and ignore their father's nonsense about the McFee blood and brains.

Her brother surprised her by doing exactly that, walking out without another word. And she couldn't have been prouder.

That night, Callie decided to skip her regular sleep dance. She would not worry about regulating her white wine intake. She would not calculate how many nights it had been since she'd last taken an Ambien. And she would find the bottle of Xanax that she'd hidden under the bathroom sink for emergency use only.

It was after nearly three a.m. when a fitful sleep finally replaced her chemically induced fog. She'd been in this state before and had often found herself immersed in vivid, incomprehensible dreams, one merging into the next with an almost painful intensity. The dreams tonight were all about Trevor. They would be together in his bungalow, with him in his gray shirt and red tie, threatening suicide and her trying to talk reason, sometimes successfully, sometimes not.

Even in the successful scenarios, she would leave Trevor in the kitchen because she needed to go have a glass of wine with Melissa on the porch. There was no logic to any of this except the logic of dreams. But when she finished her wine and remembered Trevor and returned, he would be dead, on his knees, his necktie turned in reverse, one end tied to the doorknob, the other looped tight around his throat.

As daylight and consciousness began to eke into her mind, this one scene played out over and over. His despair. His purple face. His red tie. At some point, she became aware that she was lying half-awake, cocooned in the tangled sheets and covered in sweat. But she didn't want to wake up. Just one more time, she thought. If she had the dream one more time, she would be able to save him. Just leave Melissa a minute earlier. But then she would get lost somewhere between Trevor's porch and the kitchen. Or the door would be locked. Or there wouldn't be a door at all.

Just one more time.

CHAPTER 6

CALLIE FIRST BECAME aware of the *Austin Free Press* back in her UT days. Every college town seemed to have at least one such weekly – liberal and a little funky, distributed free in vending boxes or stacked up by the doors of laundromats and restaurants. She started picking it up for the horoscopes and advice columns when there was nothing else to read. There were also coupons and reviews for restaurants and movies. At some point, she began noticing the articles. As a journalism major, she had become a newspaper snob, always ready to tear apart the style or the structure. She rarely, almost never, got through an entire *Free Press* article.

She wasn't sure when the paper changed. If she had to guess, she would say it was when Oliver Chesney took over, probably during her junior year. Suddenly, there would be an investigative piece actually worth her attention, something more important than an ill-informed op-ed about the need for more bike paths or an interview with the owner of the newest downtown bakery. She'd noticed it at the time, at the periphery of her world, never thinking that someday she would be relegated to working here, on one floor of a converted warehouse, that this would be the end result of four years at the Moody College of Communication at The University of Texas.

She hadn't intended to come in today. Everything was still so raw. But the walls of her bedroom had closed in and then the walls of the kitchen and living room. Even a day working on her laptop in a warehouse would beat doing nothing. She arrived on the floor of cubicles with her unruly hair looped back into a messy ponytail. That visual cue plus a sullen, don't-talk-to-me attitude were enough to keep the rest of the staff at bay.

She'd been ignoring her phone all morning, despite the dings of her news alerts and the pings of her texts. Now she checked. One text from Gil. Two from Oliver. The last three were from Melissa. Callie read these first. They were all under the guise of concern, but she could recognize the blatant curiosity. "Just saw on the news who your friend was. R U OK?" "I told no one about last night. You deserve your privacy. Please call." "R U OK? Let me know. Worried about U."

At some point, Callie would have to spend time with her. She would have to gauge just how much Melissa had pieced together and then explain her way around those pieces. Yes, Buddy had represented Trevor. That's how he and Callie met. Yes, they'd gone on a date, and yes, he'd been distraught. But no, Trevor had never mentioned being angry at Buddy. That's what she would say.

She was just settling behind her desk when her phone pinged again. It was her boss, his third text, asking to see her in his office.

As publisher and editor-in-chief, Oliver had the only

interior door and the only full-height walls. Callie closed the door behind her, not a typical move in their egalitarian environment but occasionally necessary. When Oliver looked up from his desk, his face assumed the expression – wide eyes, eyebrows up, tilt of the head, small, closed-mouth smile. Her name had not been mentioned in the press release. It stated only that Trevor Birdsong's body had been discovered by a female friend who had received a text from him just minutes earlier. And yet Oliver was making his sympathetic face. "How did you know?" she asked.

"I'm so sorry. That must have been devastating."

"How did you know?"

"Well…" His face and voice slowly returned to normal. "You and Trevor were seeing each other. Just the previous night."

She corrected him. "One date. Dinner only."

"Noted. May I go on?" She nodded. "The police gave out no name for his female friend – a bit unusual, implying that some sort of influence was exerted. Plus, your brother was assigned the case. And you show up here late and looking like… less than your best, no offense." Callie didn't know which was more annoying, hearing him lay out his flawless logic or hearing it done in his Amarillo twang. "You know, you can take a day off. No one would blame you."

"Does anyone else in the office know?"

"I don't think so. People have mentioned him, but no one's mentioned you. Want some coffee?"

He knew how she took it – milk, no sugar. He delivered it from his ancient Mr. Coffee and made her sit down. Then he listened as she recapped her evening with Trevor and the following evening when she'd pulled his body off the kitchen doorknob. She left out the in-between part where Trevor threatened her father. No one seemed to have made the connection between Trevor's being fired and any McFee malpractice. It was still the first day.

"This is why I showed up at the courthouse. I had a feeling that arrest would turn into something bigger." This was as close as Oliver would come to bragging. "Of course, I didn't expect suicide. He didn't seem the type."

Callie's hands cradled the warmth of her half-empty mug. "Has the company made a statement?"

"They have. Very heartfelt and short. Saying all the right things. How much Ka'Kala valued his contribution, what a wonderful fellow, how brilliant, how tragic. The company didn't go into detail. At some point they have to address it. Ka'Kala's whole brand is based on social responsibility and empathy. I suppose they're leaving that for later. A fuller response. Once they figure it out."

"And you're still a fan?"

"I am," Oliver said. "But I do want to hear more from them. I think everyone does."

"They don't happen to import coffee, do they?" Callie asked, holding up her cup and making a face. "You could use some better coffee."

Oliver's mouth turned up in a crooked grin just as they heard a knock on the door. Before either of them could respond, the door opened. Oliver's grin solidified into an almost comical grimace and stayed that way for a good five seconds. Callie turned to see a vaguely familiar man in the doorway, probably in his mid-thirties — tall, darkly tanned, with a thin face, thin lips and his long, dark hair drawn back into a man bun.

The man's most distinguishing attribute was his right arm, which tapered down to a stump right above where his elbow would have been. Despite the coolish weather, he was wearing a Hawaiian shirt, a vintage one from the look of it. The short sleeves made an obvious statement: that his arm, or lack thereof, was a point of pride. Or at least, nothing unusual or meant to be hidden. "Sorry to barge in," he said, raising his half-arm in a half-salute. "Wasn't sure I had the right door."

"You're Beau Garrison," Oliver said, prying his mouth out of the grimace.

"I am," he answered simply then looked past Oliver to the woman with the messy ponytail and cup of coffee. "Are you Callie McFee?"

"I am," she echoed. "And you're Beau Garrison." As soon as she said the name, it came to her. He was the founder, technically the co-founder, of Ka'Kala. Unlike what felt like half the population her age, she was not mesmerized by the lure of healthy lifestyles and world fellowship and eternal betterment. She remembered him mostly from a popular documentary a few years back, chronicling the adventure that led to the truncated arm and the creation of Ka'Kala. She'd never seen it, but the ads had been everywhere. "And this is Oliver Chesney," she added, finally remembering her manners.

"Oliver," he said, reaching out his left hand. Oliver jumped up to shake it. "Sorry. I was literally a block away. We're looking to expand our offices. Anyway, I thought I'd drop by and make this personal." There was a modest, unstudied naturalness to him which, Callie knew, must have taken a lot of practice. "I love the *Free Press*, by the way. We keep a stack of them by our front door. I hope that's okay."

"Yes. Wow." It was the first time Oliver had spoken since he'd informed Beau Garrison of his own name.

"Callie," Beau said, "I was so devastated to hear of Trevor's death. We're all devastated. How are you holding up?"

"I'm fine." She wasn't. At the same time, she wasn't sure she deserved any more comfort than anyone else. "How did you know? About Trevor and me?"

"I know people in the department." Beau looked embarrassed. "They showed me the police report."

"Did Trevor have family?"

"Here in Austin, yes. Mother and father. No siblings. I went to see them this morning. They were somewhat estranged. But still, their only child."

"I didn't know. We were just getting to know each other." Callie stayed seated, which went against all of her upbringing. She had never thought to blame Beau and his company for Trevor's death. She'd been too busy blaming herself and her father. But the idea of extending the blame to include Ka'Kala was irresistible.

"I can't imagine how that must have been for you, finding his body. Trevor was such a big part of the Ka'Kala family."

"And yet you fired him. Just like that."

Oliver's gasp was soft but undeniable. She was criticizing Beau Garrison.

Beau took it with grace. "We had no choice. If I'd been convicted of a felony, it would be the same. In hindsight, we should have come up with a more equitable way to deal with the stock. When we wrote the bylaws, we were young and high-minded and stupid. It cost a man his life, and that's something I'll always regret." He bit his lower lip and took a deep breath. "If Trevor had… If Trevor had lived, I would have found some way; arranged for some of my own stock to be transferred to him."

"You can give his parents the money," Callie suggested.

"I'm afraid there's no way of doing that without having it look like blood money. But we will come up with an alternative. I promise you."

There was something about sincerity that always aroused Callie's suspicions. The more sincere, the more suspicion. It came with being a McFee. "Well, thank you for coming in person," she said. "I appreciate it."

It was meant as a dismissal but Beau didn't move. "I'm hoping you can come to a little memorial we're having. Tomorrow at the office."

"A memorial." Why would they want her at their memorial? To talk to the press? To field questions about his death? To help assuage their corporate guilt? "I'm sorry, but I'm working tomorrow."

"Callie, please." He made a pleading gesture, as if pressing his hands together, but with only one hand. "We would love to have you there. I'm not sure if his parents will be having a memorial."

"You can take the time off," Oliver informed her. "No problem."

Beau turned to Oliver, obviously the weaker link in this negotiation. "You should come, too."

"Really?" Oliver sounded delighted. "But I didn't know Trevor. Actually, I met him once."

"Well, it's not so much about the deceased. It's about those he left behind. I think it would be good for Callie to have a little support there. Please join us."

"Of course," Oliver agreed. "If you put it that way."

"Wait a minute," Callie said. "I just told you I'm working."

"I get it," Beau said. "We all have our ways of mourning. But I think that celebrating his life, acknowledging his passing into another plane of existence…"

Oliver nodded. "Absolutely. We'll be there. What time?"

CHAPTER 7

AT FIRST GLANCE, the flutes appeared to contain champagne. It was of the proper orangey-beige hue, with tiny bubbles that rose invitingly to the top. Callie accepted a flute from a server who was dressed much better than she. On taking a sip, she was surprised but not really surprised, given the venue, that the inviting liquid was something non-alcoholic, veggie-like and organic – very organic and probably guaranteed to extend your life by a year. She took a second sip and pursed her lips. Probably more than a year.

The Ka'Kala offices occupied a renovated warehouse a few blocks from where the *Free Press* rented its own space. But all the similarities – the location, the open floor plan, the brick walls and industrial accents left by the interior architect – only served to accentuate the differences. This was the office that Oliver could only dream of. The Ka'Kala employees also seemed to be from a more rarefied world – all fit, young, intense and somewhat interchangeable, like the human figures drawn into an architectural rendering.

Callie and Oliver wandered the polished native wood

floor, pretending they belonged. As with their space, there was only one walled-in office. Unlike Oliver's, this was a glass cube, impossibly seamless except for the glass door. The cube stood in the center of the action, a statement of transparency, saying that Ka'Kala's CEO had nothing to hide and that his fellow workers had nothing they should hide, either. "I guess he doesn't sneak in any afternoon naps," Callie quipped as she deposited her nearly full flute on a lacquered Southeast Asian sideboard.

"I don't nap." Oliver's tone was unconvincing.

The artwork was equally impressive, if not to Callie's taste. In pride of place was a huge, framed painting of a dark-skinned tribal man with a broad nose, in a primitive thatched hut, naked except for a loin cloth, his face painted, squatting on his haunches in front of a fire, mixing a brown liquid in a small, clay pot. Oliver watched Callie as she examined the painting. "That's Ka'Kala," he murmured.

Callie had a vague recollection that the company had been named in honor of a shaman from some remote corner of the world who had supplied the original formula for the company's original product – a salve or cream or some other healing agent. "He's from a lost tribe, right?"

"Not a lost tribe. They're called uncontacted peoples."

"Is that better?" She was curious. "Is 'lost' considered a value judgment?"

"These people know where they are, even if we don't. There are quite a few tribes in South America and the Pacific. Maybe a hundred. No one knows. Because of diseases and possible exploitation, it's illegal in most countries to try to contact them."

"And yet contact was made," Callie said, tilting her head toward the painting.

"You haven't seen the documentary?" He couldn't believe it. "*Balancing the Universe*. You have to see it."

The attendees, maybe fifty in all, had gathered in the space between one side of the glass cube and the tall windows facing in the direction of the river. On the wall of the cube were mounted two enlarged photos, both portraits of Trevor, one smiling, one not, both featuring his sandy brown hair, combed back with the perfectly done highlights. Even in these close-ups, one could sense the slightness of the man. Centered between them stood a small platform and podium. Callie felt suddenly depressed. "Do you want to mingle?" she asked.

"Sure," Oliver said. "Lead the way."

"No. I mean mingle by yourself."

"Oh." He took a step back. "I get it."

"I just want to be on my own. Sorry."

"No, I totally get it." He glanced around the cavernous space. "I think I'll go take a look at the shrine."

"Shrine? Shrine to what?"

He motioned back to an area near the elevators where a decorative archway led into a separate space. *The Ka'Kala Story* was spelled out in twig-like lettering over the entrance. "They have a little museum, with displays outlining the company's history. It's been in all the press."

"History?" Callie lowered her voice. "What history? They've been around like seven, eight years."

"It's part of controlling the narrative. I think it's kind of brilliant." Oliver toasted her with his champagne substitute and walked off toward the arch.

For a minute or so, Callie entertained herself by counting man buns and ponytails. She found five, six if she included Beau, who had no doubt originated the company trend. Beau, she saw, had forgone his Hawaiian shirt and chosen a black jacket over a black V-neck. As before, his right arm was on display, protruding from the jacket's cut-off sleeve. Maybe it wasn't a statement after all. Maybe it was just more comfortable.

A videographer with a Steadicam prowled among the mourners, or celebrants, or whatever people at memorials were choosing to call themselves. They were all speaking in low tones and looking a bit somber, so perhaps not celebrants.

Among all these inhabitants of a different, much healthier and more socially aware world, Callie was pleased to see a familiar face. The person standing next to the videographer, giving him instructions, was Joey Gibson, a boy – now a soft, stylish, mildly attractive man – whom she'd more or less grown up with. All through their childhoods, they'd attended the same schools, the same parties, the same political family events. Their fathers had even had the same job. Joey's father was the current attorney general of Texas, a position that Callie's father had held just a few years before.

Joey saw her from across the room, broke into a grin and rushed over as fast as a mourner could respectfully move. "Beau said you were coming. So good to see you. Not under these circumstances, of course." They kissed on both cheeks, a ritual they'd adopted in middle school, after Joey had informed her that this was French and very sophisticated.

It had been several months since they'd seen each other. "I didn't know you worked here."

"I do," Joey said. "Beau told me you were the unnamed friend who found the body. That must have been incredibly gruesome."

"We only knew each other for a short while. But yes, the stuff of nightmares. Literally, I'm afraid."

"I'm so sorry." Joey held her by the shoulders, at arm's length and scrunched up his face. "Are you okay? 'Cause you look like shit." Joey could always make her smile, even if the smile was a sad one.

"Trevor and I met through Dad. After the arrest, so it wasn't that long."

"I know. I mean, I know he went to your dad. I recommended him. Remember that drunk driving thing on prom night? Not only did Buddy make it disappear, but he managed to cover up that I was in the car with Tad Nicholson from the wrestling team – and that we'd been wrestling, if you know what I mean."

"You and Tad? Short, blond guy with the crew cut Tad?" Callie covered her mouth. "Dad didn't tell me that part."

"He didn't tell my parents either. And he didn't lecture me. Your dad's a stand-up guy." Joey's eyes turned serious. "I guess this was one arrest Buddy couldn't make disappear."

"Could we not talk about this, please?" Callie had been so happy to see Joey and she wanted the feeling to last, for a few minutes at least.

"All right," he drawled. "But, fair warning, you may have come to the wrong event."

They found a deserted corner and faced into it, essentially barricading themselves off. Joey raised his flute and was about to take a sip when he seemed to remember the contents. "Have you tasted this muck?" he asked, lowering it again. "I think they get the bubbles from rotting turnips."

Callie laughed. "I thought you'd be into this, seeing that you work here."

"Hell, no," he scoffed. "Give me a burger and a beer. No, Dad was an early investor. I was free-lancing in graphic design and doing pretty well. But he didn't consider that a job, not for his son. So now I'm creating labels that look like something an eight-year-old aborigine would draw using berry juice and a feather."

"So?" Callie leaned in, eager for the gossip. "So, is it a fake, all these exotically sourced, free-trade concoctions?"

Joey sighed. "Wish I could say yes. But Beau and everyone else are the real deal. They do their testing and research. And they believe. I'd say they all drank the Kool-Aid, but they never would." He looked down to his flute. "God, what I wouldn't give for a good, old-fashioned Kool-Aid."

Callie thought this over. "Ethical good guys. And yet they fired Trevor."

Joey edged her even farther into the corner and lowered his voice. "Beau feels really bad about that, even after Trevor came in here and said what he said." He paused. "I shouldn't be telling you this."

But Callie knew Joey and she knew better. "You're going to tell me."

"I am. I can't help myself." Joey glanced around. The others were slowly herding themselves toward the podium and the photos. "You can imagine what it was like when Trevor stormed in that morning."

"So, he came in after his firing. I didn't know that." Beau

had given her the impression that Trevor had killed himself before they'd had a chance to talk.

"He sure did. Was it two days ago? Yeah, two days. Beau took him into the cube. We call it the ice cube. But the room isn't soundproof. And, of course, it's transparent."

Callie inched a little closer to her old friend. "And?"

He smiled. "We weren't supposed to be eavesdropping, but we were. The whole office. I think we would have all put our ears up to the glass if we could have. Trevor did a lot of yelling."

"About what? The usual 'how could you do this to me?' kind of stuff?"

"Are you kidding?" Joey scoffed at the notion. "They were genuine threats. Big ones. 'I'm going to ruin you, you fake, sanctimonious piece of shit. I know. And I'm going to tear down this whole rotten place.' He didn't say 'rotten', but my prim and proper boyfriend won't let me talk like that."

"Trevor said that?"

"Yes, he said that." Joey saw her wide-eyed reaction and dialed it back. "People say all sorts of things when they're mad. It's human nature. You get fired and lose a fortune and you make threats. That's the kind of guy Trevor was. He fought back."

Callie was intrigued. "And do you think it's true? Do you think he had some dirt on the company? Or on Beau?"

"Come on. It's what angry people say. Maybe he had photographic proof that Beau ate beef or drank a Coke. Or that the company used slave monkeys to pick coconuts in Thailand."

"Slave monkeys? Forcing them to pick coconuts? Is that a thing?"

"Slave monkeys is a thing. And we don't do it. My point is that Beau felt terrible. He didn't yell back or argue. He absorbed all the abuse. Then..." Joey took a deep breath. "Then he asked Trevor not to do anything stupid. Man, the poor guy should've listened. He should..."

Joey stopped when they saw a shadow on the wall and felt the approach of someone else into their corner. It was a slight, unassuming woman – young, and with the demeanor of an assistant or even younger, an intern. "Excuse me. Joey?" She was almost bowing. "Beau says he's going to start."

"Of course," Joey said. "Thanks, Erin."

Erin responded with a half-smile then turned to Callie. "I'm so sorry for your loss."

Callie recalled her mother's advice about manners and her father's advice about not overexplaining. "Thank you."

"Trevor used to talk about you all the time. Reggie this. Reggie that."

"Oh. That was the girlfriend before me," Callie explained. "And I wasn't a girlfriend, just a friend."

Erin gasped. "Oh, my gosh, I'm so sorry. He used to talk about her, and then when people told me his girlfriend was here..."

"I'm just the one who found his body. I'm not sure if Reggie is here or not. I don't know if anyone contacted her."

"Oh, my gosh, I'm so sorry," Erin repeated. "I just assumed..."

"No problem." The moment had been somewhat mortifying, but more for Erin than for her. "You said they were about to start?"

Callie and Joey found a spot toward the back. Oliver

joined them. Callie made the introductions and they reached around her to shake hands. Then the lights dimmed, except for two pin spots on the portraits and one on the podium where Beau stood, reviewing his notes. Callie had to wonder. Who the hell designs a workspace with dimmers and pin spots?

"Hello. Thank you all for being here." Even though it wasn't a large space, Beau wore a lapel microphone. Callie assumed it was for the videographer who had set up in a prominent position just off to the side. "Especially Gareth and Wendy Birdsong. I appreciate how painful this must be for you." He motioned to a couple in their sixties. They stood by themselves, stoically erect, neither one touching the other for comfort.

"I don't have to tell any of you this, but…" Beau cleared his throat. "Trevor was an amazing man. He was with us almost from the start. When Naomi and I were still recovering physically and emotionally…" His eyes drifted to where his right arm would have been. "When Naomi and I had that little garage in East Austin and we were piecing together the Wepapua formula from our notes and our memories, Trevor got in touch. He wanted to be part of it. It was Trevor who suggested we take our haphazard little videos and craft them into *Balancing the Universe*. That film changed everything. It took us from a pair of naïve travel vloggers with maybe fifty thousand followers to what we are today – a real presence in the world of health and eco-sourcing. Trevor helped make all this happen."

Beau inhaled through his nose, as if fighting back a sob. "But he was more than that. Trevor was a phenomenon. I will miss his energy every day, his passion, the causes he believed in so fervently…"

It was a standard but intense eulogy, in Callie's estimation, and she wondered how much of this was hyperbole. She really hadn't known him. One date and a few drop-ins for iced tea, none of them under the best of circumstances. He hadn't seemed so remarkable, but maybe he had been. She began to feel an odd sense of loss, not for someone she'd known but for someone she would never get to know. Life, for all of its ordinariness and occasional boredom, seemed to hinge on these quick, unpredictable events that change everything – running a light or staying for a drink at a wine bar.

When Beau's voice grew more dramatic and insistent, Callie tuned back in. "And that is why the board at Ka'Kala is honored to create the Birdsong Foundation. All of Trevor's stock, the stock he would have maintained, will be placed in a charitable trust, every share."

Every share? Callie was impressed. Beau Garrison was giving up tens of millions of dollars in tribute to a man who had been threatening him just two days ago.

"It's the right thing," Beau continued. "I'm sure you all agree. Trevor's parents, Gareth and Wendy, have graciously agreed to administer the foundation, in support of the causes that Trevor was so dedicated to during his life. To Trevor and his foundation." His left hand, he realized, was empty, so he mimed a toast. A handful of people toasted back.

The announcement seemed to come as a surprise, and perhaps not a universally welcome one. A smattering of applause greeted the wildly generous commitment. The applause grew healthier as the Ka'Kala acolytes realized that they were expected to be thrilled by the news.

"Ouch," Joey whispered in Callie's ear. Oliver had taken a few steps away and was focusing completely on Beau.

"Why ouch?" Callie asked.

"For the past two days, there's been nothing but talk about how Trevor's stock would get split up. People were already doing the math. No one expected it to be taken out of the company."

"But it's for a good cause."

"And the good cause, my dear, is safeguarding Beau's reputation." Joey motioned to the videographer who was now front and center, refocusing from Beau to the Birdsongs to the 'thrilled' employees who were now whooping and high-fiving for the camera.

"I didn't even think of that," Callie admitted.

"Not to mention the sale price, which could have taken a hit."

Callie leaned in. "You know, you're even more cynical than I am."

Joey shrugged. "Let's call it a draw."

When Beau ran out of superlatives to describe Trevor's legacy, he called up Gareth and Wendy Birdsong to say a few words. They were a modest couple, both larger in stature than their son, Wendy dressed in a simple black dress and Gareth in a navy-blue suit, probably the only suit he owned. Both of them spoke, but only for a minute or two.

The memorial wrapped up quickly. The pin spots faded and the general lighting returned. The platform and podium were whisked away. Trevor's photos remained on the ice cube, but Callie sensed they would be gone by the next morning.

Oliver remained silent as he and Callie walked through the Warehouse District, back to an afternoon of work at the *Free Press*. It was only when they stepped into his private office that he spoke. "That was weird," he murmured as he settled behind his desk. "I mean, the foundation is a great move. Extremely generous and striking just the right note. But…"

"But what?"

He didn't seem to have an answer. "There was just a weird vibe. I did some listening. Everyone was saying the right things, the expected things. It just felt weird." Oliver shook off the feeling and for the next hour, the two of them discussed tomorrow's staff meeting and his ideas for the next issue.

Callie stayed late and did a light polish on Jennie's piece on next month's *Netflix* releases. By that time, the downtown rush hour was almost over and she drove directly back to the Ranch. Sarah had thoughtfully placed some leftovers in the fridge – a spicy beef stew with thick-cut potatoes and a side of cornbread. As dinner was warming up in the microwave, she opened a bottle of Chardonnay and set the table. She had promised herself not to eat dinner at the kitchen counter. A person had to maintain the trappings of a civilized life, her mother had once lectured her, even when living alone.

Ever since Oliver's comments, she'd been mulling over Trevor's memorial. Like him, she had no specific reason and, like him, she'd also felt a weird vibe. Perhaps it had just been Joey's cynicism rubbing off.

The microwave beeped and she switched on the overhead light in the dining alcove. Two weeks ago, one of the light-bulbs had given up the ghost, and now its partner decided to do the same, expiring with a little pop. Callie groaned and toyed with the idea of eating at the counter after all. The stew smelled so heavenly. Or she could eat at the alcove table, in the shadows. Or in the living room by the glow of the TV. But she remembered her mother's dictum and had just enough energy to solve this problem like a civilized human being.

Foraging in the laundry room off the other side of the kitchen, she found a two-pack of bulbs. There was also a stepladder in the laundry room, but she didn't feel quite that energetic or civilized. Placing a dining chair by the edge of the table, Callie stepped up and discovered that she could barely reach over to the ceiling fixture. If she really stretched. Stepping on the small oval table was too dangerous a proposition, so she leaned over, extended herself and began to unscrew the nearest of the bulbs. It didn't unscrew easily, so she stretched even farther and applied more pressure.

That's when the chair gave way, skidding on the hardwood floor and toppling onto its side. Callie followed suit, slamming onto the floor and landing on her hip, her breath forced out of her lungs. When her breath came flowing back, she erupted into a yelp, half out of pain, half out of shock. She had barely escaped hitting her chin on the table.

For a moment, she lay there, half under the table, rubbing her hip, listening to the microwave beep its reminder. Grateful that more damage hadn't been done, she looked down at her dress and moaned. She had neglected to change out of her memorial outfit, a silk, midi-length black wrap dress, one of her favorites because it fit so perfectly. It was something she wore only on special occasions. And now it had a tear, starting just below the waist and running almost to the bottom hem. The silk would be impossible to repair.

She berated herself for being so lazy. She should have changed as soon as she'd gotten home. It was what her mother always did, wore her favorite outfits only for events then changed the second she got home.

Callie continued to moan and rub and think back. But she wasn't thinking back to her mother. The image of Trevor's body filled her mind with a crystal clarity – leaning out over the tile floor, the red tie tight around his neck, with his buttoned-up dress shirt giving him a macabre, formal look. Callie stopped moaning. The breath went out of her lungs again. And when it came back this time, she muttered, "Holy shit."

She would later consider this her lightbulb moment, although the lightbulb itself had nothing to do with it.

CHAPTER 8

The next morning, Callie had her coffee and croissant standing at the kitchen counter. The fall had left a bruise on her hip, a blue-black mark, several inches long, that stretched from her left side, just below the navel, around to a part of her back that she couldn't quite see, even in the bedroom's full-length mirror.

It was a Saturday and, according to another matriarchal rule, personal phone calls could not be made before ten. Nine a.m. on a weekday. Ten on the weekend. It was a rule that Callie often ignored, but this call would be to State, who was as aware of it as she was. At ten exactly, she pressed his number and listened as his phone rang twice then went into voicemail. After two more attempts, she came to the conclusion that he was avoiding her. He could get like that. She was tempted to call from the gatehouse phone, a number that State had no way of knowing, but then decided that an in-person visit would work better. Showing up on his doorstep, she reasoned, would make her harder to avoid.

No matter how she approached him – by phone or by

Zoom or in person over a beer – she didn't expect this to be an easy conversation. They had been on the same side, appalled by their father's outrageous, self-serving theory. But then she'd had her lightbulb moment. True, it wasn't a high-watt bulb. Barely more than a glimmer. But it might just change everything.

Callie deposited her cup and plate in the sink. Through the curtained window, from this angle, between a pair of live oaks, she could see enough of the main house to notice a vehicle parked on the gravel drive. Vehicles seldom meant good news. This was a cobalt blue, hardtop convertible and she recognized it as Melissa's Mercedes. Her immediate thought was whether or not Gil was around to run interference.

Given the condition of her hip, she toyed with the idea of driving up, but a walk might seem more casual and less intrusive. Callie put on a light jacket and hobbled up the straight drive between the oaks. The front door was wide open, as it often was on pleasant days. To the left of the main hall, the door to her father's study was closed. The door to the right led into the dayroom, and it was here that Callie found Melissa, on a coach, leafing through one of the prehistoric magazines that were always gathering dust in the magazine rack. Melissa looked up. "I think I read this same one when I was a kid." She held up a copy of *Vogue* with a young, unsmiling Gwyneth Paltrow gracing the cover. "What happened to your leg?"

"It's my hip. A home repair accident. I'll be fine." Callie walked in and scanned the room. "Does Dad know you're here?"

"Your dad's a little under the weather. We had an appointment with him, but…"

"We?"

"Aunt Dee. She's in the study with Gil."

"Oh." Callie glanced toward the study. She hadn't seen Diedre Westerman in some time, not since that horrible afternoon when Diedre, still recovering from her first bout of chemotherapy, made the trip to Oakwood Cemetery, to the family mausoleum, to say her final goodbyes to her parents and younger brother. Buddy had delivered the eulogy on that cool, windy day and fully half of Austin society showed up to pay their respects.

After Callie had renewed contact with Melissa, she tried reaching out to Diedre, but Melissa explained that the ailing woman was refusing to take calls or see visitors. "How is she?" Callie now asked. It was a question she didn't really want to hear the answer to.

"Weak," Melissa said. "She's done with the chemo, so that's a blessing."

"Done with the chemo in a good way or a bad?"

"Bad." Melissa returned the copy of *Vogue* to the magazine rack. "It took too much out of her and it's not of any use anymore. She's here to discuss some old family business, I think. It's a shame Buddy isn't feeling up to it."

Callie didn't know what story Gil had spun, so she kept her response vague. "It's just a little something. Maybe contagious. I don't know. I'm sure he's acting with an abundance of caution where Diedre is concerned."

"That's pretty much what Gil said." Melissa got up from the couch then seemed to remember that they hadn't properly greeted each other. "Callie!" She extended her arms and they shared a tepid hug. "I've been trying to contact you. Are you all right? I'm sorry I fell apart when we found him. That must have made it twice as ghastly. But I really had no idea."

"Oh, please. I'm just sorry I dragged you into it."

Melissa brushed off the half-apology. "So, what does your dad think about this? I mean, Trevor was a client, right? That's what they're saying on Twitter."

"Yes, he was a client. I'm sure Dad would have worked with him to get his job back, but…" She sighed. "Who knows why people do what they do."

"Did he leave any note? I didn't see one."

"No note," Callie said.

"Poor guy." Melissa stepped out of the dayroom and into the hall. The door to the study was still closed. "Can I go upstairs to say hello to Buddy? I'll just be a minute."

Callie was tempted to physically block the stairs but refrained. "Probably not the best idea. Contagious, remember?"

"I can keep my distance. I hope it's not something serious."

"It's not." Callie had a good idea why her father was not appearing in public today.

Melissa was already starting to climb. Callie began to follow, her hip aching with every step. And then the door to the study opened.

Gil walked out first. He saw the two women on the stairs and seemed to immediately grasp the situation. "Melissa, sorry you had to wait. I think Diedre needs to go home."

"Oh." Melissa's hand gripped the banister. "I was just going up to say hi to Buddy."

"Another time," Gil said in a way that left no room for debate.

"Melissa?" Diedre emerged from behind Gil. She looked

so much older than Callie remembered. Never a large or robust woman, she now seemed even thinner and smaller. Callie had seen her own mother's transformation. It had been frighteningly quick. And now it was happening to one of her mother's best friends.

"Diedre. Hello."

"Callie!" A delighted smile creased across the older woman's face. She had been an Austin beauty, rivaling Anita McFee, but for some reason had never married; never even been engaged. "Don't you look wonderful. Let me see." She reached out her skeleton-thin hands and held Callie lightly by the arms. Her sunken eyes stared into Callie's. "Just like your mother, except for the hair." She tsk-tsked and shook her head. "That hair is pure Lawrence."

Callie smiled back and ran a hand through her unruly mop. "So good to see you." This was the standard, acceptable phrase when 'you're looking good' was simply inappropriate.

"Why don't you ever drop by?" Diedre scolded her. "You're always so busy, I guess, with your newspaper and your life."

"I'm sorry, Aunt Dee." Melissa came down the last few stairs, crossing to the older woman's side. "Callie has asked to come by more than once. But you said you didn't want visitors."

Diedre seemed puzzled. "I said nothing of the kind. I would love to see Anita's little girl. Maybe tea some afternoon."

"Then we have to arrange it," Callie said and kissed her softly on the cheek.

"That would be marvelous. Melissa, can we go now? I'm awfully tired."

Gil and Callie walked them out to the car and waved them

on their way, waiting until they had passed the gatehouse and turned onto Hacienda Drive. "I don't know what Diedre would have done if Melissa hadn't come back," Callie said. "It's very sweet of her."

"It is," Gil confirmed. "Although I'm sure she's expecting something in return."

"You mean an inheritance? That's what everyone's saying. Is there much?"

"Enough. The Westermans are old money, but it hasn't been well managed. A lot of foolish investments over the decades. Obviously, it's enough to get a relative to move in and be nice to you. That may be all we can hope for."

Callie paused and mulled this over. "Speaking of relatives, I take it Daddy's in a mood?"

"He is," Gil answered. "He's under sedation right now."

"Why is he under sedation?"

"This morning, he was up at four, wandering the woods, looking for a treehouse he built when he was ten. Luckily, he triggered the alarm, which goes off in my room. I caught him before he reached the road. He was confused and upset and I had to get Oppenheimer out of bed. We should connect the alarm to your bedroom as well, just in case."

Callie could feel whatever distance she'd been trying to put between her and Buddy vanishing like the illusion it was. "Do you think Sarah would move back into the house?" she asked. Sarah, the cook and housekeeper, was one of the few who knew Buddy's secret – Sarah, Callie, Gil and Dr. Roger Oppenheimer, the ex-surgeon general of Texas. Even State was clueless.

"She might. She's putting a niece through college, so I think she can be persuaded."

"What did Diedre Westerman want?"

Gil turned and headed back into the house. "You know I can't discuss a client," he shouted back over his shoulder.

Callie followed. "So, Daddy is still taking clients? Haven't you two learned your lesson? When is this going to stop?"

"She was a client. Long time ago." Gil returned to the study to retrieve a yellow legal pad from the desk, the same type that Buddy always used to take his notes. "Diedre had some questions about that... situation. Unfortunately, it was before my time. Those records were destroyed, so there's only Buddy's memories. If I happen to catch him on a good day, the woman may get her answer. If not..."

Callie was intrigued. Gil had been here for nineteen years. What kind of case could Diedre Westerman have been involved in so long ago? Gil would never say, so Callie tried to put it out of her mind. The Westermans, like everyone else, had their secrets.

Gil flipped over the pad and stuck it under his arm. "I saw the press release about the Birdsong Foundation. Smart move, P.R.-wise."

"Doesn't this run against the theory that they killed him for his stock? If they're going to give it away to charity?"

"Don't scoff. Your dad has good instincts, even in his diminished state." Gil leaned back against the desk and grunted. "Okay, he could have handled your brother better. Is State returning your calls? He's not returning ours."

"He is not. But it's Saturday, so maybe I'll drop over. Unless you need me here."

"To deal with Buddy? No, I've got it under control." Gil adjusted the yellow pad under his arm and headed for the hall and the stairs. "You go make peace with State." On the third step, he stopped. "Oh, and thanks for derailing little Melissa. I don't know what I was doing, leaving her out here. I think we're all losing our edge."

CHAPTER 9

Callie followed her sister-in-law through the living room, in the direction of the dining room and the kitchen. She tried to ignore the battle of young McFees going on overhead – the shouts and screams and slams and the loud, running footfalls. "Do they have friends over?" she had to ask.

"Nope. Just the two of them." Yolanda seemed unperturbed by the unseen violence. "It's when they go quiet that you have to worry."

As they reached the back door off the kitchen, Callie paused and lowered her voice. "Is he okay?"

"For the first day or so, he was a mess. Moody, a little manic. Like having another six-year-old. Then he suddenly got very calm, almost happy. A kind of Zen-like state."

"Sounds frightening."

"Like I said, it's when they go quiet… State never really defied his father, except by marrying me." Yolanda had come from one of the oldest, most respectable Greek families in Austin, which took them back less than a hundred years. Buddy had not been a quick convert. For that matter, neither had Callie. Yolanda was small and flinty, not at all like her large, eager-to-please husband. But it seemed a good match – a happy one, in which her hard edges helped keep him safe and his friendliness gave her a much-needed social life.

Yolanda opened the door and they looked out to see State, under the spreading branches of an ornamental Chinese chestnut tree that dominated the center of the lawn. He was calmly raking the fallen leaves into haphazard piles. "Maybe you can help," Yolanda added. "I don't mean with the raking."

"I know." Callie was fairly sure that what she had to tell her brother would not help, but it would almost certainly jolt him out of his Zen-like state. "I'll do my best."

State saw his sister approaching. "Callie." He broke into a welcoming smile and set aside his rake. "Sorry if I've been incommunicado. Did Dad send you over?"

"Nope. Here on my own." She playfully kicked into a pile of leaves and retracted her Merino woolen loafer with a spikey brown ball attached to the toe. "Oops." She bent over to pick it off. "Ow, ow, ow." It was a huge chestnut, still half ensconced in its prickly, protective husk. She licked her fingertip and saw that the skin had not been broken. "They're like little land mines."

Again, she tried to remove the pieces of husk, this time nudging them with her other shoe, which only made it worse. Now both shoes had been attacked by the little brown spikes.

State laughed. "Serves you right for kicking my leaves."

"I'm injured and my shoes are ruined. It doesn't serve me right."

"Your shoes are not ruined. Just one of them."

State returned to his raking while Callie cleared spot of

grass and eased herself down, being careful about her hip, then set about picking the spikes, one by one, out of the woven fabric. In a way, she was glad for the distraction. "Don't your kids impale themselves on these things?"

"The boys learned by the time they were three."

"Great. Now I'm injured, shoeless and dumber than a three-year-old McFee."

"If the shoe fits…" State chuckled. "Thanks for the other day, by the way. I don't think I would've had the nerve if you hadn't been there. I've never done anything like that. It felt good, once I got over the shock."

"I think we were all in shock." Callie took a deep breath. "State, did you go through with it? Did you list it as a suicide?"

He glanced around, as if checking for prying neighbors in this spacious, upscale section of Old West Austin, with its wide porches and flowing lawns. "Not quite yet." He sounded childlike and embarrassed. "I'll do it on Monday."

"Well, maybe you shouldn't. Just saying."

State's mouth opened into a tiny "O" and his brow crinkled. Then he let go of his rake and crossed to his sister's spot on the grass. "What the hell's up with you?"

"Nothing's up." Callie craned her neck to meet his gaze. She had thought a lot about this since last night. "I never took a careful look at Trevor's body. He was wearing a dress shirt, as I recall. Was his top button buttoned?"

"I'd have to check the photos. Why do you ask?"

"I'm thinking that wearing a dress shirt is a little unusual for a suicide. I get using the tie. He needed something long and strong. But dressing up?"

"He wanted to wear a nice shirt."

"So, he dressed up in a shirt and tie, then used the tie to hang himself. Does that make sense?"

State shrugged. "I saw a woman who did it in her wedding dress. She was sending a message to her ex-husband. That's what the note said."

"Yes. And that's another thing. The note. Trevor didn't leave a note."

"Why are you bringing things up? Okay, there's usually a note, especially for someone youngish and not sick. But…" State raised an index finger. "The text he sent you. That's almost a suicide note."

"I guess."

"So, what's this about the button?"

Callie had not yet voiced this out loud and worried that it might sound idiotic. "Trevor said that he wore a jacket and tie only for special events and meetings. A retro affectation, he called it. So, hear me out. What if he had some meeting or special event on the night he died?"

"You mean someone was with him in the house."

"If he'd been wearing a tie, then someone could have used it to strangle him. If he'd buttoned his top button, then that supports my theory."

"Someone strangled him?" The words came out phonetically, as if he were trying to parse their meaning.

"Then set up a fake suicide afterwards."

State took this about as well as she had expected. He began to pace in little circles, changing direction again and again. "Goddamn." He lowered his voice. "Goddamn you, Callie. After I follow your lead and say all sorts of things I never would have said… You're siding with Dad now? I can't believe it."

"I'm not siding with anyone. But if Trevor wasn't alone, that's big."

"Did Dad put you up to this?"

"No. The idea just came to me last night."

"After your bottle of wine and before the sleeping pills?"

It was a low blow and Callie felt the punch. "State, come on. That isn't fair."

"Just keep your ideas to yourself, okay? I'm going to file my report and that will be the end of it. Dad and Gil will have to solve their own problems."

"Can you at least check on the shirt? If the top is unbuttoned, then I'll stop."

State considered her offer. "And you won't tell Dad?" It was like he was twelve years old and she'd just caught him sneaking into the house after curfew. "The last thing I need is him grasping harder onto this murder nonsense."

"If Trevor's top button is unbuttoned, then there'll be nothing to tell him. Deal?"

Callie could see that he was struggling, so she stood up, brushed off her jeans, ignored the few remaining chestnut spikes on her shoes and held out her right hand with the little finger extended. "Pinkie swear?"

"Don't be an ass," her brother said. "Okay. Deal." And just for good measure, he extended his own little finger and committed himself.

As soon as they walked back inside, State dealt with the second-floor cacophony by sending the twins out to the back lawn, handing them two small rakes from a rack in the garage and two sets of gloves and instructing them to take over for him.

His office was in the front of the house on the second floor. When he closed the door, he and Callie could barely hear whatever new game was taking shape, undoubtedly something that involved spiny chestnut husks.

State booted up his desktop, accessed the APD site and asked Callie to turn her back while he called up several screens and input several codes. Callie was quite familiar with State's home office. With the leather sofa pulled out, it became a guest room and was where she'd first stayed on her return to Austin. This had been a hectic, not particularly pleasant time for her, and she wondered now if she might have accidentally left a few pills – some Xanax or Ambien – behind a sofa cushion or embedded in the shag area rug under the coffee table. The odds were pretty good that she had.

"Okay. You can look," State said. On his screen was the index page of Trevor Birdsong's case file. Callie had never discussed it with her brother, but she was sure that he missed the old days of real file folders stuffed with dozens of documents and photos. That's just who he was.

With a few more strokes, he pulled up a post-mortem shot. It was a close-up of Trevor's face, his head still loosely held in the necktie noose, his empty eyes staring at the camera. Callie was jolted by the sight and turned away. She forced herself to look again, just as State muttered, "Goddamn, you're right."

There was no mistaking it. Trevor's top button was firmly fastened, just as Callie remembered. "Do you know anyone who buttons the top one without wearing a tie?" she asked.

"That doesn't mean he had a guest. Maybe he thought of suicide as a formal occasion."

"And then he turned his tie around and hanged himself."

"People do all sorts of things."

Callie scanned the index bar across the top. "As long as you have it open, can you pull up his tox screen?"

State hesitated, as if he might say no or start to argue. But he clicked on the heading labeled "Blood Work" then pulled out a second chair, so that he and his sister could sit side by side.

Callie was the faster reader. "Alcohol in his system. Nothing else. Point oh-three."

"A drink or two," State suggested. "Probably two. Not legally impaired."

"Were there any bottles or glasses around? If he'd had a drink or two..."

State didn't have to check the file, just his memory. "There were no glasses or bottles out, which doesn't mean anything. Look, Callie, you're ignoring the most obvious explanation. You."

"Me?"

"You." He paused a second to let this sink in. "Trevor texts you. He wants you to come over. He gets dressed up – for you. He has a drink or two. He cleans up because you're coming. But you don't come. Things go darker and he kills himself."

Callie hadn't thought of this, that she was the expected guest. The dress shirt. The top button. The alcohol. "No," she protested. "Trevor wasn't the type to kill himself. Someone else was there."

State swiveled his chair from facing the screen to facing his sister. "That's what Dad wants to think because it absolves him of responsibility. The same with you."

"You're wrong. I'm following the evidence."

"You're not. That text message…"

"No." It couldn't be true. "Whoever was there killed him then sent that last text. It's the perfect fake suicide note."

State nodded in a slow, patronizing way. "Okay. Then the killer's prints would be on the phone. But…" He held up a finger. "But there were no unaccounted-for prints. Anywhere."

She pointed to the computer screen. "Did you check?"

"Yes, I checked. That would be major." He moved the cursor to the index bar and opened a window. "I'll show you." Running his finger down the screen, he found the report, picking out a few items as he went. "Front doorknob, your prints, other smudged prints. Kitchen doorknob: smudges, zero usable prints. Necktie: smudges, zero usable prints. Cell phone, zero prints." His face clouded over. "Zero?"

"No prints at all?" Callie asked. "Isn't that unusual?"

"It's unusual," he had to admit. "A cell phone collects prints like a magnet. Unless someone wipes them off."

"Someone wiped his phone after that last text. That's huge."

Her brother sighed. "I'll talk to the evidence officer. But yes, it appears that way. Damn."

Neither of them said a word as State exited the APD site and turned off his computer. Then he reached down to the mini-fridge at the side of his desk, taking out a mini-can of Dr. Pepper for himself and another for Callie. They both popped the tops and took their first sips.

Callie broke the silence. "If Trevor didn't send that last text, it means…"

"I know what it means." State wiped his mouth with the

back of his hand. "I'll tell my captain about the phone. It's a high-profile case, so he's under pressure to close it."

"Dad and Gil can help ease the pressure. It's what they do."

State pushed himself to his feet. "Goddamn, why can't this be simple? All I had to do was sign off. I should have done it yesterday. Every time you and Dad get into one of my cases…"

Callie sympathized. "Look, this isn't about Dad and me. I guess we do want it to be murder. But whatever we want doesn't change the facts. You can't sign off on this, State. Not yet."

"Yeah." He knew this, of course. "We still have a problem with the locked door."

"There could be an extra key. That's easy."

"And suspects. And motive."

Callie gave her head a little nod. "I'll get to work on that part."

"No, not you. Me. I'm the police, remember? This can't be like the last time. I'm serious."

The last time had ended well, Callie recalled. Well enough. She had also nearly gotten herself killed and her brother could have been suspended. "You're right. You're the police."

CHAPTER 10

SARAH AND ONE of her brothers, Jerome, spent all morning setting up the picnic. Gil had chosen a spot beside a stream that, during the height of summer, was little more than a moist gulley. There had always been a family dispute about whether this was an actual stream, as Buddy liked to call it, or just the runoff from the underground spring farther up the hill. With the recent autumn rains, the runoff had turned back into a stream and one of its banks provided a perfect little spot, now cleared of leaves and branches and covered by a checkered blanket. A hefty, century-old wicker basket provided the centerpiece.

Gil had held off the invitations, hoping that Buddy's health would be good enough for him to extend a last-minute call to State, Yolanda and the twins, but it wasn't to be. At some point, State would have to be told, but not today. It would just be the three of them – Buddy, Gil and Callie – lounging in the dappled sunlight and grazing on fried chicken, okra cakes and potato salad, washed down with lemonade. Angus Two had come along. He nosed around the stream, walked down the middle for about twenty yards then, deciding it wasn't worth any more effort, settled into a corner of the blanket. It was probably the quietest picnic Callie had ever attended.

With lunch over, Buddy lay on his back, legs crossed, fingers laced under his head like a pillow. His eyes were closed but Callie doubted he was asleep, just enjoying the rustle of the breeze and the quick, high song of a nearby sparrow. She had fond memories of similar picnics of four, including her mother and excluding Gil. She couldn't for the life of her recall anything they'd talked about, but there had been laughter, deep discussions about life, little fights with her brother and a feeling of comfort that she hadn't felt much of since her mother's death.

Buddy had been relatively quiet all morning, his face passive, his eyes vacant. The agitation that was so often apparent during his moods wasn't in evidence today. When she saw his breathing slow and heard him start to softly snore, Callie caught Gil's attention and motioned for him to join her beyond the blanket, at the edge of the clearing that Jerome had raked for them.

"Is everything okay?" she asked.

Gil nodded. "Oppenheimer is prescribing something now. Some blankety-blank inhibitor drug. It's supposed to help with memory, judgment, that sort of thing. It takes a while to kick in. Meanwhile, he's not as edgy. That's good."

"Good." Callie felt a small uplift of hope. "But it's not a cure."

"No such thing. Not yet." Gil rubbed his narrow chin. "Don't worry. Your dad will be first on the list. On other topics…" He seemed as uncomfortable talking about Buddy's condition as she did. "Your brother. Is he going to call it a suicide?"

"He's giving you some time."

"Good. I knew he'd listen to reason." His smile was faint but obvious. "We may have lucked out with the lawsuit. I'm getting no blips from anyone in the community. If Birdsong did lawyer up before his death, we should have heard something."

"What would you have heard?"

Gil laid it out. "If he'd gone to an ambitious lawyer, it'd be all over the media, with supporting evidence from the deceased. An email or recorded conversation. 'Buddy McFee's malpractice leads to suicide.' If he'd gone to one of our friends, we would be approached, and the story would get buried in return for some favor down the road. If he'd gone to a scumbag, then the scumbag would come to us for a payout. None of this has happened." He knocked twice on the trunk of a cedar elm. "So far."

"Lucky you."

"Lucky all of us." They heard a healthy snort coming from the blanket. It had been loud and powerful enough to rouse Buddy from his post-lunch slumber. The large man rolled over, pushed himself back onto his knees and slowly got to his feet. Gil leaned into Callie. "I miss your dad," he whispered.

"I miss him, too."

Buddy stretched and yawned then focused his gaze on the wicker basket. "Dad?" Callie said. "What are you looking for?" Sarah, it turned out, had put some of her famous brownies at the basket's bottom, under a napkin. They took one brownie apiece and, as they nibbled, abandoned the blanket and began to meander back along the trail. Buddy, more energized than before, led the way, while Callie pulled Angus Two away from the crumbs and shooed him in the direction of the house. Gil, bringing up the rear, texted Jerome and informed him that the picnic was officially over.

Their little excursion had prodded Callie into thinking about family, not just hers but in generalall families. What was it about this tribal connection that superseded everything else? A kindergarten playmate that you knew better than any family member, and liked much better, didn't have the pull on you that your most disgusting cousin did. It was just a fact. A person without a good friend might be considered unfortunate. A person without a family was a tragedy. Who do you build for? What is the meaning of life, if not for someone coming after you, with your blood in their veins, to make your existence mean something?

A stark, sad example was the Westerman clan. Their lineage in Austin society was longer than the McFees'. They had been as invested in their legacy as anyone. But in one tragic moment, an accident had claimed three of them. Diedre, the only surviving Westerman, had just given up on chemotherapy and was being made comfortable while she waited to die. As for herself, Callie knew that she was expected to marry and find fulfillment in adding to the next generation of Texas McFees, but she wasn't sure how much of this she believed in anymore.

Callie fully intended to spend the quiet Sunday afternoon sitting by the Juliet balcony in her bedroom, immersed in last summer's novel. She was up to chapter five now and it was finally picking up. But halfway through chapter six, the bookmark went in, the book got set aside and, on an impulse, she called Melissa. "Hey. Sorry to bother you on a Sunday, but I was just thinking about Diedre. How is she doing?"

"Oh, thanks for calling." Melissa was sounding upbeat. "Better today, thank you. She took a walk this morning and had the strength to complain about the gardening. Even did a little weeding."

"That's good to hear," Callie said. "I was hoping to come over, if that's okay. Sometime this afternoon?"

"What a sweet thought. I'll go ask." The phone was put on mute and it was at least two minutes before Melissa came back. "Callie? I'm so sorry, but Aunt Dee says she's not up for having visitors. Even you."

"Are you sure? When we talked yesterday, she seemed very excited."

Melissa was apologetic but firm. "I'm afraid that's just something that she says. When it comes down to it, there's always some excuse. Right now, she's too tired. Come tomorrow, it'll be something else."

Callie sighed. "Oh. Well, what about you? We can have that glass of wine we never had and discuss your documentary. Do you have a title for it yet?"

"Not yet. I keep going back and forth. Look, Callie, I'm afraid today's not going to work for me either. How about next week? I'll give you a call."

"No problem."

Callie put aside her phone. She was disappointed on several levels – disappointed that she wouldn't be able to visit her mother's old friend and disappointed that Diedre had not been honest about wanting visitors. Mostly she was disappointed that she was feeling bored and antsy on an empty Sunday afternoon. Spending more time with Gil and Buddy was out of the question. State had seen enough of her lately and vice versa. And she didn't really have any women friends, outside of a few from work – women who actually worked for her.

Her last possibility, always the last, was Oliver. Their relationship was a hybrid – part work, part personal – a mix that they both felt comfortable with. More than once, she had shown up on his doorstep with the excuse of discussing next week's cover. They would wind up sharing a tofu frittata and discussing their messed-up childhoods over a bottle of wine that she'd just happened to bring along. Callie didn't do it often because she didn't want either one of them, Oliver or her, to get the wrong idea.

Oliver lived in a two-bedroom townhouse in a small complex near Tech Ridge in North Austin. It was too early in the day to show up with wine, especially after Oliver had made a comment, more of a joke gone wrong, about her alcohol consumption. And she didn't call ahead, out of concern that he, like the others, might turn her down. If he wasn't home, well, then she would drop by the Whole Foods just off MoPac, pick up dinner from their prepared meals section then return home to her book. As Callie mounted the townhouse steps and rang the bell, she realized that she was breaking two more of her mother's rules, showing up unannounced and empty-handed.

Oliver opened the door with a broad smile that instantly, almost comically, fell. Callie blushed, her hands flying up to her mouth. "Oh, my... Were you expecting someone else? You were. I'm so sorry. I should have called."

"No, no," Oliver stammered. "Well, I guess I was. But that's fine. Come on in." And he stepped aside.

Callie walked in. "I would say I was just in the neighborhood, but I don't think that's possible, since you're not near anything. No offense. I should have called."

"No, it's fine. We haven't really talked since the memorial. It'll be good to catch up." Oliver bit his lower lip then raised an index finger and dabbed the air several times, as if pushing an invisible button. "Excuse me a second. I have to send a quick text." He retreated across the living room to his kitchen counter.

"Oh, my God, I'm seriously interrupting something. Was it a date? Please don't cancel a date on my account."

"It's not a date," Oliver said as he texted. "Just someone dropping over – like you, except they called first. I can change it to dinner. No problem. Dinner had been our first idea anyway." He finished then put his phone back on the counter, screen facing down. "So…" He looked up and grinned. "Just happened not to be in the neighborhood, huh? I have a choice of water and sparkling water."

"Regular water is fine. Thanks." Another rule: always offer hospitality and always accept. On the drive over, Callie had thought of something to talk about. "I know the situation has changed, with Trevor's death, but have you thought any more about a Ka'Kala article?"

"Not really." Oliver mulled it over as he retrieved a water filter pitcher from the refrigerator and two glass tumblers from a shelf. "I'm not sure what we can add, as a weekly. The media has been all over this."

"Yes, but we have something more. I found his body. And we were both at the weird memorial."

"I never said it was weird, just that I got a weird vibe." Oliver put ice in the glasses and filled them from the pitcher. "We're going to need more than that for an article."

Callie had toyed with the idea of heeding her brother's advice, of trusting him, of leaving everything in his quasi-competent hands. But deep down, she knew she couldn't. If Trevor had sent that last, suicidal text, she would have to live with it. But if someone else did it, then that someone had murdered a flawed young man she was just beginning to know. How could State possibly think she would walk away? If State believed that, it was his own damn fault.

She accepted the water but didn't drink. "Trevor was pretty angry. Obviously. According to my friend Joey – you met Joey – Trevor walked into Beau's office earlier that day and made threats, threatening Beau about something. And then hours later, he's dead." She didn't see any coasters on the nearby side table, so she kept the tumbler in hand. "You know, the police haven't yet ruled it a suicide."

Oliver didn't drink any of his water either. "And by police, you mean your brother."

"He's part of a team. But yes, State found some irregularities with the suicide theory."

"Was it State who found these irregularities or you?" When she didn't answer, Oliver groaned. "Why does he keep letting you into his cases? It's unbelievable."

"It just works out that way," she said. "Oliver, I want to look into this."

"I assume you're talking about murder and not an accident or some sexual auto-asphyxiation thing."

"Ew, no. Yes, murder." She waited while Oliver finally took a long, deliberate sip. "The last time I talked you into covering a murder, it turned out pretty well."

She expected Oliver to smile at the memory, but he didn't. "And you want my paper to accuse Beau Garrison of murder. Based on an argument they had inside a glass box."

"Or it could be someone else at Ka'Kala. Or unrelated to Ka'Kala, I suppose. Why don't we just say murder and let the chips fall where they may?"

"No!"

"Woah." She hadn't been prepared for this single-word rebuttal. "We can at least discuss it."

"No," he repeated. "I am not doing this." Only rarely had she heard him raise his voice. "I don't know what your agenda is, but I don't want any part of it. If word leaks out that Beau is even under suspicion… You don't know." He lowered his volume to an angry whisper. "This man has been through so much. He's brought the world so much good. And then some drunk employee gets arrested and kills himself… Let me repeat that; kills himself. I can't stop the police from pursuing this if they want, but I can sure as hell stop my own paper."

"So, you're actually forbidding me?"

"You can do whatever you want on your own time. Do it in a blog and get yourself sued. But it's not going to wind up in the *Free Press*. Period."

Callie could have said a dozen things in her defense but restrained herself. She had witnessed many political confrontations throughout her childhood, spying down through the balusters into the entry hall when she should have been in bed. One of the best weapons in her father's arsenal, she'd learned, was to force yourself not to respond. "An argument hates a vacuum," Buddy had explained to her. "If you don't have a good reply, then stay engaged but silent. Often as not, your opponent will start to explain, to rationalize, to excuse himself."

Oliver waited for her to react to his tirade, expecting something. The two stood facing each other, still in the space between the living room and kitchen, only a few feet away from the front door. He was just opening his mouth to say something more when…

"Oliver?" It was a woman's voice, just outside the door. "Oliver?" Then came three tentative knocks. "You all right? I heard you yelling at someone."

"I sent you a text," Oliver shouted through the door.

"Oh. I didn't look. Give me a second."

Callie thought she recognized the voice. She glared at Oliver then swung open the door to find Jennie Larson on the other side, staring down at her phone, a bottle of wine clutched in her free hand. Jennie jerked up her head and saw Callie. "I'll come back later," she whispered over Callie's shoulder to Oliver.

"You're dating the intern from work?" Callie asked.

Jennie was incensed. "I'm not an intern."

"I'm not dating her," Oliver protested. "And I'm not dating you."

"I'm twenty-four years old," Jennie said. "And you're like what? Twenty-eight?"

"Twenty-seven," Callie corrected her. "Barely."

"So, that's three years."

"I'm not dating her," Oliver repeated.

"So, what is this?" Callie pointed to the bottle. "A friendly Sunday business conference?"

"Well…" Jennie tossed her hair and straightened her shoulders. "I guess I could ask you the same. What is this? A friendly Sunday business conference?"

"At least I didn't bring wine." Callie placed her water glass on the side table, without a coaster, and stormed out. On her drive home, she missed the Burnet Road exit leading to the Whole Foods and her prepared meal. She wasn't in the mood anyway.

It wasn't as if she was angry with them for seeing each other. A little surprised, yes. But it was the combination, one on the heels of the other; Oliver's angry refusal to do the investigative piece followed by Jennie's arrival. This combination had left her with a familiar ache. It wasn't nearly as strong as the ache when her mother had died or when she and Buddy had stopped speaking a few years back, but it was the same. The ache of abandonment. With two quick blows, Oliver and the paper had both abandoned her. At least that's the way it felt.

Dinner turned out to be a bottle of wine and the remains of a box of Cap'n Crunch from the back of her cupboard. Sugar and alcohol. It wasn't the first time she had made this menu selection.

CHAPTER 11

Monday morning dawned slowly, at least her consciousness of it did. At some point, she became aware that her fuzziness had morphed into a headache then a throb that kept time with her heartbeat in an annoying, almost frightening way. Did her heart really beat this much? Closing her eyes helped a bit, but then the dizziness took over. Callie forced herself to her feet, knowing that she desperately needed water and a couple of Advil.

When she felt strong enough, she went down the stairs and found the kitchen right where she remembered it. Coffee would be her first goal, and she was surprised to see that her phone was in the refrigerator, occupying the spot normally occupied by the cannister of coffee beans.

The cold, little rectangle still had juice and was working. That was good, although it was a mystery why she'd put it there in the first place. Facial recognition recognized her face, reassuring her that she still looked something like herself. A check of her log showed that she had indeed been on the phone last night, an eight-minute-plus call to or from a local number. No name popped up, so it hadn't been anyone from her contact list.

Her phone also told her that it was currently 9:37 a.m., a proper enough hour on a weekday. She took several deep, cleansing breaths then pressed redial. The phone at the other end rang an impressive number of times. Could it be a landline? Who on earth still used a landline? "Good morning," said a familiar voice. A woman's voice. Middle-aged or older.

"Hi. Um, this is Callie."

"Callie, dear. I hope you're not calling to cancel."

"Diedre?" It was worth a guess. She remembered thinking a lot about her mother's friend. "No, I wouldn't think of canceling."

"Good. We'll have a modest lunch and then, if you wouldn't mind, maybe run an errand together? If I can impose?" It was definitely Diedre Westerman.

Callie couldn't figure out who had called whom last night. And who had gotten whose number and from where? "Of course." She vaguely recalled the conversation now. "Around noon? Twelve-thirty? I'll come by the house."

"Noon would be wonderful."

"I'm so glad you changed your mind about seeing me."

"Don't be daft. I always wanted to see you. Melissa can be a little protective, that's all."

"Good. Then I'll see you at noon." Doing the math, she had over two hours to pull herself together and make the drive. She had done more with less. Piece of cake.

Callie felt no compunction about blowing off a morning at work. After yesterday's confrontation, it would serve Oliver right to think she was on the verge of quitting. She knew how his mind worked and skipping half a day, perhaps a full day, made strategic sense, even if she wasn't facing a hangover and a lunch appointment she barely remembered making. From the clean, unwrinkled section of her closet, she chose a blue and white floral shift, its design reminiscent of a Delft porcelain vase. It was more of a springtime choice than a fall one, but she hoped Diedre would understand. She pulled her hair back with a claw clip then added a little concealer under her eyes.

The Westerman family home was impressive, but not huge by Texas standards, perhaps five bedrooms, built in the west foothills at least half a century ago, with white two-storied columns holding up a classical pediment.

Callie parked her truck at the top of the winding drive. Diedre answered after one ring of the bell, greeted her with a substantial hug and invited her through to the dining room, which had already been set up with a cold chicken salad, croissants on the side, plated for two at an intimate end of a table built to comfortably seat ten.

The petite woman was well dressed, wore makeup and appeared stronger than when Callie had previously seen her. Callie attributed this to the end of the chemotherapy; a final, false spring of health. Diedre had served herself a smaller portion and ate most of it. The two made small talk, reminiscing about Anita McFee, sharing stories about Buddy and gossiping about Melissa. It was all very pleasant, a welcome respite for them both. But Callie sensed a nervous, unexplained energy.

They had barely finished when Diedre began to clear. Per her own rules of hospitality, she did not allow Callie to help. "I have a big favor to ask," she said as she returned for the water glasses. "Feel free to say no. I totally understand."

"I would never say no," Callie insisted, although she was wary of any request that began with a disclaimer.

"I need to visit a friend," Diedre went on. "I suppose I could drive myself, but I like having the moral support. And it's a long way, perhaps forty minutes."

"Of course," Callie assured her. "I have nothing planned."

"Oh, thank you." There was a note of relief in her voice. "Normally, Melissa takes me, but she's in classes today and… And I don't think she likes taking me, to be honest." She had returned to the dining room where she checked her hair in an old oval mirror then checked her watch. "We should hurry if we want to make visiting hours. They're very strict."

"You have a friend in the hospital?" Callie asked. This made sense, giving all the time Diedre had spent in places like that.

"Oh, no, dear. In prison." She turned from the mirror with a sheepish smile. "Is that all right? It's a long story."

CHAPTER 12

THE DRIVE TO Kyle was a straight shot down I-35, with the Kyle Correctional Center, a minimum-security prison for men, situated on a dusty access road beside the freeway. Diedre sat tall in the passenger seat, keeping her eyes on the road.

Callie promised herself not to pry. "So, tell me about your friend in prison," was not a question she was willing to ask this patrician woman she'd known since childhood.

"His name is Kyle, like the prison," Diedre suddenly volunteered, just as they turned onto Frontage Road. "We were friends in high school. Kyle got into trouble. Drugs, I'm afraid. He's been in and out of the system. We didn't reconnect until just a few years ago when his sister friended me on Facebook." She grew silent again, until a large metal sign indicated an upcoming right turn. "There's parking all along the front. Take off your jewelry. Bring I.D."

"You want me to go inside and visit?"

"I would love that, yes. I got you on the pre-approved list this morning. Using your father's name does wonders." She saw Callie's hesitation. "You don't have to say much. Oh, by the way, that's a very nice dress. Cheerful. The inmates like that."

The prison, she saw, was a low-rise series of buildings connected by enclosed walkways, centered in a treeless, nearly grassless compound surrounded by a fence topped with barbed wire. Once inside, in the small entry room, Diedre greeted the guard by name. Harvey. And he called her Deedee. Callie followed her lead, listening intently to the rules and procedures as Harvey spouted them off. She had never been in a real prison before, but if Diedre Westerman didn't act nervous then she certainly wasn't going to.

The visiting room was large, bright, painted off-white and lit by overhead fluorescents embedded in a drop-tile ceiling. It reminded Callie of her own workplace, except that here there were no cubicles, just rectangular, white tables bolted to the floor and blue plastic chairs, which were actually more comfortable than the ones in her office.

Kyle Grainger was already at a table when they walked in. Like the dozen or so other inmates in the room, he wore white sneakers, white trousers and a white, loose-fitting collared shirt over a white T-shirt. Callie's overall impression was of a factory floor where they might be making silicon chips.

Diedre's lips curved up into a grin as she headed for the table. Kyle smiled back, revealing a gap between two of his left rear teeth. He didn't stand. Perhaps it was against some regulation. Touching, as they'd been warned, was definitely against the rules. Diedre sat down opposite him while Callie sat as far as possible to one side, trying to give them a modicum of privacy.

The inmate was smallish, slight, pale and slim, with a shaved head. He looked to be about the same age as Diedre, which was probably ten years older than their actual ages. In one case, this was to be blamed on disease; in the other, prison life. He was still a handsome man with small features, wide-set eyes and prominent cheekbones.

Diedre introduced Kyle to her companion, and that was Callie's last part in the discussion. She tried not to pay too much attention, although the subject matter seemed comfortingly ordinary, as if a continuation of a much longer, multipart conversation. Was he getting along better with his cellmate? Did Kyle need anything from the outside world? You wouldn't believe what so-and-so did. Even without physical contact, there was a clear, almost heartbreaking intimacy.

As they talked, Callie became fixated on a tattoo, a crude prison tattoo on Kyle's left forearm. It was the only one that she could see: a Christian cross entwined with ivy, with a date below it. 9/23 /1991. Diedre's gaze also fell on the tattoo and lingered in a way that left little doubt in Callie's mind.

As they left the prison, accompanied by a guard, through three sets of steel gates, neither woman spoke. It was only when they were in Callie's Yukon, pulling back onto I-35 that Diedre finally said, "Thank you."

"You're welcome." Callie felt she had to ask the question. "How long did he live? Or she?"

Diedre didn't look shocked. "He. How did you know?"

This was one of those times when simple, deductive reasoning seemed like an intrusion. "It's obviously a memorial. His tattoo. It has only one date, so birth and death were on the same day. I doubt it was a sibling of his, the way you were looking at it. You said you knew each other in high school. In 1991, you would have been..." She hazarded a guess. "Sixteen?"

"Fifteen," she answered quietly, without obvious emotion, as if telling someone else's story. "The most beautiful baby. I named him Stephen and he lived for an hour and six minutes. I was holding him when he began to cry. Then a heart monitor started beeping. They took him out of my arms and I never saw my boy again. Just like that."

"Never?"

"When the doctor told me, I got hysterical." Diedre let out a soft, closed-mouth groan. "Beyond hysterical. Everyone thought it was the right choice, not to see his body. Now, of course, I regret not holding him one last time."

"What happened between you and Kyle? After."

"My parents meant well." She had turned her head and was talking into the side window. It was just starting to rain. A few heavy drops. "I know the nineties weren't all that long ago, but this is Texas and I was fifteen. Kyle was seventeen and getting into trouble even then. I hid it until I couldn't hide it any longer. Then my parents sent me to a place in Dallas. It was summer and all my friends traveled. No one suspected. Even Kyle didn't know, not that I was pregnant or any such. Not until I started visiting him here."

"That must have been impossibly hard. At fifteen?"

Diedre nodded into the rain. "You think I would have told someone – Kyle or one of my girlfriends – but I was too ashamed. And worried about my family. And feeling guilty. Did I do something wrong? Could he have lived? All those months when I went to school, pretending it wasn't happening… Maybe with a doctor and some prenatal care…"

"You can't think like that," Callie said, but she was sure she would feel the same way.

"I always meant to marry and have children. I always loved the notion of grandkids running around the same house I grew up in. But after that… At fifteen. And then never getting to talk about it to anyone… My parents never mentioned it again, like it never happened."

"You're talking to me," Callie pointed out.

"Yes, you and Melissa. I never even told your mother. She and I didn't meet until years later, but even then I was too ashamed."

"Was Kyle the love of your life?"

Diedre's chuckle was barely audible. "That would not have been a good marriage. Can you imagine? But he was my first love and we had a beautiful child together." She turned away from the window. Together they listened to the swipe-swipe of the windshield wipers. "What about you? Do you have a love of your life? Your father mentioned this young publisher you work for."

"Oh, God, no!" Callie was startled by her own vehemence.

"Well, don't wait too long. What about using one of the websites? A lot of people meet that way."

"I tried one of the websites," Callie said, shaking her head at the unpleasant memory. "Who knows? Maybe I'll try again."

For the next half hour, they fell into an easy pattern of small talk – the weather, politics, and their fond, funny memories of Anita McFee. By the time they reached the Westerman house, they had driven through the rain, and the sky was starting to clear. They both spotted the blue convertible at the top of the circular drive. "Oh, dear," Diedre said, almost under her breath. "Looks like we've been found out."

Callie was just helping Diedre out of the truck when

Melissa stepped out onto the portico, brushing her short hair back over her ears. She had a talent for smiling and saying the almost right, almost gracious thing while maintaining a certain coldness around the eyes. "Callie. Thank God. I thought Aunt Dee might have gotten herself kidnapped. Guess you two were just out for a little joy ride."

Almost instantly, Diedre was apologizing. "I'm sorry, dear. I should have left you a note, but I didn't think you'd be back. Callie was sweet enough to take me to see Kyle."

Melissa seemed to take a moment to process this statement, her smile freezing then unfreezing. "Callie, you didn't have to do that. But it was so nice of you to look after her."

"My pleasure. It was a great afternoon." Callie gave an arm for Diedre to lean on. Halfway up the steps, Melissa offered her arm and took over, like someone accepting a package for delivery. At the top, Diedre turned to Callie, said a soft, simple 'thank you' and disappeared into the house. Melissa followed.

Callie stared through the open, empty doorway, feeling somewhat awkward. Should she drive off? Should she join them inside? Should she wait a minute or two and then text Melissa? Callie was still weighing her options when her phone rang. She was surprised to see it was her brother. "Hey," she said. What's up?"

"Just checking in." From the background noise, predominantly male voices echoing off the walls, she assumed he was at the police substation. "I called you at work and your boss said you didn't show up today."

"What? You're checking up on me at work?"

"Wanted to make sure you're not doing anything stupid."

"No, I'm not doing anything stupid. If you must know, I spent the day with Diedre Westerman, mother's friend."

"Oh. Well, that was sweet of you. How is she?"

"Today was a good day," Callie said. "And a very interesting one. If you like, I can put her on and she can verify my whereabouts."

"Don't get snarky," State said. "Oh, I thought you might like to know, before it hits the press, that the case is now officially labeled suspicious. Warranting further investigation, as we like to say." He paused. "You're welcome."

"Thank you."

"You can pass this on to Dad, if you like."

"Why don't you pass it on? I know he wants to hear from you."

She could almost hear him considering it. "Nah, I think we'll let this rest for a while."

"Well, Dad will be glad to hear it. Was there anything besides the wiped cell phone?" She wondered how much further State would go with his revelations, if there was anywhere further to go.

"Nothing much," he replied. "Some bruising across the fingers of both hands. Could be signs of a struggle. Also, fibers under his fingernails. From the tie. On the negative side are the ligature marks across the front of his neck, a V pattern, in keeping with a hanging suicide."

"Right." She had already looked this up online. "Those marks could mean he was strangled from behind by anyone a little taller. With Trevor, that's a lot of people."

She heard a page turn and visualized her brother flipping through his notepad. "There's also the house key. It's one of those complicated 'do not duplicate' numbers. We talked to the locksmith who installed it and examined his records. He made two spares, both of which we found in a kitchen drawer."

"Any key can be duplicated. We're not talking Fort Knox." Callie had not looked this up. But it made sense.

"I suppose," State half agreed. "But that would necessitate having one of the keys to start with and then taking some time to make the copy. We have no indication that this happened."

"Was there anything else in Trevor's house?" Callie was vaguely aware that she was crossing a line, that she was asking State to tell her things he probably shouldn't.

"That I can't tell you," State confirmed. "But rest assured. We spent the whole day there and got everything we could."

Had they gotten everything they could? Callie doubted it. She leaned up against a pillar and sighed. "So, basically all you have is Trevor's wiped-off cell phone. And your lieutenant is willing to call that murder?"

"No," he reminded her. "Just warranting further investigation."

"Got it." Callie pushed herself away from the pillar and looked off to her left. "Oh, shit."

"I thought you'd be happy."

"No, it's not that. It's something here. State, I have to go."

"Okay… Is everything okay?"

"Not really. Look, I'll tell Dad the news. And I'll call you back when I can. Bye."

Callie pressed the screen's red circle then returned her gaze to the open doorway. Melissa stood there, mouth hanging open. How much had she heard? How much had there been to hear? "You're saying Trevor was murdered? That's crazy, right? How?"

"Absolutely crazy," she answered reflexively. "Actually, it's not crazy."

Melissa stepped out into the portico. "Sorry if I was listening, but… You said Trevor's phone had been wiped? You mean like fingerprints?"

If Callie had had a few minutes, she might have come up with a convincing lie. If this were anyone but Melissa, the person who had discovered the body with her… She came closer and spoke in a whisper. "You have to promise not to tell another living soul. If my brother finds out that I told you…"

"I absolutely promise."

"Good," Callie said. "It will be good to talk this over."

And with that, the two childhood friends settled onto the steps of the Westerman home and talked through the events of that evening, from Callie's multiple attempts to contact Trevor, to his first, unexpected text when she was just sitting down, to his last, right after Melissa had joined her at the wine bar. Melissa asked to see the texts and Callie saw no reason not to show them to her.

"So, who sent the texts?"

Callie shrugged. "I don't know. Maybe Trevor sent the first ones and the killer sent the last one. That's just a guess."

"Or Trevor sent them all, and the killer wound up touching his phone for some reason."

"What reason?"

"To check Trevor's messages. To see who he'd been talking and texting to. Then he wiped off his prints."

"That's a possibility," Callie allowed. "There were several minutes between us leaving the bar and breaking into his house. A lot could have happened during those minutes."

Melissa thought over the possibilities then broke into a sly grin. "Are you going to investigate?"

"Investigate? No. I mean, we are planning a story about Trevor's company. It's newsworthy."

"So, you are going to investigate." Melissa glowed with an almost childlike excitement. Callie had rarely seen her so engaged. "I so admire what you did with that murder last spring. Truly. Let me help."

"Help? No, no. I'm just writing an article."

"An investigative article. Meaning you're investigating. Come on. We found the body together. I'm part of this." Melissa leaned in. "Do you think they did it? Someone from Ka'Kala? Beau Garrison? I love their sunscreen moisturizer, by the way. You should try it."

Callie ignored the veiled suggestion about her skin tone. "Absolutely not. Aren't you busy with classes? And your project?"

Melissa waved it away. "Oh, they can wait. I'll file for an extension. It's not nearly as exciting as this."

An extension on Buddy's documentary? An extension sounded good to Callie. "How could you help?"

"Well, first of all, two heads are better than one."

"It depends on the heads."

"And you're a well-known reporter. People are going to be wary, talking to you. Me, I'm just an adorable college girl."

Callie took a moment to consider the advantages: having a partner to help bounce around ideas, now that Oliver had refused to help; also, giving Melissa a project to take her mind off her documentary. Callie took an extra moment. "Let me think about it."

CHAPTER 13

That night, Callie set two alarms, her clock alarm and her phone. Tomorrow, Tuesday, was going to be the first day of her investigation and she was determined to get it right this time. No drunken impulses or half-baked ideas. At least not on Day One.

On her drive into the city, she made a detour south to Davis Street and cruised by Trevor's bungalow three times, at five-minute intervals. From what State had said, his crew had spent all of yesterday here and may well have released the site by now. On her third pass, Callie confirmed that there was no police presence and no activity in the house.

Even after taking the time for her surveillance, Callie was the first to arrive at the *Free Press*. She had never arrived first before, and it took her a while to figure out where all the light switches were. When the others dribbled in, she made a point of being seen. Oliver greeted her with a meek "good morning" as he scurried past. Jennie's greeting was similarly meek and quick. Callie didn't care. Her aim was to make herself as obvious as possible – dropping by cubicles, discussing assignments, brainstorming ideas – before sneaking off to an early "lunch".

The Birdsongs lived on the other side of the river, in a modest ranch-style house on a modest street in the relatively modest neighborhood of Barton Hills. She had called ahead, with her story all worked out. She had been a friend of Trevor's toward the end, she told them. And just for good measure, she mentioned her father's name.

Wendy Birdsong didn't offer her anything to drink but welcomed her in and told her to make herself comfortable in a tattered club chair facing the sofa. Callie expressed condolences for her loss and Wendy accepted the sympathy without comment.

"Excuse me," Wendy said then crossed to the hallway leading down the length of the house. "Gareth!" A few more shouts down the hall brought Gareth Birdsong into the dimly lit, low-ceiling room. He also accepted Callie's sympathy then felt compelled to explain why he was at home in the middle of the day. "I just retired. A little over a month. Still getting used to it. Probably napping more than I should." He covered his mouth and suppressed a yawn.

"Where did you work?" asked Callie.

When Gareth hesitated, Wendy jumped in. "The Austin Country Club. Gareth worked security. I worked in the kitchen years ago, until Trevor came along."

"Oh." Callie smiled. "My family belongs." It was the oldest, most exclusive club in Austin so, of course, the McFees belonged. "I must have seen you there a dozen times."

"Maybe," Gareth said. "I used to see your father but never actually met him. Good security stays in the background."

"He seems like a very charismatic man," Wendy added. "When Trevor told us Buddy McFee was handling his legal problems, we were impressed."

"It didn't turn out so good." Gareth lowered himself into one half of the deeply cushioned sofa, pulling his polo shirt down to cover his girth. "That wasn't Mr. McFee's fault. He didn't have a lot to work with."

"Trevor was always headstrong," Wendy said. "I know the police are holding off calling it a suicide, but it obviously was."

"Suicide is a very selfish act," Gareth added.

Callie didn't know what to say. Beau Garrison had mentioned that Trevor and his parents hadn't been on good terms, but she hadn't been prepared for this. From what she knew of their son, he was many things. But he was nothing like these straitlaced, hard-edged people. "He was your only child." She tried not to make it sound judgmental.

"We never thought we could have children," Wendy said as she joined her husband, sinking not quite as far into the folds of the sofa cushions. "Trevor was like an answered prayer. We did everything we could to create a good home, a loving environment." This was as emotional as she would let herself be.

"We shouldn't bore our guest." Gareth reached over for his wife's hand and gave it a squeeze.

Wendy winced and nodded then looked up, straight into Callie's eyes. "Someone pointed you out at the memorial. Our boy was dating Buddy McFee's girl," she said with a note of pride. "Little Trevor."

"I liked Trevor. A lot of people did." Why did she have to defend their son to them? "That memorial was quite a tribute. And that foundation! Think of all the good you can do."

Gareth seemed to agree, at least partly. "It's a big responsibility. No matter what Mr. Garrison said in his speech, Trevor didn't have a lot of causes he was gung-ho about. Nothing he told us. I suppose some liberal, earth-saving eco thing. I know that's what Garrison and his folks are into." He turned to his wife. "We can always give it to the church."

"Now, honey…" They had obviously had this discussion. "It's supposed to be about Trevor, not us. Besides, I'm not sure what Pastor Tom would do with thirty-six million dollars."

"Thirty-six? That much?" Callie was impressed.

"That's the current number," Gareth said. "They say there's a bidding war. Not that it affects us. All it means is more work and worry."

"Well, I'm sure the foundation can hire a director to handle it." Callie had some experience dealing with foundations, mostly on her mother's side.

"We're already hearing from people," Gareth said, a wry smile lifting the corners of his thin mouth. "We got an email from a native bird preservation society. Guess they think the Birdsong Foundation is about birds."

The three of them shared a little laugh. "Callie, dear?" It was the first time Wendy had used her name. "Do you have any ideas? What was Trevor interested in?"

"We didn't know each other that well," Callie confessed. "He was still getting over his last girlfriend, so things never got very serious."

"You were the one who tried to save him," Gareth said. "That's what the police told us."

She nodded. "I got there too late."

"It's not your fault in any way." Wendy leaned forward

and reached across the coffee table. Their hands met halfway but for just a second.

Callie took a deep, focusing breath. Now seemed like the right moment. "I'm afraid I did leave a few things over at his house. In all the confusion. The police said I couldn't remove anything from the scene, so I was wondering if…"

"Well, your timing is excellent," Wendy said. "An officer dropped off Trevor's keys just this morning. Gareth can go with you to pick up your things. Can't you, Gareth?"

"Sure. I suppose."

Callie had been afraid of this, but it was still workable. She would go with Gareth and 'retrieve' a few innocuous items from the bungalow. When Gareth's back was turned, she could simply unlatch a side window for a future, less formal visit. It would add one extra step to her plan, plus an act of breaking and entering. "Or… Or I could borrow a key," she suggested. "If that would be easier. I can drop it back this afternoon. Or have a messenger drop it off. It's really no bother."

"I hate to make you come all this way," Wendy protested.

"I can ask a messenger from work to do it. They enjoy getting out of the office." She had no intention of doing this, of involving a witness to her possession of Trevor's key. She would return it herself.

"All right." Gareth seemed more agreeable to this arrangement. "Sounds like a plan." Before Wendy could protest again, he forced himself up from the folds of the sofa and crossed to the end table by the front door. When he opened the junk drawer, Callie could see him pull out a small manilla envelope with the APD logo emblazoned on it. He poured the three 'do not duplicate' keys into his other hand then handed one to Callie.

"Thank you so much," she said. "I'll make sure to have someone get it back to you. Is tomorrow morning okay?"

CHAPTER 14

It was slightly after five when she parked in the lot on Driskill Street and walked. Neither of them would be parking in front of the bungalow. No reason to draw attention. Melissa was already waiting on the corner of Davis, looking casually, effortlessly elegant, even in her black sweatshirt and black skinny jeans. She took a few steps toward Callie and twirled. "You like? It's my cat burglar outfit."

Callie winced at the implication. "No, technically, this is legal. His parents gave me permission and we have a key." When exactly, she wondered, had she gone from 'this is the right thing to do' to 'technically, this is legal'?

"But we'll still be burgling," Melissa said.

"Only technically."

Callie had gone back and forth about bringing her along. In the end, she'd decided that another pair of eyes and ears would be an asset, as long as Melissa treated their mission seriously. This would be a test.

It was early on a Tuesday evening, and foot traffic on the two-block-long street was nearly nonexistent. Callie had the key in her hand, ready to use, as the two women hurried through the gate and up to the porch. The broken sidelight by the door had been covered over with a piece of plywood nailed in place. Once inside, Melissa locked the door behind them. Her hand hovered by the wall switch. "Lights or no lights?"

"Let's try no lights," Callie said. The house wasn't quite as dark as she remembered. "If you need to use a flash, I guess that's okay."

"Got it. Now remind me. What are we looking for?"

"Anything about Ka'Kala. If Trevor had some dirt on the company, or on Beau, he wouldn't keep it at the office. Photos, documents, letters. Take a lot of pictures and we'll sort it out later."

"Wouldn't the killer have found this thing and taken it with him?" Melissa asked, not unreasonably. "Or the police? They've been combing the place for days. Don't get me wrong. I like a good break-in, but…"

"I don't think we'll find a big clue," Callie admitted. "But maybe something small will lead to something else. This is the first time anyone's been in here besides the cops and the killer."

"And us. Twice now." It was a sobering thought.

Melissa started in the living room while she took the kitchen. Neither were rooms where they anticipated finding a clue, but it was good to get them out of the way. Callie tried not to think about the last time she'd been in this kitchen.

Trevor had been well-organized, from the look of things – spices lined up in a neat row in a cupboard, coffee cups with their handles all facing the same direction – not quite what she expected from a young bachelor. Callie photographed the contents of the shelves, the cupboards and the fridge. The oven and microwave were empty and the cookie jar contained nothing but cookies. It had been a while since lunch, so she helped herself to two small chocolate chips.

Callie returned to the living room just in time to find Melissa posing by the boarded-up window, taking a selfie and grinning broadly. "Are you crazy? No, no, no. No selfies."

"I'm not going to post it," Melissa said. "It's for posterity."

"No. Come on. Take this seriously or get out." She watched as Melissa reluctantly deleted the last four shots on her phone. "Good. I take it you didn't find anything."

"Nothing. Where to now?"

Callie assigned Melissa to the master bedroom while she took the second bedroom, now outfitted as a home office. This would be the logical place, she thought as she started from the doorway and worked clockwise, taking photos every step of the way. The desk, a metal, glass-topped model, was nearly bare. Trevor's laptop, she assumed, was now at the forensics lab, being examined meticulously. There were two notepads near the desk's top edge, each one holding a few scribbled phone numbers and scratched out reminders. She took photos of the top pages then leafed through each pad, making sure there were no other notes.

Above the desk was a long, narrow shelf, holding perhaps a hundred DVDs between a pair of metal bookends. They were mostly vintage films from the eighties and nineties, the collection of cheap horror movies that Trevor had been so proud of. She took more photos. She removed three magazines from the magazine rack, leafed through them and took more photos.

On the floor, in the corner by the window, were three

stacks of books, most of them on marketing, and a side table held Trevor's printer.

She was just checking the printer to see if anything had been left in the feed when she heard a noise from another room. What the hell was Mel up to now? It sounded like someone prying off the top of a wooden box. Okay, she had told Melissa to make a thorough search, but really? Was she pulling up the floorboards?

Callie made a mental note of where she was then turned to find Melissa standing in the office doorway, looking terrified. "Someone's trying to get in," she whispered. "What do we do?"

Together, they tiptoed into the living room. The street-lights had just come on and, through the sidelight on the other side of the front door they could see the shadow of someone at the plywood barrier. The plywood shook, as a nail in the upper right corner screeched its way out of the window frame.

Melissa seemed to be about to shout something to the intruder, but Callie stopped her. "We have a legal right to be here," Melissa whispered. "We have a key."

"It could be dangerous," Callie whispered back. "It could be… you know."

"Oh." Melissa understood. "What do we do?"

The last nail began to come out of the plywood. "We go out the back."

The light from the broken window came pouring in just as the two of them hurried toward the back of the house. Any second now and a hand would come through to unlock the door, the same way they had gained entry a few days ago. They were in the kitchen when they heard the door open. A second later, Callie slid the bolt on the rear door and began struggling with the doorknob, the doorknob that had supported Trevor's dead weight, but the mechanism wouldn't give. Something had been twisted – twisted and pulled. She put down her phone and used both hands, trying her best to stay silent. Melissa was right behind her, extending her hands, offering to take over. Callie brushed her away.

In one last twist and pull, the mechanism gave, emitting only the faintest squeak and a pop. Once outside, Melissa eased the door shut, not quite engaging the latch, but good enough. Instinctively, they lowered themselves onto the broad top step, Callie on her haunches, Melissa kneeling down, both below the edge of the door's square window. Callie breathed once more and congratulated herself for having had so much foresight – for not parking right in front, for not turning on any lights, for not leaving anything… Damn, where was her phone? Where the hell was her phone? "You didn't pick up my phone, by any chance?"

"No." Melissa groaned. "You left your phone?"

Raising her head just enough to see through the gauzy window curtain, Callie peered inside. There it was, face down in its shiny red case, on the table in the middle of the kitchen, right where she'd left it. "Damn it to hell."

"Maybe he won't see it."

"Maybe," Callie said, not believing it for a second. Before she could reconsider, she got to her feet, pushed open the door and slid back inside the shadowy house. She had taken just two steps and was just reaching out for her phone, when a tall, thin figure passed by in the doorway. Callie stopped.

She'd seen him for only a second, but the fleeting image

was burned in her brain. The man was taller than average, thin, his dark hair drawn back into a bun. She hadn't focused on his face. But since he was crossing from left to right, from Trevor's living room past the kitchen doorway toward the office, and, since he was wearing a shirt with the right sleeve cut off, it was easy to see that he was missing the lower half of his right arm.

It took several seconds for her to unfreeze. Her first instinct was to take her phone and retreat. That would be the easy and safe thing. She didn't need to verify that the man was Beau Garrison. Beau Garrison was the only tall, thin man she'd ever met with a bun and only half of a right arm. But that would leave the big question unanswered, the whole reason why she and Melissa had come here themselves.

Callie stayed in the kitchen, inching toward the doorway then positioning herself behind the door. From here, standing by the hinges, she would have a sliver of a view into the hall. Beau was clearly in the office. She could hear him muttering to himself as he looked around. There was no way that she could actually see what he was doing, but perhaps she could hear something or catch a glimpse as he left – to see what he was carrying, if he found whatever it was he was looking for.

At some point, Beau stopped muttering. Had he heard her? Had he somehow sensed her? Then he laughed to himself, a soft, short chuckle. "Gotcha, you sneaky little bastard."

Callie focused her senses, but all she heard now was a soft rustle. Was it paper or fabric? Or was it just her imagination? Then, in a blur of color and motion, he was back in the hall, striding past the sliver of an opening and vanishing from sight.

By the time she'd slipped out from behind the kitchen

door, the front door was closing. By the time she got to the living room doorway, Beau was outside. She could see his face come into view through the broken glass, with an expression that was smugly, maddeningly self-satisfied. Then the sheet of plywood slid back into place and was secured with a couple quick taps of a hammer.

Callie often found herself thinking peculiar little things during moments of stress. Right now, she was thinking about the hammer. Had Beau left the hammer outside on the porch or had he brought it inside with him? Had it been in his hand, his only hand, the entire time he was in the house? And what exactly would he have done with that hammer if she'd been just a little more careless or a little more daring?

CHAPTER 15

SHE WAS STILL thinking about the hammer when she sensed someone else, someone directly behind her. Callie spun and found herself staring at a tall, silhouetted figure in the hallway, perfectly still, poised with a long, large knife. She let out a short, piercing scream. And the silhouette screamed back.

"Sorry, sorry, sorry." Melissa dropped the kitchen knife and took a step into the light.

"You scared me to death," Callie gasped. "What's with the knife?"

"When you didn't come back, I got worried. Sorry."

"That's okay." Callie had both hands pressed to her pounding heart. She tried to laugh but it came out more like a whimper. "So, what was your plan, to come in and save me? Thanks."

Melissa glanced at the knife on the floor. "Probably more for self-defense. I didn't think it through. Are you okay?"

"It was Beau Garrison." With a shaking hand, Callie pointed to the boarded-up window. "I swear it was him."

"Beau himself? Are you sure? Did he see you?"

"He didn't see me. I saw him."

"What was he doing?" Melissa asked, gripped by the same excitement. "Obviously, he was looking for something. Did he find it? What was it?"

"He found it. I don't know what." Callie led the way into the home office, stood in the center of the room and slowly turned. She did two full circles, trying to take it all in: the glass-topped desk with the notepads, the narrow shelf with the old books and DVDs, the marketing books in the corner, the leather loveseat that might have doubled as a pullout bed, the matching, modern floor lamps. The room seemed just the way she'd left it. "Luckily, I have photos," she said. Then she took her phone and started all over, photographing every inch of the room.

"All we have to do is compare them," Callie said at the end, as she slipped her phone into her jacket pocket. "Like one of those games in the back of supermarket magazines. 'Can you spot the difference?'"

"I've always been good at that," Melissa said. "If you need help."

Callie gave it only a moment's thought. "Sure." Melissa, she felt, had earned it, even if she'd been wielding the knife just in her own defense. "But not here. The police have been gone for half a day and the place has already had two break-ins. How about tonight? My place."

"I would absolutely love that."

They agreed on a time, 7:30, at the gatehouse. Since Callie didn't cook, she would text Sarah and ask her to throw together a dinner and leave it warming in the oven. The two would make an evening of it. A little food, a little wine, a little detective work. It would be as close to a girls' night as she'd had in a while.

That evening, Melissa showed up with a bottle of red, which was not Callie's poison of choice, but it was a dry Malbec and went well with the leftovers of roast pork and green beans from Buddy and Gil's dinner the night before. Before opening the bottle, they worked on the photos. Callie had downloaded them to her computer, which had a decent-size screen, and set it up in the living room.

It wasn't as easy as she'd anticipated, since the angles were not the same. Neither was the lighting. The *befores* had been taken in the fading light of day, the *afters* with the lights on. And Beau had done some rearranging as he was searching for whatever it was. The three stacks of books had been rearranged, for example, but every volume seemed to be there. Callie called out the titles and Melissa checked them off a list.

"My eyes are blurring over," Melissa finally said. They'd been at it for well over an hour. She stretched, arms over her head. "What he took had to be pretty small, right? Something he could fit into a pocket. I mean, you didn't see anything. And we're talking about a man with one and a half arms."

"A document?" Callie guessed. "Or a photo or a DVD or a small book? Something either valuable or incriminating. I'm guessing incriminating."

"Augh," Melissa said as she stretched again. "This detecting is tough."

Callie was ready to call it quits as well. "Maybe in the morning when we're fresh. I'll send you the file and we'll take our time. Are you hungry?"

Callie closed her laptop and retreated to the kitchen, where the aroma of yesterday's roast pork was making her suddenly ravenous. She uncorked the Malbec and pointed Melissa to the cupboard with the plates and wineglasses. "Do you think he did it?" Melissa asked.

"The white plates," Callie instructed her then went in search of placemats. They were hiding in a bottom drawer, where they'd been residing, unused, since Callie first moved in.

Callie was piecing it together, combining the known facts with her suspicions. "Trevor gets fired because of the company bylaws. He threatens Beau. They set up a meeting. Trevor dresses up. The meeting doesn't work out. Beau feels angry enough or threatened enough to strangle him."

"What about the texts to you? Trevor's texts?"

Callie shrugged. "That part I don't have figured out."

"But you will," Melissa promised.

"Thanks for the vote of confidence."

Melissa started opening kitchen drawers, searching for silverware. "If I was Beau, I'd be feeling pretty sweet right now. He found what he was after."

Callie arranged the mats on the table in the dining alcove then went in search of the oven mitts. They were on a hook by the microwave, the most used appliance in her kitchen. "I think we need to learn more about Beau Garrison."

Melissa delivered the plates and silverware then went back for the wineglasses. "We should re-watch *Balancing the Universe*. I wouldn't mind seeing it again."

"I've never seen it," Callie admitted.

"You've never…" Melissa was aghast. "Callie, you absolutely have to. It was nominated for an Oscar."

"Well, some of us aren't into documentaries. Not so much." She raised her hands in apology. "No offense."

"None taken, I guess. But now that Beau's our prime suspect..." Melissa set down the stemmed glasses and looked around for the bottle of Malbec. "I'm pretty sure it's on *Netflix*. You want to watch it with dinner? Or after?"

Callie proposed starting the movie with dinner and went to get her computer from the living room. Somewhere around the halfway point, they would move from the kitchen into the living room and finish it up on the big screen.

Balancing the Universe was better than Callie expected. The film, and the story it was based on, had gotten a lot of press seven years ago, when she was still in college. It was one of those things that everyone in Austin talked about so much that she quickly developed a contrarian attitude and refused to pay any more attention.

It was the tale of Beau Garrison, back when he'd had two arms and a gorgeous girlfriend, a Black woman in her twenties named Naomi Pauling. Beau and Naomi had been travel vloggers, based in Austin, with a devoted following of young adventure seekers, or at least young followers of real adventure seekers. The couple perfectly embodied what their corner of the market wanted – beautiful, reckless, in love, and with a sense of entitlement that was the bane of tourism boards in nearly every country worldwide.

Their escapades had included skateboarding on the Great Wall of China and wall climbing the Grand Bobo-Dioulasso mosque under the light of a full moon. That last stunt would have landed them in prison for years or even worse, except that they were careful not to post anything until they arrived back in the U.S., which – they'd done their homework – did not have an extradition treaty with the devoutly Muslim nation of Burkina Faso. These assorted stunts took up the first ten minutes of *Balancing the Universe* and left the typical viewer, Callie among them, with a strong, visceral need for Beau and Naomi to die, or at least get severely injured.

That opportunity came with their visit to West Papua in Indonesia. Their plan, the most reckless and ambitious one to date, was to trek through the island's rainforests in search of an uncontacted tribe. According to the grinning, two-armed Beau, there were at least forty such tribes on the huge island, each with its own fascinating culture and completely unknown to outsiders. He and Naomi, alone, would hack through the jungle – perhaps a day's journey, according to the locals – make contact with a tribe and video the whole experience for their worldwide audience. A GoFundMe campaign had raised more than enough to finance this expedition.

As the world was to learn later, the endeavor went insanely, terribly wrong, almost from the start. Beau and Naomi began in the village of Tege and drove their Jeep along the one good road into the mountains until the road turned into rocks and petered out. From then on, it was backpacks with everything they needed, plus an inflatable raft for whatever rivers they might run into. After the second day of slogging through the rain and mud and the undergrowth of vines, their global, state-of-the-art satellite GPS ran out of its signal range. A day later, their solar-powered camera charger stopped working. Their video journal got spottier as they tried to conserve power. But the camera did happen to record the exact moment when Beau fell sideways and a snapped branch drove itself all the way through the lower part of his arm. His howl of pain was extreme.

In the shorter and shorter video snippets, Callie saw the handsome couple growing sicker, more dehydrated and more and more desperate. The camera, almost out of battery life, did manage to get one final shot. The very last snippet that Naomi recorded was of a man in a loin cloth and a painted face, in a thatched hut, preparing the ointment that would save Beau's life.

Meanwhile, back in the world, fifty thousand fans were starting to worry, and the story caught traction. Some saw Beau and Naomi as young explorers, well worth saving, while others labeled then the victims of Darwinian laws and thus ripe for extinction. The Indonesian government didn't care one way or the other.

Three weeks after the couple disappeared, an adventure tour group from Germany spotted an orange inflatable raft, barely afloat, spilling over a whitewater section of the Baliem River. Beau and Naomi were clinging to the sides, alive but weak and delirious. From the moment of their rescue, Naomi began muttering about a wise, miraculous shaman who had brought them to his village and nursed them back from the edge.

The couple's recovery, in an Australian hospital, was a slow one. Naomi seemed to be suffering from hallucinations and Beau's injured forearm had developed gangrene and needed to be amputated in order to save his life. It wasn't until well after they returned to Austin that they posted the first in their series of vlogs and revealed to their stunned fans the harrowing adventure they'd been through.

Beau and Naomi themselves narrated the last part of the documentary, speaking over stock footage, each of them giving details of their unrecorded time with the shaman and his tribe. Melissa was sniffling all through this part, and even Callie found herself moved. Gone were the obnoxious, entitled thrill-seekers, replaced with two humbler, simpler people, awed by the grandness of nature and grateful for all the small wonders of life.

At the end, it was Beau and Naomi who decided to inflate their raft and take their chances on the untamed river that cut through the island's interior. They took with them the memory of what they'd learned from this wise, kind shaman and a firm commitment to help connect the rest of the world to his vision, imbued with the hope of one day... *Balancing the Universe.* The final shot was a repeat, showing Ka'Kala as he squatted over his fire, the same scene portrayed on the wall of the company headquarters.

Okay, Callie thought as the credits rolled. A little hokey but heartfelt. She closed her laptop and split the last of the wine between the two of them. "And this came out just after they started Ka'Kala?"

Melissa wiped away a tear and took a sip. "They had only the one thing, the Wepapua ointment. We Papua. Get it? Ka'Kala had given them some to take with them. It didn't reverse the gangrene, but it probably saved his life."

"And everything else came from that." It made sense. A saga like this was the perfect vehicle for an eco-sourced line of just about anything: supplements, essential oils, even sunscreen moisturizers, with the coconuts definitely not picked by Thai slave monkeys. "By the way, what happened to Naomi? She's not with Ka'Kala anymore?"

"She and Beau split up a few years ago and she left the company. That was in the news."

"We need to check on her," Callie said, not knowing what good that could possibly do. She eyed the miniscule amount of Malbec still in her glass. "Want to open another? I've got a passable Sauvignon Blanc."

Melissa demurred. She had to drive home, she said. Plus, she had a class in the morning and half a bottle was pretty much her limit on a school night. Melissa thanked her for dinner, and Callie thanked her for helping with the photos and for making her watch the documentary.

Callie stood on the front steps of the mini-chateau, waving goodbye, when she noticed someone on one of the stone benches in the rose garden on the far side of the drive. She knew instantly that the dark form, with its bulk and relaxed presence, was her father. Her first thought was that he must be in a "mood", perhaps at risk of wandering off the property. But then she saw the cigar between his fingers, coming to his lips and down again, leaving no smoke in its wake, and breathed a sigh of relief.

On her deathbed, Anita McFee had made her husband promise never to smoke again. Buddy was a man of his word, especially where his wife was concerned, so for the past few years, whenever the impulse grew strong, he would bring out a wooden cigar, perfectly detailed, from the hole through its center to the carved bit of ash dangling from the end. Buddy liked the familiar feel and the rhythm of smoking it. For Callie, the wooden cigar was a signal. It meant that he was engaged enough in the present to remember his promise.

"Daddy?"

He looked up and smiled at the woman crossing the gravel drive. "Sweetheart. Come to check up on me?" Callie didn't answer but motioned him to scoot over on the bench then eased in beside him. "This was your mom's favorite spot," he added. Gil had mentioned that Buddy was now on some medication. She'd looked it up. A cholinesterase inhibitor.

"I see you had company. How's her school project going? Am I going to have to grow a beard and change my name?"

"I didn't ask," Callie admitted. "We were occupied with other things."

He considered this for a second. "Good. You need to have friends, regular friends to spend time with, not just your job and your boss and these fellas who get you all tangled up with..." He flicked away an imaginary ash. "You know."

"Death. I know." She'd had the very same thought. "This was a nice evening. Mel can be good company when she relaxes, even though... Even though we did talk about murder."

"I see. In a broad sense or a specific sense?"

"Specific." She smiled. "I'm afraid you may have been right after all."

Buddy chuckled. "That's nothing to be afraid of."

"Daddy?" Callie hadn't intended to tell her father any of this. "Trevor may have been murdered." She watched his posture straighten and his face light up. "We're working under that assumption."

"Ha! No kidding. Didn't I tell you?" Buddy crowed, loud enough to echo off the row of live oaks. "You scoff at my professional opinion, but I've been dealing with matters like this for a long time."

"Forgive me for doubting," she said. "But your professional

opinion, in my opinion, seemed greatly influenced by your need for self-preservation."

"But I was right. That's my point." He slapped his leg. "What does State think?"

"He agrees, to an extent. The department is looking into it."

"Don't tell him you told me," Buddy said, still savoring the news. "I want State to have to tell me himself. After the things that boy said…"

"Don't be mean, Daddy."

"You're right," he mumbled with reluctance. "Not mean. I should be the bigger man."

"However you want to put it."

Together, they gazed out at the last of the summer roses, the dry petals barely hanging on. The gardener had already mulched the beds with cocoa bean hulls, giving the air an exotic yet familiar pungency.

"Is there something I can do?" Buddy asked then took another puff. "I know you're going to do whatever you're going to do. But Gil and I can help. We have connections. And if you need some discrete protection, we can supply that."

"Dad!" She drew out the word. "I'm not doing anything dangerous. It's just an article."

He waved away her rationale. "Don't be too proud or stubborn. There's no upside to that. And don't give me that condescending look." Without even glancing her way, he knew. "You're like me, you know, more than your brother ever was."

She couldn't argue with that. Truth be told, she didn't want to. She just sat there, matching his breaths one for one and taking in the scent of cocoa bean hulls.

CHAPTER 16

THE NEXT MORNING, over two cups of coffee and a cranberry muffin, Callie created a Dropbox file, uploaded all the *befores* and *afters* from the bungalow office and shared the folder with Melissa.

Her night had been no more sleepless than usual but no less either, which had given her plenty of time to think about her brother and his assertion that he was the police and that she needed to stay away and let him do his job. She agreed with parts of that statement, enough to persuade her to make an unpleasant call. "Hey, State." From the young, raised voices in the background, she assumed he was still at home. "Is today not a school day?"

"They have colds," he said grumpily. "So, in three days we'll all have colds."

"That's too bad. Look, I'm afraid I have some information. No, I said that wrong. Great news. I have some information."

He managed to squeeze a world of apprehension into his one-word response. "What?"

She told him the same lie she'd told before, of having left

something at Trevor's bungalow – her favorite baseball cap, she decided. She would have asked State to pick it up, but he'd already returned the keys to Trevor's parents, so she went to visit them. From that point on, her story stuck pretty much to the truth, except for Melissa being there and the two of them taking two hundred photos apiece.

State listened without interrupting. "You're sure Garrison took something?" he asked.

"I'm positive. And I told you what he said."

"I wrote it down." State cleared his throat. "Okay, I'll get the key and reopen the house."

"I already have a key," Callie reminded him.

"Well, you need to return that to the Birdsongs. And then I'll borrow it. That keeps it official. Luckily, we took a ton of photos. We'll compare them to the house's present condition."

"Right. Like one of those puzzles in the back of magazines."

"What? Oh, yeah. I guess. And I'll need you to make a statement. You can meet my new partner."

"Oh, you have a new partner."

"Yeah. He's a peach."

They kept in touch throughout the morning, and when it came time for lunch, Callie left the *Free Press* and met her brother at the bungalow. He was waiting in the living room.

"Don't touch anything," he warned her. "And don't go into the office."

Callie put her hands in her skirt pockets. Inside the office, a crime scene technician was dusting the surfaces. A second officer, a male detective in a suit, was holding up an iPad screen, comparing an image to the shelf above the desk. "Was

Garrison wearing gloves?" State asked. "We didn't find any-thing on the plywood."

"Glove," she corrected him. "I didn't notice. Sorry. Do you think a stump would leave a print?"

State seemed intrigued by the thought. "Well, a print is made from body oil, so it would leave some trace. I honestly don't think we could I.D. a stump, but it's something to keep in mind."

A chuckle emerged from the other room. "I'll keep an eye out for a stump print," the technician called out.

"My prints will be in there," Callie told her brother. "And Mel's, maybe. From when she was here before. Remember?"

"Okay…" State gave her a slant-eyed glance. "We'll question Garrison about his break-in, tell him a passerby rec-ognized him coming out. See what he admits to. I won't tell him about you."

"I would appreciate it."

"Did you find it, by the way?"

"Find what?"

"Your baseball cap. It must have been your favorite, to make you go to all the trouble."

"My absolute favorite," Callie said and proved it by reach-ing into her bag and pulling out a teal blue cap that she'd bought at a Lululemon just an hour ago. She'd been smart enough to remove the price tag. "Nice, huh?"

"Nice." State sounded skeptical. "Where was it?"

"In a corner of the kitchen. It must have fallen off when I tried to get Trevor's body off the doorknob."

State, still skeptical, seemed willing to let it drop. "Did you tell Dad? About the murder possibility?"

"No," she lied. "I figured you would, when the time is right."

"Right," he echoed. "Although I wouldn't mind if you said something first."

Callie was about to respond when the other detective walked in – Black, probably in his forties, well-built, in a slim-fit gray suit and sporting a no-nonsense kind of demeanor. "I think I found something," he announced. "One of the DVDs is missing."

"Way to go," State said. "Oh, Randal, this is Callie. She reported the break-in. Callie, this is Randal Greene, my partner."

"I know who Callie McFee is," Randal said, sounding uncordial and unimpressed. "Should we be talking in front of her?"

"If it wasn't for her, we wouldn't be here," State said. "So, yeah. What about the DVD?"

Randal shrugged then went on. "He's got quite the collection. In the photos, there are ninety-seven of them. Now there are ninety-six. I counted twice."

"Which one is missing?"

"I can't make it out from the spine." Randal displayed the image on the iPad, enlarging it until the definition went fuzzy. "The word *blood* is in the title. Something blood or blood something. It looks pretty gory. When we manipulate the image on a high-def monitor, we'll be able to see more."

Callie wanted to say something, to congratulate Randal for finding what she and Melissa hadn't been able to, but it felt safer to just blend into the background.

"Good job," said State. The two detectives headed back

into the home office. "Now we just have to figure out why Beau Garrison, grand guru of natural healing, is breaking into houses and stealing cheap horror flicks."

151

CHAPTER 17

"I CAN'T BELIEVE we didn't see it." Melissa grimaced then checked her speed and slowed down to a reasonable five miles over the limit.

"Well, the police had better cameras and better lighting, all of that."

"Why would Beau go to all this trouble for a DVD?" Melissa asked. "Aren't they all mass produced?"

"According to Trevor, some are pretty rare, although it's hard to imagine anything disappearing completely. Let's hope there's at least one more copy."

"And we're not even sure the movie's important," Melissa pointed out. "There could have been something else in the DVD case."

"That's true." Callie settled back into the black leather passenger seat and tried not to think about it. "Hey, I love your car."

Her friend responded with a gratified grin. "I always wanted one. I bought it used, but I tell people I got it new a few years ago. Oops, I shouldn't have said that. Do you want the top down?"

"No, this is fine." Callie was looking for a chance to chat, and a windy car would not be as conducive. "How did you find where Naomi was? There's nothing on social media or on Google."

"Just call it brilliant detective work." Melissa eased onto the entrance ramp of I-35 South. "I found an article, around the time when she and Beau were lost in the jungle. It mentioned her family back in Boston. A mother and two brothers. One of her brothers, it turns out, is heavy into Instagram. A year or so ago, on a vacation, he posted several videos of a flower shop in Buda, Texas. The Living Garden."

"What are you saying? Naomi Pauling owns a flower shop in Buda? That did not show up on my search."

"That's because..." Melissa was savoring the moment. "Suzanne Pauling owns it. Naomi's mother. So... why would Naomi's mother move to Texas and open a flower shop fifteen miles from Austin?"

"I get it," Callie said. "Good work. I should have thought of that."

"Well, you were busy dealing with your brother. Did you mention me?"

Callie laughed. "He barely believed my story about the baseball cap. If I told him that I'd brought along an accomplice to help me find it..."

"Ooh, I like that title. Melissa Miller, Accomplice."

Ten minutes later, the blue Mercedes edged onto the Main Street exit, took a right and continued straight for half a mile. Buda was an old railroad town that had been absorbed into the Austin suburbs. It still sported a quaint downtown district, now studded with antique stores and coffee shops.

They located The Living Garden on Main, just past a small park. The shop occupied all of an old stone building with arched doors that had been converted into display windows. It seemed extravagantly large for a flower shop in a town this size. Melissa found a parking spot a few doors down.

"I called about an hour ago," Melissa said. "A woman answered and said they were open until six. I'm guessing it was Suzanne." She checked her watch. "We have a few minutes."

"We're not just going to talk to her?" Callie hated being behind the curve. Melissa had obviously thought this through.

"It may be hard to get to Naomi. No one just disappears from social media, especially someone who made her living by it. We're better off following her mother."

"Makes sense," Callie said as she eased down into her seat. She glanced up and down the half-empty street. "If I'd known this was going to be a stakeout, I might have suggested my truck instead of a Mercedes."

They didn't have long to wait. It was still a few minutes to six when a largish woman, perhaps in her sixties, with a mane of long, wild hair, turned the hanging sign from "open" to "closed", emerged onto the street and locked up. During all of this, she had a phone to her ear. She didn't seem to notice the two women motionless in the cobalt blue sports car as she ambled to the dusty pickup truck parked directly behind them.

Following her was easy. The pickup made a right turn past the Buda water tower and just two turns after that, made a left onto Windmill Way. Melissa stayed back a good hundred yards, but thanks to the flat terrain and scruffy vegetation, always had a clear view. The "way" did turn out to have at least one resident windmill, turning lazily in the low Texan sun. As they approached, Callie was delighted to see a lush, irrigated rectangle of green, an oasis, surrounding a cozy, two-story farmhouse just a few dozen yards from the windmill. A row of tall, fading sunflowers prevented her from seeing that the pickup had stopped by the front gate. By then it was too late. The largish woman was still in the driver's seat, waiting for them, looking peeved.

"Are you from the bank?" she demanded before Melissa could even cut the engine.

"We're not from the bank," Callie shouted through the open window.

"Are you reporters?" When they didn't answer, she reached across to her glove box and brought out a handgun.

"We're not reporters," Callie shouted and then remembered that yes, she was.

The woman emerged from the pickup, brandishing the gun, her arm extended. As handguns went, it didn't look all that threatening, probably due to the pink casing and the small daisy decals along the barrel. The woman saw Callie's reaction and smiled. "Used to be my daughter's, but I know how to use it. Who are you?"

"I'm a friend of Trevor Birdsong's." Callie got out of the car, at the same time reaching out her arm and signaling for Melissa to stay put. She had a feeling that, in this situation, one intruder might be better than two.

"Trevor." The hardness in the woman's face began to fade. "I heard about Trevor. I am so sorry. That goddamn company does things to a person. That man, Beau…" She sighed and lowered the gun. "Why are you here?"

"It's selfish of me, I know," Callie said, improvising as she warily approached. "I was hoping your daughter might be able to help me understand."

"I haven't told her about Trevor," the woman said. "My daughter doesn't watch television or go online. She likes her plants." With the tilt of her head, she showed off the gardens, the fall blooms now replacing the summer ones. "It was my idea, this and the shop, from her share of the company."

"It's beautiful. And so peaceful."

Suzanne's smile turned sad. "I don't know how much longer I can keep it going. Do you know anyone who wants to buy a flower shop?"

"Afraid I don't," Callie said. "I don't mean to intrude, but… would Naomi have any idea why Trevor would kill himself?"

Suzanne shook her head. "It's been four years. She should have left that place before, but she thought things would get better. It just made her worse."

"I'm sorry. I didn't know. Is your daughter better now?" Callie realized that she hadn't bothered introducing herself. Now wasn't the time. She didn't want to remind Suzanne that they were strangers who'd just met.

"She is better," Suzanne answered. She reached out and leaned against the picket gate. "Naomi was such a carefree girl. He made her into this thrill-seeker, a person she has never been, not in her heart. Their time in the jungle. I don't know what happened there, but it was bad."

"Mamma." The voice was soft and breathy, little more than a whisper. Callie turned to see a woman, mid-thirties, medium height and thin, emerging from the depths of the garden. She was dressed like a professional gardener, wearing a long-sleeved shirt, a wide-brimmed sunhat and gloves. On one arm hung a woven basket overflowing with stems of purple salvia. Callie recognized her at once. "Mamma, who is this?"

Suzanne caught Callie's eye in a stern, unmistakable warning to keep back. Then she reached through the truck's window and returned the pink pistol to the glove box. As she passed through the gate and approached her daughter, Suzanne lowered her voice. Naomi spoke in quick, nervous bursts; her mother in quiet, soothing tones.

Something behind Callie moved. It was Melissa, she saw, stepping toward the gate, holding Callie's phone. Suzanne might have become aware of the fourth person, but Naomi's eyes were downcast as she focused on her mother's voice.

"Your brother texted you." Melissa held out the phone. "They found the movie."

"That's great." Callie glanced at the gardener and her mother then back at Melissa. "Maybe Naomi knows about it."

Melissa nodded. "That's what I'm thinking. Do you want to ask her?"

Callie took the phone and opened the message. "Doesn't look worth stealing," her brother had texted. "Randal is tracking down a copy." The text was accompanied by a screengrab of a movie poster from what looked like a cheap, independent horror film. Perfect for Trevor's collection. It showed a gray, grotesque, zombie-like face, overlaid with a splatter of the reddest blood. The title was also in blood, dripping almost illegibly. "*Zombie Blood*," Callie said then said it louder. "*Zombie Blood*." She was hoping for some reaction. "A movie called *Zombie Blood*."

"What are you saying?" Suzanne jerked her head around, annoyed by the intrusion. Naomi's eyes were still lowered, hidden from view by her sunhat.

Callie walked through the gate into the garden. She enlarged the photo and tried to sidestep Suzanne's protective barrier. "Hi, Naomi," she said, mimicking the mother's calming tones. "I'm a friend of Trevor Birdsong."

"Trevor," Naomi said. She looked up, her expression turning warm. "I love Trevor. How is Trevor?"

"He's fine." Callie enlarged the photo and turned the phone around. "Trevor told me about a movie he likes. Did you see this movie? *Zombie Blood.* I know it sounds pretty dreadful." She faked a laugh.

"Trevor likes this?" Naomi accepted the phone and held it in both hands, with the basket of purple stalks dangling from the crook of her arm. She squinted at the image, not comprehending, not at first. The first reaction Callie noticed was the purple stalks in the basket beginning to quiver.

It came slowly. The other three women could sense it coming and all were powerless to intervene. Even Naomi's protective mother stood frozen, watching as her daughter's hands began to shake uncontrollably, her eyes widening and her mouth falling open.

Naomi dropped the phone then fell to her knees, the basket still stuck in the crook of her arm. A sound gurgled up from somewhere deep in her stomach, through her chest and throat, hitting the air as little more than a gasp. After that, it grew quickly, and within seconds had turned into the most heartbreaking scream Callie had ever heard.

CHAPTER 18

After Naomi's breakdown, after her mother had ordered them off the property and threatened to have them arrested, Callie and Melissa drove straight back to Austin. The situation should have given them plenty to talk about. How could the sight of a trashy horror flick have sent a person over the edge like that? But they were left feeling too stunned – stunned and ashamed of whatever it was they'd done. Despite the traffic, Melissa managed to drop Callie off at the gatehouse by seven. Neither one of them wanted to hang out.

Callie was not in the mood for food or TV, but there was a barely-opened bottle of Pouilly-Fuissé in the fridge that shouldn't go to waste. Having poured herself a healthy glassful, she sat by a front window and watched the sky grow darker, dipping the room into deeper and deeper shadows. When she found she could no longer take the silent introspection, Callie got up, switched on the lights and took her wine upstairs, into the second bedroom, now serving as a home office.

For the next hour, she sat at her laptop, organizing her sketchy notes for an article that might never get published.

Perhaps Oliver would change his mind if she came up with an airtight case against Ka'Kala's chief executive. It was worth a shot. The one good thing about Naomi's breakdown was that it proved that she was frightened of *Zombie Blood* itself and not of some other DVD that might be hidden in the case. It was one of the few things she knew with any certainty.

All evening long, her phone pinged with messages from State. She had called him from the car, to tell him about Naomi, and had been lucky enough to get his voice mail, where she left a concise retelling of their trip to Buda. Since then, she'd been ignoring his flurry of calls and texts. His last one had been over twenty minutes ago, which meant either he'd given up or was on his way over.

When the front door opened, Callie remembered that, as usual, she'd forgotten to lock it. "Up here," she shouted out the door and the stairs. For a second, she half-hoped it might be a serial killer or Beau Garrison trying to shut her up, but it was her brother after all.

"I just came from the flower farm," he said, walking in and looking calmer than she expected. "She won't talk to us. Not voluntarily."

"I had no idea she was so emotionally fragile," Callie murmured. "How is she now?"

"Don't know. Her mother won't talk to us either."

After closing her laptop, she turned to face him. "You know, it could have been even worse with you there. We were a couple of harmless girls. Imagine if we'd been a pair of burly detectives."

"First of all, you're not girls and we're not burly. Second, because you did it behind my back, there's no official account of her reaction. If it comes to an actual case, the DA will flip out. And third, you just reinforced everything horrible my new partner thinks about us."

Callie took a sip of the Pouilly-Fuissé. "A rocky start with you two? I could tell."

State eyed the second chair by the desk but didn't sit. "Randal is fifteen years older but we're the same rank. He came up the hard way. And now he's partnered with a privileged white kid with a powerful dad. And then there's you, which doesn't help – showing up at Trevor's house, then making a potential witness hysterical."

"He doesn't like me being involved. Point taken." Callie nodded thoughtfully. "So, what's the deal with *Zombie Blood*?"

State bit his lip and clenched his fists. "Goddammit, Cal. I can't give you departmental information. We're not a team. That's what I'm saying."

"You didn't give me information. Naomi is co-founder of the company I'm doing an article on. Mel tracked her down. It's simple reporter stuff."

"Yeah, let's talk about Mel. How the hell did she get involved? Was it her bright idea to show it to Naomi?"

"Does it matter?" Callie demanded. "You're the one who gave me the photo."

He sighed and wagged his head. "You're right. That's Randal's argument. I gotta stop doing this."

"I'll tell you what I know. From the worldwide web, not from you." She swiveled her desk chair and looked up. "*Zombie Blood* was a small indie, filmed here in Austin about five years ago. It never got distribution. You must have contacted the director or the producer by now and they're sending you a copy.

Am I right?" State nodded, but just barely. "Good. You're going to watch it. And then you're going to check with everyone – writer, actors, costumer – and see if anyone has a connection to Beau's little eco-health company. Is that where you are?"

"I can neither confirm nor deny," State said. "But yeah."

"Of course. You must have interviewed Beau by now, right?"

"Not at liberty to talk about it."

"Does he know that you know about the DVD?"

"I cannot divulge that information."

"Does he have an alibi for the time of Trevor's death?"

"Cannot divulge."

"Does he have a believable, innocent explanation about why he broke in?"

"Ha!" State scoffed at the thought. "It's about as believable as you and your baseball cap."

"So, he has an explanation, which is a lie, of course." Callie got up from the desk and wandered into the living room. "I get it. You can't share. And I shouldn't share either. Fair is fair."

"Deal," State agreed then thought about it for a second. "Deal," he reconfirmed. "Unless you uncover information that's pertinent to the crime, in which case…"

"No, no, you can't have it both ways. If you can keep information from me, I can keep it from you."

"Okay." He grunted his displeasure. "I'm glad we agree. Now I have to get home."

"That's it? You came all this way just to yell at me?"

"That's what brothers are for." As he started down the stairs, State paused and looked around. "How is it, living in the shadow of the family manse?"

"Not bad. Makes it harder to avoid dinner invitations."

State understood. "I've always loved this little house," he said. "George the gardener and – who was the handyman? Hank? They had a real bachelor pad here. Used to let me hang out in high school, when I was supposed to be getting tutored."

Callie followed him down the stairs to the living room. "Hank used to smoke pot, didn't he? I could smell it on his clothes."

"He used to grow it. Mom's cutting garden. That ended when Sarah accidentally added a few stems to a flower arrangement in the front hall. Mom didn't recognize them, but Dad did. So did the governor. They all had quite the laugh."

"No!" Callie put a hand over her mouth. "I don't remember any of that."

"Good times," State said then eased open the front door and gazed out into the shadows. "Did you know Dad is out in the rose garden? By himself?"

She wasn't surprised. "I think it's becoming a habit. You want to go chat?"

"No. One family drama is enough. Two, if you count me coming home late again. Let's save Dad for later."

She smiled and waved him on his away. "Say hello to Yolanda and the boys."

Callie watched her brother drive off between the stone posts. The evening was chilly, so she grabbed a sweater from a hook and wandered out. Buddy was not smoking his wooden cigar tonight, but he seemed calm enough. "Hey, Daddy."

He looked up from the bench, his expression laced with confusion. "Calista? What are you doing here?"

Callie had learned the hard way to be as unspecific as possible at moments like this. "Do I have to have a reason to come visit my dad?"

"I thought you were..." He scratched at the short silver hair above his ear. "No matter. I'm glad you're here. Have a seat." He had never liked having people loom over him. "My mind gets fuzzy. I was never fuzzy. I was like one of those waiters who never writes anything down. You want to say to them, 'Write things down, for God's sake.' I used to be like that waiter, except I wrote things down." He scooted over and she joined him. "What have you been doing? Not that I'll remember. The art of conversation..." And he blew gently into the air, like blowing the fuzz off a dandelion.

Callie tried to think of a safe subject for conversation – nothing about State or her mother or anything work-related or even school-related, nothing to contradict wherever he might be now. "I saw Diedre Westerman the other day," she offered. "We went for a drive. Had a nice talk."

"Diedre," Buddy said fondly, using three syllables. "She and your mother. A few years younger than your mother, right? I haven't seen her... I don't know when I saw her. Diedre of the Sorrows, I always think, like the character. Poor girl wanted a family. Real shame she never had another kid."

Callie was perplexed. "How do you know about that?" According to Diedre herself, no one outside her family knew of her secret.

Buddy chuckled. "You're talking to Buddy McFee. I arranged it. The clinic in Dallas. The payoffs. She was what? Fifteen? Hardly old enough to be saddled with a child."

"Saddled... I'm not sure I'd say saddled. Her son died."

"Died?" Buddy seemed confused. "When did he die?" His confusion took on a note of paranoia. "And how do you know him at all?"

"When did he die?" Callie repeated. "Daddy, you know when. You were probably there."

"You mean in the clinic? That's right. In the clinic."

It was clear that he was lying, and Callie felt a sick churning in the pit of her stomach. "Are you saying the baby didn't die in the clinic?"

Buddy squirmed. "I'm tired, sweetie. You know how I get things mixed up."

"So, if he didn't die in the clinic…" She thought back to Diedre's story. About the baby and the heart monitor and never seeing her little boy again. "What happened? Did you get him adopted?"

"Adopted?" He scoffed. "Don't be daft."

"Then what? Did you just give the baby away? Please tell me you didn't."

"I didn't do it," Buddy growled. "Sean and Pegeen did. Pegeen begged me to make it happen. You knew the Westermans. Snooty and superior as all hell."

"I can't believe… That is so heartless and wrong."

"It was the right thing."

"You faked a baby's death and just gave him away."

"To a good family who would love him and bring him up right."

"Oh, my God." She could barely catch her breath. "He's out there, alive. All these years she's been mourning her boy. And he's alive."

Buddy pushed himself up from the bench and began to

wander. "It's what they wanted. What was best. She was young and her boyfriend was no good."

Callie stayed seated, unable to move. "Her son is out there, not having a clue about his real mother. How could they do that? How could you?"

"It wasn't my choice," he spat back. "I expedite things. That's what I do."

"Yes, I'm sure. Out of the goodness of your heart. The Westermans were big donors to your campaigns, weren't they?"

He stumbled back in her direction, pointing a finger. "Don't you do that. Don't you dare."

Callie stood, now matching his height and his intensity. "Even now? Now that her family is gone and Diedre is dying? You never told her a thing?"

"I didn't…" He reached up and rubbed his temples. "That was so many years ago. There were so many secrets."

Callie thought back to their conversation in the truck, of Diedre's dream of grandchildren running through the old family home. "She has to know. Who did you give him to?"

Buddy grimaced. "I forget. My notes are in my files. I'll look in the files."

"Okay." At some point, on a good day, he would remember that all his files had gone up in flames. "Think, Daddy, think. Were these people in Austin? In Dallas?"

"Goddammit, am I supposed to remember everything? I can't remember."

CHAPTER 19

THE INTERNET SPEED was faster at the *Free Press* than at the gatehouse, which was reason enough for her to get into work at a decent hour and pretend to be writing the first draft of an op-ed piece critiquing the Texas state policy on renewable energy. It was more of an Oliver piece than a Callie piece, but she agreed with most of his points and could easily channel her publisher's voice. All the notes were there and, in a day or so, when push came to shove, when the deadline had already passed and Oliver was knocking on her cubicle wall, she could easily deliver a thousand words of intelligently phrased outrage.

Meanwhile, she spent her first hour trying to make sense of the maze of Texas childbirth laws and regulations. Then she compiled a list of clinics that might have been in operation back then. When that became overwhelming, she switched gears and started googling all the available information on *Zombie Blood*, which wasn't much.

It had been an attempt at a cheap but profitable horror film written and produced by a group of middle-aged Austin businessmen with no connection to the film industry. Their old Facebook page was full of misplaced hype and hope. The last *Zombie Blood* post, she noticed, had been over four years ago when they offered sample DVDs to potential investors and were still trying to secure any kind of a distribution deal. The sad, amateurish nature of this Hollywood misadventure stood in sharp, mystifying contrast to the death of a young man and the theft of one of the film's last remaining copies.

Callie couldn't wait to see it. She even toyed with the idea of contacting one of the producers and claiming to be – just as an example – an executive at the Horror Channel, in search of content, perhaps even holding out the possibility of turning *Zombie Blood* into a series. Of course, they would have to send her a copy in order for any of that to happen. Her scheme, she felt, had a high probability of working, given everyone's desire to be part of the next zombie franchise. But then she considered her brother and his partner and their towering rage if they were to ever find out, so she forced the idea to the back of her mind. Not right now, she thought. Maybe later.

"Callie?" It was Jennie Larson, leaning against the doorway of her cubicle, arms folded, looking annoyed and superior. "The staff meeting? You're late? Everyone's waiting?" Jennie had the maddening habit of turning nearly every sentence into a question.

"Sorry," Callie said. "Just working on the op-ed." Then she closed her laptop and followed Jennie to the conference table located in the middle of the warren of cubicles.

Today's meeting, a regular Friday confab, centered on new ideas for articles. Her absence last Friday had been noted by much of the staff, invariably in the guise of, "We really missed your input." She realized that she not only had to show up this Friday but had to participate and make some meaningful contribution, which did not mean that she'd actually taken the time to come up with anything to contribute. She had other, more critical things on her mind.

Oliver was good at these story meetings. He listened, asked probing questions and was decisive. Four new, good-enough ideas were approved and assigned when Oliver's eyes finally fell on her. "You've been quiet," he observed. "We can always count on Callie McFee to give us something exciting. What have you got?" He probably didn't mean it to be confrontational, but that's the way it sounded.

Callie met his gaze, her mind racing. For a long second, she considered making a pitch for the Ka'Kala exposé, just to get a rise out of him.

"What if…" It was an idea that had just come to her, but a good one. "What if – and I know this has been done before – but what if we investigate abuses in the adoption business?" Then she took a deep breath and dove in. "It wasn't all that long ago that teenage mothers were forced into giving up their babies, legally and illegally. In one case, a fifteen-year-old was told that her infant died in childbirth."

"Did that really happen?" asked a shocked, young staffer.

"Yes," Callie stated. "But my angle wouldn't be historical. It would be about birth mothers, thirty or forty years ago, who have no idea that their children are alive, adults now with no clue about their pasts. How many of them are there? And who was responsible?"

Oliver seemed intrigued. "Do you have a source?"

"An anonymous source," Callie said. "Her parents felt it was for the best. Better than having their little girl refusing to give up her baby."

"Wow." The publisher leaned across the table, eyes widening, definitely hooked. "Can you tell me the source in private?"

"No," she told him firmly. "I promised. I want to spend time on this, Oliver. It may turn into nothing, but I think it's worth pursuing."

Callie had been kept awake half the night thinking of Diedre and her high school boyfriend with the prison tattoo and the child they thought was dead. It was dangerous ground, but she thought she could handle it. There was no way on earth that she would implicate her father, but she needed to do something. And that something was bound to involve spending even more time out of the office.

Several editors and writers had opinions and suggestions, but Callie knew that Oliver would have the final word and that the word would be *yes*.

"I'll give you a few days," he finally said. "No questions asked. Do you need to start today?"

"Yes, thanks," Callie said and instantly got to her feet. "I'd like to start now."

"Okay," Oliver said. "'What? You mean now? I know that's what you said, but… Um, sure." He shrugged. "But don't forget the op-ed piece."

"Nearly done," she said then began to make her way out through the cubicle maze. She called out over her shoulder. "Sorry about the meeting."

*

Callie did not phone ahead. That would have involved thinking and planning, and she didn't want to do either, just to go with her instincts. As she drove out of the city and off the highway, she took comfort in the familiar, twisting back roads leading to the long white structure with its white pillars and aura of security and tradition.

Diedre answered the door herself. "Callie. How wonderful of you. Come in." She seemed a little unsteady on her feet but alert and relatively cheerful. "Did you come to see Melissa? She should be home any minute."

"No, I came to see you." Callie had been mulling it over ever since last night, weighing the pros and cons of this visit.

Diedre led the way into the house. "Isn't that sweet. Can I get you some lemonade?"

"That would be lovely."

They settled into rattan chairs, in a light-filled, plant-filled room overlooking the rear gardens, a room the Westermans had always called the conservatory. The two women made small talk and toasted their lemonades. Diedre took a sip then waited expectantly for her guest to start.

"I don't know how to say this," Callie said then pressed on in a single breath. "I think… I think your son is alive. Your parents arranged to give him away, and they kept it from you because they knew you wouldn't agree to an adoption."

Diedre reacted with the slightest of smiles. Then she inhaled and seemed to grow as the air entered her body. "I knew he wasn't dead. After I was diagnosed, I had this strange feeling, like little Stephen calling out to me. I just knew he had to be alive. Do you know where he is? Who he is?"

"I don't know," Callie admitted. "I tried to look into it, but I need more information. Do you remember what hospital it was?"

Diedre put down her glass and pressed a bony hand to

her temple. "I don't think it was a hospital. It was a painful and confusing time, as you can imagine. But it seemed small, like a clinic."

"That makes sense. They would want to manage the situation, have as few moving parts as possible."

Diedre thought this over. "Was your father involved? Is that how you found out?"

Callie had known this would be an early question. "Yes. Daddy arranged it. He kept records of all these things, but the records went up in a fire. I'm so sorry."

"Yes, of course. I heard about the fire."

"Daddy doesn't remember the details anymore. He's worked on so many things."

Some of the air went out of the older woman. "I understand. And my family won't be able to help either, will they?" Her little chuckle turned into a sigh.

Callie was outraged that Diedre didn't seem to be more outraged. "Aren't you angry for what they did? They took your baby and told you he was dead."

"They did what they thought was best," Diedre said evenly. "I was barely fifteen and in love. Who knows what would have happened? Would Kyle have married me? The second time Kyle went to prison, it was for beating up his girlfriend. My parents thought I would make a real family one day, make a new start. Then the years passed by. How could they tell me then?"

"But it's not over." Callie inched her chair a little closer. "You can still find him. Your son is out there, maybe with a family of his own."

Diedre's face creased into a smile. "Yes, that's thrilling to know. Do you have any leads?"

"No," she had to admit. "That's why I came here, part of the reason, to see if you remembered anything."

"Glenda," she replied. "She's the person you should talk to. She has all the information."

"Glenda?" Callie wasn't sure she even knew a Glenda.

"Glenda Tilley. The private investigator I hired."

"You hired someone to find Stephen?" Callie had not been prepared for this, a private investigator who just might expose everything and implicate her father. This wasn't good.

"Melissa thought it was a waste of time. But Glenda came highly recommended."

"Has she gotten very far?"

"Glenda says that if it happened – and now we know it did – that it was professionally done. She's the one who mentioned your father's possible involvement. The man with the connections and the smarts."

"You came to see Daddy last week at the Ranch," Callie recalled.

"Yes. Glenda's been trying to meet with Buddy, but Buddy and his little henchman keep putting her off. I thought that I could persuade him, as your mother's old friend. But he wouldn't even see me."

"Daddy was under the weather that day. He really was."

Diedre brushed away the excuse. "I don't blame him. His job – maybe not his job, but his calling – was to solve problems for people like my parents."

A series of sounds from the front of the house alerted

them. "Melissa!" Diedre called out. "Hello, dear. We're back in the conservatory."

"Aunt Dee?" The voice echoed through the house. Seconds later, Melissa joined them. She seemed pleased to see Callie, although Callie did note a slight hesitation as the younger woman took off her jacket and set it down on an empty chair. "I'm so glad Aunt Dee has a little company."

Diedre Westerman rose half out of her seat, so intensely eager to spread the news. "Oh, Melissa, it's just wonderful. Stephen is alive. I was right. A mother knows."

"Your baby's alive?" Melissa beamed. "That's wonderful."

"Callie's father arranged it, just like Glenda thought."

Callie shrugged apologetically. "I'm afraid that's all I know. Daddy doesn't recall the details. It was a long time ago."

"Well, we have to find him, that's all there is to it." Melissa rushed over, planted a kiss on Diedre's cheek then turned to her jacket, looking for her phone. "I'll send Glenda a text right now. She'll definitely want to speak to Buddy."

"I'm not sure..." Suddenly, Callie was second-guessing her decision to come here. "I don't know if Daddy will talk to Glenda or not."

"Of course he will. He has to."

"No," Callie answered emphatically. "No, he doesn't have to."

"Hey, Siri," Melissa said. "Text Glenda Tilley."

A disembodied male voice answered. "What do you want to say?"

Diedre didn't seem to hear any of this. "I wonder if he has a family. Who knows? I probably have grandkids. Can you imagine?"

Melissa held up a finger, calling for silence then spoke into her phone. "We have new information about Stephen. Call me as soon as you can."

Callie tried her best to suppress a groan. The last thing she wanted was for Siri to accidentally transcribe this unhappy sound emanating from her throat.

CHAPTER 20

It began as a simple plan, to let Diedre Westerman know about her son. This was a secret that Callie felt she had no right to keep. But now it had devolved into this situation with a private investigator – a very good one, according to Diedre – who already suspected Buddy's involvement. Plus… Plus, she had gotten her boss excited about an article centered on the same secret. Every step had been reasonable at the time, but combined they seemed to equal some sort of death wish, like a lemming racing to the edge of a cliff, leading all of its relatives along for the run.

This morning, Callie hoped to distract herself by focusing on something that felt less dangerous than a missing son. A murder investigation, perhaps. But State had reiterated his decision not to share any more information about *Zombie Blood*. And it was already the weekend, the time when normal people like State had lives and families.

Callie spent the morning in an act of workplace penance, driving to the Warehouse District and actually doing her job. Several other staffers were in the *Free Press* offices, all of them astonished by her appearance there on a Saturday. She spent the first hour or so advising them on various approaches to their articles, then retreated to her cubicle and pounded out the op-ed on renewable energy. Along the way, she received a text invitation from Joey Gibson, inviting her to a spur-of-the-moment brunch. She loved his brunches, usually at a table full of his irreverent, loud, fun-loving friends. This time she declined, with the proudly stated excuse that she was in the office, working. He tried twice more to convince her and each time she demurred.

At 12:23, when Joey showed up at the doorway of her cubicle, she wasn't surprised. He had never taken rejection well. He held up a large white takeout bag with the Tommy on the Lake logo, printed in bold red. "If Calista won't come to the brunch, then the brunch will have to come to Calista," he announced, an obviously rehearsed line.

"Joey, Joey, Joey." He could always make her smile.

"Please don't tell me you've already had lunch."

"I have not," she admitted.

"Good. Then I won't be forced to eat two portions of huevos rancheros with chorizo right in front of you."

"Huevos rancheros! That is so sweet."

"Isn't it?" He perused her cubicle office with its one desk and two chairs. "You must have a lunch area or a kitchenette or something."

"We have vending machines, a fridge and a microwave," Callie said. "But the publisher has a room with a little more space. He's not in today. Will that do?"

She led the way to Oliver's private sanctum. Along the way, her old friend took in the rest of the converted warehouse.

"This is like our offices," Joey whispered, trying not to let the other Saturday workers hear.

"There are similarities," Callie agreed.

"Except that yours is the creepy *Twilight Zone* version," he said, causing Callie to erupt in a wicked little yelp.

The two of them closed Oliver's door and settled in, pushing aside the recycling bins, clearing the cluttered desk and rearranging the chairs. Callie laid out the food on paper plates. Joey had brought along two chilled longnecks of Lone Star, which he jabbed open on the edge of Oliver's desk, an expert move that didn't leave a mark. "So, what is it that brings you in on a Saturday when you can't even go to brunch?"

"Just deadline stuff." Callie tore off a piece of tortilla and piled it with salsa and rice and a generous swipe of yolk. "Nothing exciting." She took a bite. The dish had traveled well; still warm and not too soggy. It had been so thoughtful of him to bring it. "Shouldn't you be out having brunch with your friends?"

"That's Sunday," mumbled Joey, also between bites. "I thought today should be just the two of us. We didn't get a chance to really talk at the memorial." He took his time swallowing then took a long pull of his Lone Star. "Did you know Trevor well?"

"Not really," she said. "A few nice conversations and one official date, during which he kept talking about his previous girlfriend. So, no, not close."

"Do you think he killed himself?" Joey assumed a serious tone. "I mean, at first it seemed obvious. But then your brother and his hunky partner came by the other day and had a long talk with Beau. That got everyone excited."

Callie made a face. "His partner's like forty-five."

"That doesn't keep him from being hunky. Unfortunately, they kept their volume down, so no one heard a thing."

She smiled. "You need to hire someone who's a lip reader."

"I'll mention it to H.R." Joey sawed through his egg-topped tortilla then put down his plastic knife and fork. He sighed heavily, staring down at his plate. "Was there something you saw at Trevor's house?" he asked meekly. "Is that why you think it's murder?"

"I never said it was murder." She had said it, yes, but not to Joey. "Do you think it was murder?"

He looked up, his eyes meeting hers. "I'm so sorry, Callie. I shouldn't have come."

Callie toasted him with her longneck. "What are you saying? This is wonderful. Thank you so much."

"No, I mean I…" The words came out in a stammer. "I shouldn't be asking you questions."

Callie was puzzled. "You can ask me anything you want. We've known each other forever."

"That's the point. We should be able to trust each other."

"What are you saying? You don't trust me?" Callie went over in her mind any way she might have betrayed his trust. "Is there some question you want me to answer? Ask and I'll answer. Honestly."

"Okay." Joey toasted her in return but didn't drink. "Why are you after Beau?"

The question had come out of nowhere. "After Beau?"

"Let me rephrase. Is it about the company? Is it about Trevor? Beau knows you and your paper are after him."

"Interesting," she said slowly while her mind raced to try

to connect the dots. "State didn't tell Beau about me," she muttered. "Daddy didn't tell Beau. Mel didn't. So, who else knew? Naomi and her mother, of course."

Joey was straining to listen. "Did you say Naomi? Naomi Pauling? I've never met her."

She ignored him. "Naomi must have called Beau. Described what I looked like. And Beau obviously told you. So, why did Beau tell…" Her eyes widened. "Oh, my God!"

"I'm so sorry, I really am," Joey moaned through a thin smile. "On the plus side, Beau's paying for brunch."

"He sent you to spy on me?" She couldn't believe it. "And you said yes? You're spying on me?"

"Callie, you have a track record with killers and scandals. He's worried."

"He should only be worried if he's guilty."

Joey made a face. "You know that's wrong. People can have their worlds ruined and not be guilty of anything. Especially in a business like this."

"Beau knows what I'm up to?" It was bound to have happened sooner or later. "Then he knows that I know about the movie."

Joey looked confused. "You made a movie?"

"Damn it. I need to stop thinking out loud." Callie pursed her lips and made serious eye contact with her childhood pal. "Are you going to tell him this?"

"No." He looked insulted. "I do have some sense of loyalty. Do you really think he killed Trevor? Isn't that a leap?"

"I don't know," Callie said. "But he's up to something."

"Like what?" Joey winced at her glaring, unspoken reply. "Okay, you're right. Better that I don't know."

"What exactly did Beau tell you?"

Joey pushed aside his paper plate. "Beau knows we're friends. He called me into his ice cube. He said you and your paper were cooking up some exposé. He didn't know what about or why you would do it, but it might be something that could affect our sale – unless he can get on top of it, he said. Damage control. And since you and I are old friends…" Joey winced. "This sounded less horrific when he said it. Can you forgive me?"

"Of course." Callie put her own plate aside and laid a comforting hand on Joey's knee. "I'm glad you couldn't go through with it." She was very much her father's daughter, and once the shock subsided, she pushed aside her qualms about Joey's intent. She was onto the next step; how she could use this. "I guess the question now is can I trust you?"

Joey bristled. "Yes, you can trust me. I just told you I was a spy."

"What are you going to tell Beau about our conversation?"

He gave it a moment's thought. "I'm going to say you refused to talk about it. You changed the subject. Is that good?"

"Good," she said. "That will do for now. At some point, I may need you to tell him something else. Is that going to be okay?"

"Tell him something else? You mean a lie?" He preened. "What am I, like a double agent?"

"That's a great way of putting it. You were his spy, a crappy spy. Now you're a double agent." Callie frowned. "At some point, what I do may affect the company's sale. I'm sorry, Joey. I know that's real money for you."

Joey waved away her concern. "Oh, don't worry. I turned

down the stock participation. I've been kicking myself ever since. Hell, I'll actually feel better with no sale."

She chuckled. "That's the boy I know and love." They shared a grin then both returned to their huevos rancheros.

For the next half-hour, they polished off their brunch, complete with slices of Tommy's decadent blueberry cheese-cake, as they gossiped about old high school friends. Once or twice, Joey circled back to his mission with Beau, reassuring Callie that he would be a convincing double agent, that he wouldn't let her down.

"If you slip, that's okay," Callie told him. "Well, not okay, but not the end of the world. Just tell me if it happens."

"I will. I promise."

Back in her cubicle, alone again with her thoughts, Callie drained the last of Joey's Lone Star and debated whether or not to leave for the day. It was Saturday, after all. When her phone rang, she eyed the unfamiliar number, most likely a telemarketer from Bangalore. It was a testament to her need for distraction that she answered it.

"Callie McFee?" a woman's voice asked.

"Who's calling?"

"This is Glenda Tilley from Tilley and Associates. Ms. McFee, how are you doing today?" This was said in a warm Texas accent, not much different from her mother's.

"Doing well. How can I help you?" She had just asked the question when she recalled how she knew the name. "Oh, Ms. Tilley."

"Glenda. I believe Ms. Westerman mentioned me. I apologize for calling on a Saturday, but I'm helping out on a Westerman family matter and would love to sit down with you. Today, if at all possible."

"Glenda." Callie paused, eyeing the Lone Star and wishing there were even one swallow left. "I'm not sure what help I can be."

"Why don't you let me be the judge? Unless there's some reason why you don't want to meet with me," she added sweetly. "Is there a reason?"

"Um, no."

"Good to hear. Shall we say four o'clock? We can make it earlier if you're in the neighborhood."

CHAPTER 21

Tilley and Associates was headquartered in the Frost Bank Tower, a massive, modern cathedral to commerce, topped off by a jagged, lighted spire. The office itself was impressive, with a reception area opening onto a single corridor, opening onto a total of six small, private offices. A receptionist, probably annoyed at having to work on a Saturday, greeted Callie then ushered her down the corridor. Glenda Tilley had chosen the corner for herself. Again, the space was not huge, but her desk was centered between two sets of floor-to-ceiling windows, making it seem larger than it was.

Glenda got to her feet, full of energy, and offered a warm double handshake. "Callie." Glenda was what her father had often referred to as ample, an attractive woman of about 50 with no hard edges to her. Soft brown hair, soft colors, muted makeup. "You probably don't remember, but I've been to a few parties at the Ranch. You and your mother and your brother. What a lovely family. And Buddy, of course." Her laughter was bright and efficient.

Callie was offered a coffee or tea or water and, for the first time in a while, didn't accept the gesture of hospitality. "You wanted to see me about a family matter?" Her nerves were already getting the better of her.

"I did." Glenda took her time returning to the other side of the desk. "Callie, dear, the last thing I want is to make trouble for your father. He's a good man and a talented one – back in his heyday. He could cover things up with the best of them."

Callie didn't respond. She had nothing to say.

Glenda went on. "For example, there's no death certificate for little Stephen Westerman. No adoption papers listing the birth mother. I had people scour medical clinics in the Dallas area. We found nothing matching the facts and dates as we know them. Diedre's parents are unfortunately dead, so we have no witnesses to confirm anything. It's almost as if Diedre fantasized the whole thing. From an evidentiary point of view."

"She didn't fantasize it," Callie said.

"I don't mean to brag, but my firm has access to a very expensive, very extensive tracing system. I was expecting for something to pop up. Paperwork. DNA records. Something. Teenage girls, troubled girls, can invent their own realities, you know."

"Is that what you think happened with Diedre?"

"I did entertain that possibility," she admitted. Her smile was wide and thin. "And then you came along, with your statement of what your father told you. I must thank you, Callie. For verifying her story."

Callie stiffened. "I deny making any such statement."

"I have two witnesses who say you did. But I think we're getting off track, don't you?"

The investigator settled back into her cushioned chair, folding her arms across her midsection. "I'm not after your father. First of all, Texans have long memories. They're still quite fond of Buddy, and I can't be the one to ruin that. Plus, he and I are somewhat similar. People value my discretion. They trust me not to tell the world about love affairs and family secrets and business chicanery. Exposing Buddy would make people think twice about hiring me."

Could she be right? Was this smug, manipulative woman in her shiny tower just another version of Buddy McFee, a version stripped of the politics and the pretense of public service? Callie did not want to think that. "So, what do you want from me?"

"I'm going to continue to pursue our regular avenues of information. Something may appear. But Buddy is our best connection to Stephen, and Buddy won't talk to me. That leaves you, dear." Her tone turned sincere. "You obviously care about Diedre."

"She was my mother's best friend."

"So I understand. I'm not asking you to do anything you wouldn't do anyway. Records of what happened probably don't exist, and I'm sure your father's memory is hazy. But if you could prod him a little. You live at the Ranch, correct?"

"I live on the property, not in the house."

Glenda leaned across the desk. "Do you think there are any records in the house? Any old photos, for example, from thirty years ago that might point me in the right direction? Things in the bottom of drawers. It may be something you've seen your whole life and never thought twice about." She chuckled. "I can't tell you what to look for, but everything leaves a trace somewhere."

"You're asking me to implicate my father."

Glenda shook her head. "I'm not interested in some old crime. That's not my job. I'm asking you to help your mother's best friend find her only child."

Callie mulled over the request. She did want to help. This was a dying woman's desperate wish. But she already felt like a traitor – mentioning her father's slip of the tongue to Diedre, proposing some half-baked article about adoptions.

"No," she told the president of Tilley and Associates. "I'm afraid I can't help you."

CHAPTER 22

STATE TIPTOED DOWN the stairs in a jacket and tie, stepping as lightly as a solider making his way across a minefield. Callie was waiting in the entry hall. "They should be tuckered out," he whispered, making sure to move the conversation away from the echoes of the hall. ""Yolanda made me play tag and catch with them for a full hour." He suppressed a grin. "We don't play hide-and-seek anymore, not since Larry got his head stuck in the storm drain and the fire department had to come. That was a full afternoon."

"I don't need them to be comatose," Callie protested. "I've done this before." She actually hadn't. The closest she'd come was in high school when she and a few others sneaked into a house where their friend Patty was babysitting for the evening.

"Well, we can't thank you enough." State stopped by a mirror, checked his tie and straightened his jacket.

Callie hadn't exactly volunteered for the job. For some reason, Yolanda blamed her for the cancellation of their previous date night, as though State's last-minute assignment to the Trevor Birdsong case had somehow been her fault. When

Yolanda called this morning and mentioned that their last reliable sitter was not returning their calls, she made it clear that, if Callie was any kind of decent sister and aunt, she would sacrifice her own Sunday evening, take on the twin six-year-olds and give their parents the break she owed them.

"Yolanda will be down in a minute," State added. "She's printing out the instructions."

"Instructions?"

"She's a little skittish about leaving them with you, to be honest."

Callie was about to offer a sarcastic observation, but a stern look from her brother stopped her. "Oh, by the way, a head's up," she said, making a diplomatic change of subject. "Beau Garrison knows that we know about *Zombie Blood*. Either Naomi or her mother gave him a call. Probably her mother."

"How do you know that? Never mind." State waved away the question. He didn't care to know. "*Zombie Blood* was a dead end, anyway. The producers were amazed that anyone wanted to see it. They burned us two copies and messengered them over to the substation."

"And?"

"Randal and I watched it two times each. We questioned the director, the lead producer, all of the actors that we could get a hold of. Not one of them has a connection to Birdsong or Ka'Kala. We can't even figure out under what circumstances this piece of crap could be relevant to a murder. Do you have any clue? Give me a 'for instance'. A cheapo horror film that never saw the light of day. How is that relevant? What should we be looking for?"

"I don't know what to look for," she had to admit. "But Beau did steal the DVD. And his old partner did go crazy when she saw the title."

He shrugged. "Okay, that I can't explain. As far as evidence goes, all we have is a wiped phone and some suspicious behavior."

"So, dig a little deeper."

"There is no deeper, okay? Whatever respect my new partner had for me is gone. My lieutenant is making noises about manpower hours and caseloads. Your necktie murder theory? That was a long shot that didn't pan out. It's a suicide." State switched to his calm, brotherly tone. "Cal, I know you're emotionally invested. You were the last person he communicated with and the first person to find him. You feel responsible. But that doesn't change the facts."

Callie knew he was right. She needed it to be a murder, just to help her sleep at night without the dreams of Trevor dangling from the doorknob. "So, that's it?"

State nodded. "If something changes, we can reopen." As for Dad, it looks like he doesn't have to worry. Trevor's parents aren't making a stink about whatever drove him to kill himself. No one is, to be honest."

"A man is dead and no one's making a stink." This had to be the saddest thing she'd heard in a while.

"Keep your voices down!" Yolanda was halfway down the stairs. Her whisper may not have been any louder than theirs, but it carried. She was wearing a print maxi dress, knotted at the waist and with a stylish slit up one leg. In one hand was a small, sparkly clutch, in the other several pages of a printout, stapled together. She hugged her sister-in-law then handed her the pages. "Callie, thank you so much. The boys should be out for the night, but just in case, on page two, I've written out…"

"Don't insult her. She'll be fine." State was checking his watch. "Come on. They're not going to hold our reservation forever."

"If you're hungry, there's a Tupperware of mac and cheese in the fridge." Yolanda turned to her husband. "Okay, okay, I'm coming." Her final glance at Callie was out of the corner of her eyes, a wordless admonishment not to screw this up.

Callie watched from the window as they backed out of the driveway then gave the printout a quick perusal before setting it aside. The house was silent now, a rarity, and she was tempted to check the fridge, not for the mac and cheese but for an open bottle of wine. She'd just stepped into the kitchen when a light thumping sound caught her attention. It was coming from overhead, a light thump every ten or twenty seconds. She postponed the wine and went to investigate.

In their earlier years, Larry and Brad had shared a bedroom, a normal thing for young boys, especially twins. But somewhere around their fifth birthday, out of sheer desperation, State and Yolanda experimented with separate rooms. The first night or two were rough going, with the boys pounding on the walls and shouting through the vents to communicate. After the novelty wore off, however, it was like a miracle. Gone were midnight pillow fights and shouting matches and coordinated raids on the kitchen. Also gone were Brad's bed-wetting episodes and Larry's teasing him about the bed-wetting episodes. It was almost as if the separation gave each one a chance to be an individual. State joked that he was thinking of getting them separate houses.

Brad's room was at the top of the stairs. Callie eased open the door and, by the glow of the nightlight, saw that he was fast asleep, curled in a ball in the middle of his bed.

When she opened Larry's door, she found him also in bed, but face-up, tossing a rubber ball, trying to see how close he could get to the ceiling without having the ball touch. He saw her and made one more toss before stopping. "Mom said you were gonna be here."

"Hey, Larry."

"Can you call me Buddy? I want to be called Buddy."

"Sure," she readily agreed. "Do your parents call you Buddy, Buddy?"

"Not yet. I'm doing a kind of grassroots thing. You're my first grassroot."

"Well, I'm honored." Callie wasn't sure how State and Yolanda would react to the name change, but she loved that a six-year-old was using words like grassroots.

Larry and Brad were fraternal twins. The plan had always been to name one after their paternal grandfather and one after their maternal. Larry had arrived first, with a tuft of red curls clinging to his skull. Brad's locks started to come in a few days later, mimicking the dark straight hair of Bradley Adamos. It was obvious which name belonged to which twin, even before their personalities began asserting themselves. "Do you want to be like Grandad?" Callie asked.

Larry looked embarrassed. "I just like the name."

"Well, it's a very good name, Buddy. Your grandad would like that." She held out her hand and Larry "Buddy" McFee handed her the rubber ball. "But now I think it's time for sleep. Okay?"

"Okay." Larry/Buddy eased down onto the pillow then raised his head again. "Aunt Callie? Are zombies for real?"

"No, zombies are not for real. Zombies are made up, just like Sant…." She stopped herself just in time. "Like the sandman."

Buddy was confused. "What's the sandman?"

"He's the guy who comes into your bedroom at night and helps little children get to sleep."

Her nephew did not like this idea. "Someone comes into my room?"

"No, I just told you. There is no sandman, I swear. Now get to sleep." She pulled the covers up to his neck. "Larry… Buddy…" she remembered. "What made you ask about zombies?"

"I don't know," he said, looking down, avoiding her gaze.

"Did you see your daddy watching a movie about zombies?" He didn't answer. "You can tell me."

"It was last night," the boy finally confessed. "Please don't tell Daddy."

"I won't," she solemnly promised, at the same time suppressing her excitement.

"I was supposed to be in bed, but I heard people screaming on TV, so I sneaked down. Zombies eat people, you know. They're very scary."

"I know they're scary," Callie agreed. "Which TV was he watching? The one in the living room?" Little Buddy nodded. "Well, just remember. Zombies aren't real. And this will be our little secret, okay? I won't tell your daddy you saw it and you won't tell your daddy anything. Okay?" She gave him a reassuring kiss on the forehead, deposited the rubber ball in a bureau drawer and headed directly down the stairs.

Zombie Blood was in its case, barely hidden under the front edge of an elderly DVD player. It served him right, she thought, bringing his work home and then inviting her in to babysit. Callie inserted the disc and made sure the volume was on low before pressing "Play".

The plot, what there was of it, was so derivative that it seemed to be cobbled together from the worst moments of every other horror movie. A lonely cabin in the woods. A cemetery scene with the undead crawling out of their graves. Zombies shoving past each other to get to a squirming torso, like rude, hungry diners gorging themselves at a buffet. No wonder Little Buddy had been traumatized.

What made *Zombie Blood* almost unforgiveable, for her at least, were the abysmal production values. Plywood walls in rooms with no ceilings. Bad sound effects. Wigs that looked like they'd been ripped off of department store mannequins.

She had grabbed a notepad and pen before starting, fully intending to jot down any possible connection that came to mind, no matter how ridiculous or small. But the notepad sat on her lap, empty. She recalled what Trevor had said, that you can learn a lot from a bad horror movie. She hoped it would be true.

Callie was halfway through the cemetery scene when a crazy idea began tickling at the back of her mind. It was a random thought, prompted by… She wasn't quite sure what. She had no idea how this wild idea could possibly apply to Trevor's murder, but…

She was in the middle of rejecting the whole notion when

she became aware of the soft whimpering off to her left. Little Buddy stood frozen in the doorway, helpless and horrified but apparently unable to look away from the bloody gore on the huge, hi-def screen. "Oh, Buddy. I'm so sorry." She put the DVD on pause and rushed to his side. "It's not real, okay? You need to get back to bed."

The scene had frozen on the image of a terrified mourner standing alone by a headstone. The boy stared. "What if the zombies come?"

"They're not going to come," she vowed then knelt down and hugged the shivering boy. "They're just make believe." She had already explained this but her logic didn't seem to resonate with the six-year-old. "I can protect you, okay? But you have to stay in your room." She got to her feet, took her nephew by the hand and led him up the stairs.

"Can I lock the door?" he asked when they reached the top. "Please?"

"Um…" On examining the bedroom's doorknob, she saw it was the usual thumb-lock mechanism, equipped with an emergency pinhole, allowing it to be opened from the outside. "Good idea. Zombies can't open locks. You'll be safe in here. "

"But they're not real, right?"

"No, they're not real."

Callie tucked Little Buddy in, stuffing the sides of the bedspread reassuringly under the mattress. On her way out, she made a point of securing the thumb lock, knowing full well that he would be up the second she left, just to make sure it was locked.

Back in the living room, she found the remote then tried to recall what she'd been thinking when Little Buddy interrupted her.

What was it? She furrowed her brow. Something about the actors. State had said they'd contacted all the actors from the movie, all the ones listed in the credits. This had not been a huge challenge, considering the limited size of the cast. But there had been other people, too. Something she'd seen on the screen, or someone, right before Little Buddy started whimpering, had made her think about these others – the assorted zombies and background extras. What had made her think of them?

Callie pressed *stop*, then forced herself to start *Zombie Blood* from the beginning, this time with the sound on super-low, just above mute. She let herself fast-forward over some scenes and focused this time on the zombies and the extras, the forgotten players in this deservedly forgotten film.

About twenty minutes into the DVD, just as the undead began wandering through the cemetery, growling ominously, arms outstretched, lumbering from side to side, she saw it. This is what had planted the forgotten idea in her head. This particular face.

Callie froze the screen then inched the scene backward and forward, trying to find just the right frame, hoping for a clearer shot. She stared at the best shot she could find, baffled by the image, not quite sure what to make of it.

An hour or so later, as Callie was dozing through a *Friends* marathon, she noticed the headlights turning into the drive-way. She switched off the TV then grabbed an icepick from the kitchen and ran up to unlock the door to her nephew's room. She had just returned the icepick to the drawer when the front door opened.

"How did everything go?" Yolanda's voice was tinged with concern.

"Perfect," Callie replied. "Didn't hear a peep."

"Thank you so much," Yolanda said, trying her best to make it sound casual and sincere. "I'll just go up and check, if you don't mind." She didn't even take the time to remove her wrap before she went bounding up the stairs.

"She just gets skittish." State kept his voice to a hush. "We had a lovely, much-needed dinner out, thanks to you."

"I had a great evening as well," Callie said. She kept a straight face, wondered when the best time would be to tell State of her discovery.

"State?" Yolanda was at the top of the stairs, looking and sounding panicked.

"What?" State went instantly into cop/dad mode. "What's wrong?"

"Larry barricaded himself in his room."

"Oh, my God," Callie moaned under her breath.

"I can't get in." Yolanda was halfway down the stairs. State was halfway up. "I pushed. But his bureau's in front of his door. I don't know what's happening." Instinctively, she looked to Callie. "What the hell did you do?"

"Was he trying to keep you out?" State demanded. "Callie? Why would he do that? What did you do to him?"

"Me? No, I didn't do anything. Why would you assume that I did something?"

"Because he barricaded himself in his room," Yolanda answered.

"Good point," Callie allowed. "Um, maybe he's afraid of monsters or something."

State was immediately suspicious. "Since when is he afraid of monsters?"

Callie gave up trying to explain. "I went upstairs and I tucked him in bed. That's all I know."

"Did you tell him a story about monsters?" Yolanda asked.

"No. I mean, I don't know. You'll have to ask Little Buddy."

Both parents looked confused. "Who?" asked Yolanda.

"I mean Larry. He wants to be called Buddy now."

"Buddy? Is this your doing, too?" Yolanda had never been Buddy Senior's biggest fan. "You renamed our son? My God, we were gone two and a half hours."

State shot his sister a deadly look then continued up to Larry's bedroom. Callie could hear him knocking gently on the door. "Larry? Little Buddy? This is Daddy. Can you push the bureau out of the way? We can push together."

Callie waited until Yolanda had joined her husband upstairs. Then she slipped the DVD out of the player and into her bag. This was not in any way her fault, she told herself, growing angrier by the second. State had been the first one to let his son see a zombie movie. And Larry himself had suggested the name change, not her.

Her brother would have to apologize, Callie decided. Only after he had issued a full, heartfelt apology would she let him in on her little breakthrough. Maybe not even then.

CHAPTER 23

Callie spent the first half of Monday morning at home on her laptop, piecing together the photographic proof and contemplating her next step. She knew now, or at least thought she knew, the reason Beau had been so anxious to get Trevor's copy of *Zombie Blood*. But there were still missing pieces and she wasn't quite sure how to proceed. She needed to get someone else involved, she realized. The one previous time she had tried her hand at investigative reporting, she'd flown solo during one of the most critical moments. It hadn't been the best choice.

For a micro-second, she considered enlisting her brother. But she was annoyed with him from last night. Plus, she didn't want to have to deal with the constant arguing and the whole sibling thing, not to mention State's fussiness about police procedure.

Melissa was a possibility. She had texted several times, curious to know how the case was going. Callie had not responded. Her childhood friend had proven to be an enthusiastic partner in crime and certainly deserved to know the reason behind Naomi Pauling's wild reaction. But Callie had qualms. She wasn't sure how close she should get to Melissa, given her documentary on Buddy. Too many moving parts, she thought. Too many things that could go wrong, especially for her father.

That left Oliver as the obvious choice, but still a difficult one. She would need his cooperation to write her investigative piece, the one he had forbidden her from writing. She would also need to convince him that Beau Garrison, his lifestyle hero, was something of a fraud, perhaps a murderer. That might take some convincing, given that her total amount of proof were two screenshots taken from two videos. Callie printed out the screenshots, then packed them and her laptop into her shoulder bag and headed into work.

The *Free Press* offices were on the third floor of the old warehouse. If they'd been on the second, she would probably reject the single, painfully slow elevator and take the stairs every single time. That's what she told herself. But the third floor was just far enough to turn this into a daily decision, a test of her good intentions in which her good intentions lost more often than they won.

Today, she pressed the up button and waited, noting that the elevator light seemed to be stuck on three. She waited thirty seconds. Still stuck. Still on the third floor. So, she did the math. It could start moving at any moment. Should she quit and take the stairs and thereby lose out on the thirty seconds of wait-time she'd already invested? Or should she wait another minute and, when it still didn't budge, face the harder decision of a ninety-second investment. Callie cursed under her breath and opted for the stairs.

A reinforced glass panel gave a glimpse from the stairwell into the *Free Press*'s reception area just opposite the elevator. On the top landing, when she stopped to adjust her shoulder bag, she had just enough time to glance through. It was exactly what she'd expected; two people waiting by the elevator and one of them – in this case, Oliver – rudely holding the door open, allowing him time to have a last few words with a departing… Callie caught her breath. It was Beau Garrison, unmistakably him, gesticulating grandly with his one-half arm. This was the very last person she wanted to run into, especially now.

Instinctively, she ducked below the panel, then raised her head. The lighting in the reception area was a glaring fluorescent, much brighter than the single bulb illuminating this part of the stairwell. If she stepped back a foot and didn't move, then she probably couldn't be seen.

This was the second time in a week that she'd wound up spying on Beau Garrison, which made her feel vaguely guilty, even though he was the guilty one, she told herself. Of something or other. The men's conversation was soft and garbled but their body language was clear. Beau was the alpha, dominant and secure, taking up space, no doubt pontificating on some great, ethereal secret. As for Oliver… It was painful for her to see her boss, a sweet, unpretentious man, reduced to the role of a lifestyle fanboy.

For a frightening moment, it seemed like Beau might be gravitating toward the stairwell, but he eventually stepped into the warehouse elevator and disappeared. Oliver stared at the closed doors then reluctantly turned back to rejoin his own, less bright, less important world.

Callie dropped her jacket off in her cubicle. She gave

Oliver a few minutes to decompress then took her printouts and marched over to his door. As usual, it was open. Oliver looked up from his desk, speechless and expressionless. "Close the door," he finally said. She had already been about to close it, but to have him say it… Callie did as she was told.

"You're trying to take him down, aren't you?" The accusation caught her off-guard. "Beau Garrison was just here. He asked about the piece you're doing, the piece I said you couldn't do."

"I was working on my own time."

Oliver wasn't buying it. "Really? And what about your piece on shady adoption practices? How is that coming?"

"Um…" She shrugged. "I got kind of sidetracked."

"Did the story even exist, or did you just make it up?"

"It existed. It exists."

"Beau says you tracked down Naomi Pauling and made her go hysterical. What did you say to her?"

Callie paused and counted to ten – closer to an actual five than a ten. "Oliver, I know you admire him. Millions do. But Beau Garrison is a fraud." She kept her voice steady and calm. "The man is desperately hiding something. And I know what."

"Okay." Oliver swallowed hard. "Okay, I'm listening."

"Who is this?" She handed him a printout of a screenshot.

Oliver took one look. "It's the shaman, Ka'Kala."

"Right. I found it online. The last piece of video they got out of the camera before it died – according to their documentary." She paused for effect then handed him a second screenshot. "Now who is this?"

Oliver looked then focused his eyes into a squint then looked back to the first screenshot. "Where did you get this?"

It was a still from *Zombie Blood*, the best shot Callie had been able to find of a middle-aged Black man standing at a gravesite, looking genuinely horrified at three zombies who had just stumbled out of the bushes. "Ignore Ka'Kala's face paint. It's the same man, isn't it?"

"It looks like the same man," Oliver allowed.

"It is. Look at that horizontal scar on his chin." She pointed it out on both photos. "Here. There. Same scar."

"Where did you get this?" Oliver repeated.

"Trevor Birdsong once told me that you can learn a lot from a bad horror movie. I think this is what he meant."

"You got this from Trevor?"

"In a way. Your friend Beau broke into Trevor's house and stole a copy of the DVD."

"He stole…? How do you know?"

"Because I saw him do it." She waved away his next question. "Never mind how. That's a still from *Zombie Blood*. It was filmed a few years after Beau and Naomi stepped out of the jungle with their story."

Oliver's brow furrowed in confusion. "It could be someone else. It has to be."

"Even if that's true, which it's not, it doesn't explain why Beau would break in and steal that particular movie."

Oliver went from one photo to the other, his eyes focused on the scar. "So…" He was still piecing it together. "The actor in this movie also played the role of Ka'Kala. So, there was no real Ka'Kala. Is that what you're saying?"

"There was no real Ka'Kala."

"No. No way. There's got to be an innocent explanation. Did you ask Beau?"

Callie tried not to roll her eyes. "Even if there is an innocent explanation, it doesn't change the facts. The video was supposed to be of a real shaman in the rainforest. Imagine what that would mean to Beau's brand if this got out."

Oliver understood. "They've already arranged a sale. Beau told me. It's being signed next week. A story like this…" He shook his head. "Beau lost a hand, for God's sake. None of that was fake. And they came out of the jungle with the Wepapua ointment. How do you fake that?"

She pointed to the photos. "This is all speculation on my part, except for the fact that Ka'Kala is not any kind of a tribal shaman. You want to know when Naomi went hysterical?" Callie didn't wait for an answer. "It was when I showed her the promo page for *Zombie Blood*. I'd get hysterical, too, if something like this suddenly came back to haunt me."

Oliver scratched at his permanent stubble and sighed. He was being swayed, she could tell. "Who else knows? Your brother and his people?"

"Not really," Callie said sheepishly. "State has the movie. Well, he did until I borrowed it. But he hasn't seen *Balancing the Universe* in years, if he ever saw it. I don't think anyone else has made the connection."

"Except Trevor Birdsong. Trevor made the connection." Oliver scrunched up his face. "I can't believe Beau's that kind of person."

"This is the same guy who rock climbed the wall of a sacred mosque. He may have changed his game, but do you think he's really changed? Deep down?"

"Okay. Maybe. But murdering Trevor?" Callie could have said a dozen things to heighten the moment and get him onboard. But she knew this man. Whatever she could say, he was already thinking it. "Okay." His voice was barely audible. "It's something we need to investigate. And I apologize. I should have trusted your instincts."

"Thanks," she replied. "I could have been nicer about it."

"True." Oliver bobbled his head and gave out a little smile. "But that's a discussion for another day. What now?"

Callie had already figured it out. "We need to learn as much as we can about that trip."

CHAPTER 24

It was a few minutes before five p.m. when the call came from Joey Gibson. "All clear," he whispered. "All clear."

Callie could barely hear him. "What's all clear? Joey?"

Joey sighed. "I was trying out my spy voice. Beau left around four. The last stragglers left a few minutes ago."

"That's pretty early for an office."

"Well, Beau believes in this whole quality of life thing. And to be honest, we're just kind of treading water. No new products or campaigns. Not until this whole sale thing goes through. Are you coming or not?"

"We'll be there."

Callie and Oliver arrived in under fifteen minutes. The building itself was larger than theirs, with Ka'Kala occupying the entire warehouse. Receiving and shipping were on the ground level while the offices were on two and three. Joey met them on the street and quickly ushered them in. If he'd been wearing a trench coat, the collar would have been turned up.

"Thank you so much for doing this," Callie said. "I owe you."

"Beau wants me to take you to dinner," Joey said as the elevator doors closed. "He says I should get you drunk and get you talking. Can you believe that?"

"I don't need your help to get drunk."

"I know. That's what I told him." Joey chuckled nervously. "I'm not going to ask what you're up to."

"We're just here to visit the museum," Oliver said.

"You mean *The Ka'Kala Story*?" Joey looked crestfallen. "Really? You could have come in anytime for that. Technically, it's open to the public. For tax reasons, I think."

"If Beau knew we were interested in the museum..." Callie realized she had to be cautious, even with Joey. "We would prefer he didn't know."

"Fair enough." The doors opened onto the third floor, the one with the museum and the ice cube. "I thought you were going to plant bugs or hack our computers. Not that you can, but it would be fun to see you try."

"We're not going to do anything illegal," Oliver assured him, not realizing how disappointing this might sound.

"But it's still a secret mission," Callie said. "Please don't tell Beau."

"Got it." Joey led them to the arch just a few yards from the two elevators. "So, what are we looking for?" Callie and Oliver stopped in their tracks, causing Joey to erupt into a little bark of a laugh. "Just kidding. I'll let you guys at it. I suppose you want electricity." Joey flipped a row of switches, bringing to life the displays inside the arch, complete with the muted sound of rain and assorted jungle noises. "When you want to leave, just text me," Joey said. And with that, he headed jauntily back into the offices.

Neither one of them knew what to look for, only that Beau's secret lay somewhere in the rainforest of West Papua and that the museum, *The Ka'Kala Story*, was a shrine to that time and place. Directly inside the arch, the story began with video clips of the younger, cockier versions of Beau and Naomi prepping for their journey into the land of the uncontacted tribes, in one of the most remote spots in the world.

Callie had brought along her laptop. She set it down on a display cabinet, booted it up and connected it to her phone's Wi-Fi hotspot. "You said the museum was all about Beau controlling the narrative," she reminded Oliver. "I'm just curious to see how that narrative has changed over the past eight years."

Oliver was intrigued. "You think it's changed?"

"Let's see."

Callie had bookmarked many of the early articles on the couple's jungle misadventure. Now she pulled them up and began comparing them to the official museum version. Near the arch was a screen, highlighting a video/audio clip from one of the German tourists who'd rescued Beau and Naomi from the white waters of the Baliem River. In the clip, Naomi was mumbling about a magical shaman who had saved their lives. "Can you pull up *Balancing the Universe*?" she asked Oliver. "It's on *Netflix*."

Oliver took over her laptop while she watched the museum's clip three more times, looking for anything.

"It's not on *Netflix*," Oliver said.

"Yes, it is," Callie answered. "I watched it last week."

"Well, it's not on now." Oliver spent another thirty seconds checking. "I don't think it's streaming anywhere. Someone must have pulled it."

"Pulled it? Interesting." Callie knew that things like this happened. Movies go in and out of availability on all sorts of platforms. And it was still possible to find *Balancing the Universe*. Amazon must have dozens of copies. But the timing was interesting.

Oliver pointed down into the cabinet. "That's the bowl Ka'Kala gave them," he said. It was a small, hand-carved bowl, holding pride of place in the lighted display, like a precious, ancient artifact. It was the same bowl featured in the only existing video of the shaman. "There was some ointment left in it. It's how they worked out the formula for the Wepapua."

"Did the Germans take any videos of that bowl? When they came out of the jungle?"

Oliver shrugged. "I don't remember. Maybe not."

"Interesting," Callie repeated as she left her laptop and wandered around the next few displays. One of them, an enlarged photo, showed the couple, bedraggled and covered with sores, but looking grateful in their hospital beds. "Beau and Naomi went into silence mode during their recovery in Australia," she said when Oliver joined her. "It was only later, when they were back home, that they started vlogging again. Plenty of time to embellish – and invent some miracle lotion."

"They invented the ointment?" This seemed to disturb Oliver as much as anything. "No, that's not possible. Wepapua is an absolute wonder."

"I'm not saying it's bad. It could be great. But there's probably some placebo effect. You're convinced it works wonders, and it does."

"So, there was no shaman at all?" Oliver demanded. "No

uncontacted tribe? Just some actor in a loin cloth? In a hut? In Austin?"

"If the guy in both videos is the same guy, yes."

"And they were doing what? Just stumbling around the jungle for three weeks?"

"If it's the same guy, yes."

Callie took the screenshots from her computer bag and went out through the arch into the actual offices, not far from the glass cube. She stood in front of the Ka'Kala painting, held up both photos and compared them to the man dominating the huge frame. Oliver, as usual, followed. "Damn," she said with just a touch of admiration.

"Damn what?"

"The artist changed Ka'Kala's face." She handed one of the photos, the one in the hut, to Oliver. "See?" The painting had been taken from the video and they were meant to be the same, the same man in the same hut, laboring over the same medicine bowl. But she was right. The faces were different. The nose was a little broader. The forehead narrower. The hair slightly longer.

"It was done by an artist," her boss argued. "You know, like Paul Newman's face on his salad dressing. Artistic license."

Callie wasn't convinced. "It was done on purpose. This is the image they use now, the one people remember. They altered his features just enough. Their new, improved reality." She stopped Oliver before he could counter. "And don't give me that Paul Newman bullshit. Paul Newman on the salad dressing still looks like Paul Newman."

From what they could see as they continued to wander through, the rest of the museum held nothing new, nothing that stood out, just a chronicle of the world's instant fascination with the couple's jungle adventure and how Beau Garrison and Naomi Pauling had generously shared their story – and the Wepapua ointment and their ever-growing line of holistic products – with the rest of the world.

Callie packed up her laptop, thanked Joey effusively and turned her attention to her growling stomach and her need for a good glass of white. She invited Joey to join her – his choice of restaurant, her treat. But Joey had to get home to celebrate his six-month anniversary with Patrick. "I wouldn't take it so seriously," Joey explained. "But neither one of us expects this to get to the one-year mark, so we have to enjoy it while we can."

Oliver had been within easy earshot and was therefore prepared. "Sorry," he told Callie when she turned in his direction. "I have plans, too."

"What made you think I was going to ask?" she countered. "Do you have a date, is that it? With Jennie? A date with young Jennie?"

"Yes," he said without a hint of an apology. Then he checked his watch. "Sorry. Let's talk first thing in the morning. I think we have some promising leads. Good work." Callie's ego prevented her from delving further into Oliver's plans for the evening.

All the way home, she ruminated over the current state of her freezer, wondering if there might be a leftover from the main house in there or maybe a Lean Cuisine nestled in the back. She had wanted company and conversation and now would have to make do with something out of the microwave. How pathetic! And did Oliver actually have a date with

Jennie? Or had he just been miffed that she'd asked Joey before asking him? And what the hell was with the 'promising leads' and 'good work'? She was leading him straight into a high-profile exposé involving fraud and murder, and all he could think to say was 'promising leads' and 'good work'? Douche!

CHAPTER 25

By the time Callie turned off Hacienda Road and drove onto Ranch property, she was prepared for a wine-fueled night in front of the TV. And then she saw the lights up at the house – porch lights and interior lights and lights in the back garden, reflecting off the trees. An oversized, white SUV stood in front and, though she couldn't make a positive I.D. from this distance, she was sure it was State's. Callie ignored the gatehouse turn and drove straight down the avenue of live oaks. After parking by the edge of the house, she walked around the flagstone path to the rear. This was where all the action was.

Once around the corner, Callie had time for a good look before anyone there looked at her. The stone firepit was alive with healthy flames and the unmistakable scent of hickory. Buddy and his red-haired grandson stood in the fire's glow, roasting hot dogs on wooden sticks while State stood several yards off, arms folded in a protective posture, observing carefully. Gil Morales, a few yards off on the other side mimicked State's protective posture. The rest of the family, Yolanda and

Brad, were setting the stone slab of a table under the lights of the veranda.

"Callie, honey." In her focus on the scene, she had failed to notice Sarah. The older woman approached, wiping her hands on her apron. "I was hoping you'd show up."

The household's one full-time employee had been at the Ranch for as long as Callie could recall, but it was only in the past few months that, at Callie's insistence, she had stopped wearing her traditional white and gray uniform. Any woman who was as much a family member as Sarah shouldn't have to dress like a servant. Sarah had been reluctant at first, but Gil and Buddy both pretended not to notice the change.

Sarah glanced back over her shoulder, not looking at all pleased with the proceedings. "They showed up without warning, bringing this damn picnic dinner. Casual as all hell."

Callie smiled. "No one's going to blame you if the potato salad is a little under par."

"It's not the woman's damned Greek potato salad, which you can't even call potato salad. No, honey, it's your father."

"Oh." Callie knew instantly what she meant. "How bad is he?"

"Well, he's not belligerent, thank the Lord. But he's not himself."

"Is it obvious?"

Sarah's grin was familiar and endearing, harkening back to earlier, simpler times. "Let's just say your brother noticed. So, yeah. Obvious."

"Well, it was bound to happen." Callie sighed. It was almost a sigh of relief. "You should go home. Gil and I can handle this."

"You sure?" Sarah sounded hesitant but was already taking off her apron and folding it. "I was supposed to leave at five. I do have a schedule, although you wouldn't know from looking."

"You should go home," Callie repeated. "There won't be much cleanup."

"And now Mr. Gil wants me to move in and live here. Imagine that? Like the old days when I was always on call. I don't know if I want that."

"They'll pay you a lot more, I can guarantee." She regretted the words as soon as they left her mouth. "I'm sorry. I know it's not about the money."

Sarah shook her head. "Only rich people say it's not about the money. Are you sure it'll be okay for me to go?"

"I'm sure." The two women shared a quick hug, then Callie watched as her childhood confidant, a woman who'd been like a second mother, quietly made her exit across the veranda and through the house.

Callie maneuvered slowly out of the shadows and into the flickering light. The air was rich with the tang of hickory smoke. Her mother had never approved of installing a firepit. Not in keeping with the spirit of the Ranch, she would say. But one weekend, when Anita was off on a shopping trip to New York, Buddy and two pals from the governor's office swooped in and built it themselves, using stones they had carted up from the riverbed. Buddy later calmed her down by saying it was a temporary installation, easily removed, just to see if the family might enjoy it. That was well over twenty years ago.

Gil was the second person to see her. He made eye contact, took a swig from something in a rocks glass and ambled in her direction, swaying ever so slightly. "We have some wine in the cooler," he offered, "courtesy of the invading forces. We also have hot dogs, although between Buddy and Larry's current skill levels, I'm not sure I would recommend."

"Not right now," Callie said. "You seem in a good mood, given the situation."

"I suppose I am more relaxed," he admitted. "It was a trauma when they drove up, I'm not going to lie. But now the whole family knows."

"Sarah told me. It's a good thing, no?"

Gil turned to observe the three generations of McFee males around the fire. "A burden shared is a burden halved, as the saying goes. Your dad made me promise never to tell State. Now I don't have to."

"How did he take it?"

"Too early to tell. Your brother doesn't always react the way you think he should. It's part of his macho training."

"And Dad's behavior?"

"Well, your father didn't strip to his skivvies and jump into the pond. But his mental state was pretty clear from the moment they ambushed us. Your poor brother makes a big deal about coming here to reconcile with the old man and then he finds this."

"The twins must be confused."

"At the moment, they have another playmate, so all is good." Gil dipped a finger in his drink, swirled the ice cubes and eased out a final sip. "I won't ask what you've been up to."

"Good. I won't have to lie."

"A little birdie tells me the *Free Press* is looking into Trevor Birdsong's death. Is that wise?"

"You used to think so." Callie had no idea how Gil knew, but she wasn't going to give him the satisfaction of looking surprised. "Isn't that what you wanted? No one even mentioned murder until you and Dad brought it up."

"We did indeed," Gil said. "But that moment has passed. The young man did not initiate his lawsuit. And his death, his suicide, did not initiate any waves."

"So, you never really thought it was murder." It had been such a typical move, to delay and distract. "You harangued State into keeping the investigation open, but it was all just an act."

Gil shrugged. "Please excuse me for not having a crystal ball. We did what we had to at the time."

"Well, I happen to think you were right. I think he was murdered."

"That's what my little bird says. And that's why I'm warning you to be careful."

"You're warning me? That sounds a little ominous, Uncle Gil. What are you warning me about?"

"Calista." Gil's sudden, Cheshire cat grin was probably intended to seem disarming. "When you talk about murder, it includes a murderer. The two go together; that's been my experience. That's all I meant. Be careful, girl."

"I'll be careful."

Callie glanced at her empty hands then over at the red cooler by the table. She wished now that she'd accepted Gil's offer of wine. Gil was examining the bottom of his empty rocks glass, probably with a similar thought in mind. Then he looked up, scanning the veranda and the firepit for someone. "Where the hell's Sarah?"

"I told her to go home," Callie said.

Gil grunted. "You're right. Good idea. It'll be easier when she moves back in. Easier for everyone." A second later, he headed for the veranda doors leading to the sunroom and the wet bar.

Callie didn't follow him physically but followed his lead, crossing to the stone table and the red cooler. Yolanda and Brad had finished with the place settings and were making their way to the firepit. By the time Callie took her first sip of the slightly chilled, screw-top Chardonnay, State had joined her. She took her time, fighting her urge to talk, knowing it would be better for him to speak first.

"I'm gonna need that DVD." Instead of a beer bottle, her brother was holding a rocks glass; golden brown liquid, half full, no ice. From his slow, slightly slurred speech, she guessed that it wasn't his first.

"It's in the gatehouse," she said. "Did Larry tell you what happened?"

"He's Little Buddy now. Yolanda absolutely hates that name, but… so what. Yeah, Little Buddy told me about the movie. We're keeping it from his mother, since I'm partly at fault."

"He saw the zombies first on your watch."

"That's what I'm saying," he snapped. "Did you see anything? In the movie?"

Callie debated for a second then went back to her original decision. "Nothing you didn't see." Which was true.

"What did I tell you?" He swirled his drink and a drop of it splashed over the side.

"Are you okay?" she asked, taking a step closer. "And don't pretend you don't know what I'm talking about."

He moved his head, not quite a nod, not quite a shake. "Still processing, I guess. When we got here, he didn't know our names, not even mine. Gil claimed it was a senior moment, but please…"

"Dad's on some medication now. It should be helping."

State looked back at his father and his son together, chatting like two six-year-olds. "It's so hard seeing him like this. I came over to set things right. And now…"

"I know it's a shock."

"When did you find out? How long ago?" State had suddenly raised his voice.

"Since I moved back from Dallas. He didn't tell me, honest. He didn't want either of us to know."

"Then how did you know?" he asked. "And how didn't I know?"

Callie recognized his resentment and countered with some resentment of her own. "Good point, State. How didn't you know? There were plenty of times when you should have. Did it never occur to you?"

Her brother made a face, but he knew she was right. "I realized he was slowing down. Getting erratic. I mean, the man's in his seventies. Maybe I didn't want to ask."

"It's something no one wants to ask."

State cocked his head at the dawning of a new, disturbing thought. "Good God. Why is he still working? How is he still working?"

State was asking the same questions that she'd asked all those months ago. "Because he has to," she answered. "Gil and I have tried to get him to stop. But he has to be Buddy McFee. Who else can he be?"

"And his clients are okay?"

"Most of the time, it's nothing that Gil can't handle. A little influence peddling or advice. And Daddy still has enough good days to keep up the illusion." She took another sip then delivered the reality check. "Of course, there is the odd case when a client commits suicide or gets murdered."

"Oh, my God." Callie could see her brother, the big, strapping homicide detective, literally go weak in the knees. "Please tell me he didn't do anything to cause that. Even if he did do something, please don't tell me. I can't know."

"He didn't do anything," she swore.

"Thank you for saying it."

"He didn't," she insisted. "Look, you'll sit down with Gil and Dr. Oppenheimer. It will be good to have you in the loop. Yolanda, too."

"Yolanda, too? That's a lot to chew on."

Callie had to laugh. "I'm serious. We have our differences, but she's a much better caregiver than either one of us."

"She is." State took another healthy swallow then turned in search of his wife. She was arranging the last of the blackened hot dogs onto a platter and trying to usher everyone toward the stone table.

Buddy had an arm sloped over his grandson's shoulder. "Your name's Buddy?" he said in jovial, booming voice. "That's incredible. My name is Buddy. We got two Buddies here. How did that happen?"

Little Buddy giggled. "You know. They named me after you."

"Who named you? Your daddy?" He pointed to State. "Is that your daddy over there?"

The boy's giggle grew. "Yes, that's my daddy. My real name is Larry."

"No!" Buddy gasped, his free hand flying up to his mouth. "Are you kidding me? My real name is Larry. How did that happen?" Then both Buddies giggled together.

To Callie's surprise, the potato salad and hot dogs wound up being edible. The apple pie, bought from a farm stand and served with ice cream, was delicious. By the end of the evening's picnic, she had screwed the top off a second bottle of Chardonnay, which she begrudgingly shared with Yolanda, while Gil and State made two more visits each to the bar in the sunroom.

Everyone helped in the cleanup, even Gil, filling the cooler and the wicker basket with the leftovers and carrying them out to the oversized SUV. State was in no condition to drive. It wasn't until the kids were bundled in the back seat and his wife was behind the wheel that he changed his mind about leaving. "Can you put them to bed?" he asked, leaning into the driver's window. "Please? I'll be home in a little while."

Yolanda had found just enough empathy at that particular moment not to question him. "Just let me know," she said softly then kissed him on the cheek and drove off.

Back at the firepit, Buddy had put on another two logs and was watching, mesmerized, as they slowly took the flame, spitting little bursts of embers into the night sky. State set out two Adirondacks, offered one to his father and settled into the other.

Callie was tempted to join them, but she resisted. Her brother needed this more than she did. She'd already had her quiet evenings with Buddy, engaged in halting, meaningless conversations or, more often, no conversations at all, just the physical proximity. The silence could be quite wonderful, pretending to be back in the old days and able to carve out some quality time with the great, busy man –your father, the man everyone in Texas wanted to be with.

Callie took her own chair and watched from a distance as the new logs were reduced to old logs and the flames began to fade. At some point, Gil, who must have also been watching from the shadows, came to escort his boss into the house and up to his bedroom.

"Want me to drive you home?" Callie stood over her brother, wobbling from side to side. "On second thought, it might be safer to call a car service."

State looked up. It had not been that chilly of an evening and fire had made the whole area quite toasty. "I want to spend the night here."

"You can't stay here. It's going to get cold, and you'll be sore as hell in the morning." She reached for his hand with both of hers and began to pull him up.

State stumbled to his feet. "No. I mean in my old room. Do I still have an old room?"

"Mom left it as a shrine when you moved out. I imagine it's the same. The cleaning service comes twice a week, so the rooms should be in good shape. Want to check it out?"

His had been the room at the end of the balcony hall on the second floor. They both knew what to expect, but opening the door and turning on the light still provided something of a revelation. Many of State's favorite things were gone – the framed posters that he'd taken with him to college, the football trophies, the layers of clothes strewn over the floor. But the curtains were the same, and the bedspread, and the wallpaper. "Has anyone else ever used this room?" he asked.

"I doubt it."

"Good. We probably don't even need to change the sheets."

"We're changing the sheets. End of discussion."

State had no idea where the linens were kept. He had probably never known. His sister led him to a closet just off the laundry room where they found a clean set on a shelf labeled "Full Fitted". They were both just sober enough to strip the bed and, after a few tries, get the new sheets fitted in the right direction.

State sat heavily on the bed's edge. "Thanks, Cal. I mean it."

Callie had no idea what he was thanking him for, but she appreciated it deeply. "Don't forget to call Yolanda. Given the time, maybe a text is better."

"Right." State reached into his jacket for his phone. "What's going to happen to Dad?"

"A lot of people go through this," she said, using her most comforting voice. "Other Buddy McFees go through this, as scary as that is to believe. We just have to make it through with the least amount of damage. That's how I see it."

"Damage?" he asked.

"Suicides. Murders. That kind of thing."

"Jesus!" State dropped his head to his chest. A few seconds later, he began to chuckle. It seemed to last longer than any healthy chuckle should. "Ahhh, Cal," he said at last. "You have a good way with a bedtime story."

"Happy dreams," she replied with a snarky grin then left the room and closed the door.

Her own childhood bedroom was right next to his. The

door squeaked as she edged it open. Then she reached around the corner for the light switch. One of the overhead bulbs was out. But by the light of the other, she looked around at the most familiar room of her life. It was slightly smaller than State's and not particularly girlie in either the colors or furnishings. Callie eased down on the slate gray bedspread then lay back and felt the reassuring push of the old mattress springs.

The next thing she was aware of was the daylight streaming through the open curtains. She was lying in the center of the bed now, still fully dressed and on top of the bedspread. Somehow, without the benefit of her pills or her Marpac sound machine or her two special pillows or any of the other nighttime rituals she'd created for herself, she had managed to sleep through the night.

CHAPTER 26

CALLIE LOOKED AROUND the bedroom for her phone, then seemed to recall having left it outdoors. Had there been any rain? She didn't think so, but of course there was always the humidity. She had heard of phones being put out of commission by the heavy Austin dew. As she walked out, she noted that the door to State's bedroom was open. He was nowhere in sight. All that remained was a large, impressive imprint on the top of the bedspread.

Outside, the hickory fire was long cold, but the overhead lights by the veranda were still on, piercing through the remnants of morning mist. Her phone, in its ruby red case, was on the stone slab of a table, face down, its top covered in a layer of moisture. She picked it up, wiped it off and found it was low on power but still functioning.

"How's your head?" It was Gil Morales, out by the firepit, piling leftover bottles and glasses and napkins on a tray. "You and your brother were sure throwing 'em down."

Callie paused and focused on her head. "Not bad. A little

throbbing, but nothing outside the normal parameters. How is Dad?"

"Haven't heard a peep from him; thank you for asking. I imagine he'll have no memory of last night, but you can never tell. Life is an adventure." Callie's phone pinged with a text message and she reflexively glanced at the screen. "Go ahead," Gil said. "Don't mind me."

The text was from Oliver, as were the previous three. "Meet me at Austin Memorial Park. ASAP. Let me know." She scrolled up to the others. "I think I have a lead. Call me," said the first. "Where are you?" had arrived nine minutes later. And five minutes after that: "I don't want to do this without you."

"Any problems?" Gil was a legendary poker player and had a way of seeing through even the blandest of expressions. At one point, he'd been banned from the weekly good ole boy games, carried on after hours at the Texas Statehouse.

"It's my boss," she said, flashing a disarming little smile. "Apparently, I'm late for work."

"Okay," Gil drawled and returned to the firepit and his cleanup efforts.

Callie exited through the house and was surprised to find her truck parked off to one side. She'd completely forgotten that she'd driven here. It had been that kind of a night. Leaning on the hood, she began texting Oliver – manually, not by voice – since she didn't want to say anything out loud. "You mean the cemetery? That Austin Memorial Park?"

"FINALLY," Oliver texted back. "Already here. Meet me at the administrative office." And he listed the address for her to put into her GPS.

The cemetery was a straight shot up MoPac, just a few

turns off the Hancock Drive exit. Callie found the small stone visitors' center and office just inside the gates and parked right behind Oliver's gray Prius. She was just getting out of her truck when Oliver emerged from the building. He waved and smiled then waited until he came within easy speaking distance. "What do you want to hear first, the good news or the bad?"

"Bad." Callie always liked to get it out of the way.

Oliver crinkled his face and sighed. "Actually, I can't tell it that way. I shouldn't have even asked. I'll start with the good news. I recognized the cemetery."

"From *Zombie Blood*?" Callie asked, just to make sure. She had thought about it on the way over but had no idea how this could be a substantial lead.

"It's in section eight," he said, pulling a little map out of his pocket. "You can drive."

As Callie's truck made its way around the irrigated lawns and the gentle, rolling curves, Oliver explained. "I kept studying the shot you grabbed from the movie. I have an aunt buried here, so the landscape looked familiar. Take the right fork here. Good." He looked up from the map. "Luckily, there's an obelisk kind of monument in the background of the shot, so it took me less than an hour to track it down."

"Track what down?"

"The grave. The grave where Ka'Kala was standing in the movie." He seemed quite proud of himself. "There's the obelisk. You can pull over here."

Callie hated being the one to ask the questions, especially when it might be something that she should have figured out. She had barely shifted into Park when Oliver opened his door and started marching up the slight incline of grass. Callie recognized it, too – the spot where the three zombies had stumbled out of the brush and startled the hapless mourner, otherwise known as Ka'Kala.

Oliver stopped by the headstone and pointed down. It was a modest piece of dark granite. "Georgia Andover. 1970 – 2009. Beloved Wife." A single red rose in a small, metal bud vase was spiked into the ground. The rose looked fresh, just coming into bloom. There was even water in the bud vase.

Callie examined the simple marker, reading it over and over. "Okay, I give up." It wasn't an easy thing for her to admit.

To his credit, Oliver didn't gloat. "One thing that bothered me – about Beau using an actor to play Ka'Kala. Even someone who just did extra work. Why would Beau take the risk? If I was trying to pull the wool over the eyes of the world, I certainly wouldn't hire an actor to play my shaman. I'd want someone completely unknown. So, maybe…"

She was following his logic. "So, maybe he wasn't an actor. Maybe the guy just happened to be here, putting flowers on a grave, when these amateur filmmakers came around. Is that what you're thinking?"

"Exactly," said Oliver. "My guess is they didn't even bother to get him to sign a release. Maybe the guy mentioned it to Beau and Naomi. Maybe he didn't. But it never became a problem until Trevor stumbled across it.

"Wow." *Wow* was a top-end compliment in her vocabulary. Callie focused again on the granite headstone. "Beloved Wife. And a fresh rose." She gasped. "Maybe he was here today. Or yesterday. Ka'Kala was here."

"I know," Oliver agreed. "At least there's a good chance."

Callie's excitement grew. "I think there was a rose in the movie, too. A red rose. Maybe not. I can't remember. But if we can track down the guy… Georgia Andover's beloved husband, maybe? We could be so close. Ooh!" She snapped her fingers. "They must have records. Someone who paid for the burial. Or maintenance fees. Or a contact name and number. Did you check with the office?" She looked up at Oliver. His hangdog expression said it all. "Oh. This is the bad news, isn't it?"

He nodded. "They can't give out that information. Privacy."

She understood. "Of course. And I don't suppose there's any way we can trick them into it."

Oliver rolled his eyes. "You know? I didn't even think of that."

"Well, it's probably too late. You already put them on alert."

"I apologize," he said. "Lying and scheming don't come naturally to me."

Callie shrugged. "It's a skill. You have to put in the hours. Meanwhile…" She expelled a sad little breath. "Are you hungry? I haven't had a thing all morning."

They took photos of the grave marker and noted its location. Then Oliver searched for "restaurants near me" on his phone. The closest was a cute little place called Debbie's Diner, right on Hancock Drive, barely a block from the cemetery grounds. The photo showed it to be an actual lunch car diner, shiny with aluminum, dating back to the heyday of the railroads.

Debbie's Diner was nearly empty when they arrived. Callie imagined the place might be packed on Memorial Day or after a funeral service, but not today. They settled into a booth with red leatherette banquettes. A friendly, middle-aged waitress wearing a Denise nametag handed them menus the size of photo albums. When she returned with their water and silverware, Callie ordered the full Rancher's Breakfast while Oliver requested a veggie Egg Beaters omelet, heavy on the veggies and no cheese or toast.

By the time Denise returned with the coffee cups and the carafe, Oliver had brought out his gravesite photo of Ka'Kala or, as they were starting to call him, Mr. Andover. "Maybe we should do a stakeout," he suggested. "Of the cemetery."

"Do you know how long that would take?" Callie asked. "We don't know if he comes every day or once a week or in the morning or afternoon. We don't know if it's even him, after all these years. He could be dead."

Oliver disagreed. "If he was dead, he'd be buried with Georgia, don't you think? Beloved wife?" It was only then that he became aware of a pair of eyes behind him, staring over his shoulder.

"Sorry," said Denise. Then she turned and walked away. "Your meals should be out in a few."

Oliver waited until she was out of range. "We can't just leave it like this. He's so close. I can feel it. Maybe you can find some way to get those cemetery records. Your dad has connections. Your brother's a cop. If you tell State what we're doing…"

"I prefer not to go there," Callie said. "If this becomes a police investigation, we'll get frozen out. State's new partner will see to that."

"Then what do you suggest?"

"Give me a minute to think." She saw him eyeing his watch. "I didn't mean a literal minute. Go check your phone. Jennie probably needs your advice on an article."

Oliver didn't take offense and did as he was told. The two of them sat in silence until Denise returned with a veggie omelet looking lonely on its plate. On the other plate was a huge mishmash of eggs and pork and hash browns and whole wheat toast. "Enjoy," she said, centering the plates with a towel. "Let me know if you need anything."

"Excuse me, Denise." Callie adopted her friendliest, most guileless smile. "I couldn't help noticing when we were talking. The way you looked… Does Mr. Andover come in here often?"

"Who?"

Oliver instantly understood and took the *Zombie Blood* photo from the banquette beside him. He put it down for her inspection. centering it on the Formica tabletop.

Denise stared at the photo. "Is that Henry?" She examined the candid, close-up shot of a middle-aged black man, his face awash in bewilderment.

"That was taken a few years ago," Callie said. "Do you know Henry Andover?"

"Henry comes in for breakfast. You just missed him, maybe half an hour."

"Henry," Callie repeated. At least they had a first name. It seemed almost miraculous, but also logical. Even mourners have to eat. "Is he a favorite of yours?"

The only other two customers were seated at the counter, each nursing a cup of coffee, one on his phone, the other with a paper. Denise relaxed. "Henry's a sweetheart. Do you know him?"

"From a long time ago," Oliver said. "Around when that picture was taken. Does he still visit Georgia's gravesite?"

"At least once a week," Denise confirmed. "He visits her then he drives here on his little golf cart. He gets exactly the same breakfast. Two poached eggs with white toast and hash browns. Tea, not coffee and a bottle of Tabasco. How do you folks know Henry?"

"We're family." The words were out of Oliver's mouth before he realized the problem. "By marriage. We're related to Henry by marriage."

The waitress nodded sagely. "World's made up of all kinds of families, ain't it?"

"That's the truth," Oliver agreed. "We haven't seen Henry in years. How's he doing?"

"Henry?" Denise didn't seem to know the proper answer. "He's good. He's a very sweet man."

Callie recognized 'sweet' for the euphemism it was. That combined with the man's expression in the photo… "Henry is a little slow," Callie said softly, "if you don't mind my frankness. He's always been like that."

"But very sweet," Denise repeated. "And harmless. He tells the same stories all the time."

"Oh, no." Callie pretended to blush, her hands flying up to her cheeks. "I hope he doesn't talk about us. That would be so embarrassing."

Denise's laugh was good-natured and substantial. "Oh, no. He talks about his wife. Old stories. How they met. Her favorite food. Sometimes he'll talk about what he had for dinner last night or a show on TV. Sometimes about his sister."

"Which sister?" Callie asked, trying to keep the conversation going.

"He only talks about the one. She lives in the area."

Callie ventured a wild guess. It couldn't hurt. "Do you mean Suzanne? Suzanne Pauling. That's her married name. She runs a flower shop."

"It could be Suzanne." The waitress scratched at her temple and laughed. "Henry doesn't speak the clearest. Are you trying to get in touch with him? I heard y'all talking."

"Yes, we are," Oliver said. "My sister and I…" He shot Callie a warning glance. "We have some family business to discuss with Henry."

"My brother and I…" Callie was having fun with the concept. "We're trying to track Henry down, but no one's heard from him. You wouldn't happen to know where he lives? Denise?"

"Sorry." There was a hint of suspicion in the woman's voice, just a hint. "If you want to leave your information, I can give it to Henry on his next visit. Will that be okay?"

Oliver said it would be fine, even though it wasn't. He borrowed a guest check from Denise's order pad, wrote down a half-fake name, Oliver Andover, and his real cell number. He handed it over, holding out little hope that it would ever get into Henry's hands or, if it did, that Henry would ever call a stranger claiming to be an unknown white relative.

Their breakfasts were slightly soggy by the time they got around to them. Neither had much of an appetite now, but they put in a good effort and kept their conversation as innocuous as possible, since they never knew when the eagle-eared

Denise would be making a flyby to refill the water glasses. Oliver paid in cash and left a generous tip.

They were saying goodbye to Denise who promised again to give Henry the message, when Callie happened to have a long shot of an idea. She turned to Oliver, beaming with the imitation of good will. "I think we should pay for Henry's breakfast today. Don't you think that would be nice?"

"Very nice, Sis," said Oliver, barely skipping a beat. He was learning quickly. "A really cousin-like thing to do."

Denise purred happily and clutched her heart. "Aw. That is so sweet of y'all," she said. "Henry would just be tickled to death."

"Then we'll do it. How does Henry usually pay?" Callie asked. "Cash?" She hoped it wasn't cash. "Credit card?" There might be something on a credit card receipt that could give them a clue, although she didn't know what. "Check?" That was the long shot she'd been thinking of. She had a distant McFee relative in Oklahoma, a sweet, harmless man like Henry, who lived in a group home and was never trusted with cash or credit cards.

The waitress chuckled. "He does pay by check. It takes him about five minutes to fill it out. I'm not joking."

"Wonderful." Callie couldn't believe her luck. "You should tear up that check and let us pay."

"Tear up the check?" Denise made it sound dangerous, like an act of pure rebellion. "I don't know."

Oliver pulled a billfold out of his back pocket. "It's up to you. What do you say?"

Denise thought it over. "You know what? Okay. I'm going to do it." And with that, she wiped her hands on her apron, scurried behind the counter and opened the register. By now, the diner's only two other customers had put down their coffees and their reading material and were watching, little smiles etched on their faces.

It took her only a few seconds to reach under the cash drawer and find the check. "This is like one of those stories you read on Facebook." She held it out with both hands. "Here you are. Henry C. Andover. Nine dollars, including tip."

Callie and Oliver leaned in to inspect the check. "Nine bucks, to the penny," Callie said. "Look at that handwriting. You can barely make it out." Denise laughed along with her.

"Only nine dollars?" Oliver took a closer look. "We should buy him two breakfasts. What do you say?" He produced a twenty from the billfold. "For the next time he comes in. From Oliver and Calista."

"Two breakfasts. Done." Denise accepted the bill, placed it in the drawer then tore up the check with a flourish. "And I'll make sure Henry gets your contact info, like you asked. You folks are the sweetest, you know that?"

"Nonsense," Callie said, trying to match her enthusiasm. "Henry is such a darling man."

Oliver grinned but said nothing. He waited for a minute or so, until they were safely out in the parking lot, standing between Callie's Yukon and his Prius. Then he grabbed his "sister" and impulsively hugged her. "You were absolutely brilliant," he gushed. "I never would have thought of that."

"1527A Bull Creek Circle," Callie mumbled, reciting the home address that had been printed on the check's upper left corner.

"1527A Bull Creek Circle," Oliver confirmed. "It can't be all that far, if he gets here in a golf cart."

CHAPTER 27

Bull Creek Circle was one of several similarly named streets in Vista Verde Mobile World, just off Bull Creek Road. To Callie's eye, it didn't look like a popular mobile home park or a particularly well-maintained one, but it was within an easy drive of the cemetery. Number 1527A, an aging single-wide, stood at the end of a gently curved cul-de-sac and, since the lots on either side were vacant, enjoyed a fair amount of privacy. Almost directly in front, by the set of metal stairs, was a battered Yamaha golf cart, plugged into an outlet on the lower edge of the trailer.

They had parked behind a utility shed, out of the line of sight of the windows. As they stood behind the shed, Callie tried to tamp down her excitement. "My phone's almost out of juice, so you should bring yours. Your voice memo app should last at least ninety minutes."

"And we don't have to tell him we're recording him?" Oliver asked.

Callie grunted. They had been through this before. "In

the state of Texas, you need consent from only one party to record a conversation."

"I'm talking ethically, not legally."

"You? You're the guy who told a waitress we were brother and sister and related to a black family, so I think your ethical ship has sailed."

"Okay, okay." He could see her point. "But he may not want to talk at all."

"And that's fine," Callie said. "If he's related to Suzanne and Naomi, we can make the connection through legal records. But we need a photo. That will be plenty damning. The uncle of Ka'Kala's co-founder bears an uncanny resemblance to the jungle shaman."

Oliver hesitated. "I'm not sure how I feel about grilling someone with diminished capacity."

"Don't overthink this." Then she grabbed her boss by the shoulder, pushing him past the utility shed and into the open. "Henry did nothing wrong."

Callie led the way, impatient but in control. She mounted the metal stairs, took a deep breath and knocked politely but firmly. When she heard no movement inside, she knocked again. "Henry? Hello?" A third series of knocks. Nothing.

"He's asleep on the couch." Oliver was halfway down the length of the trailer, his nose to a grimy window, shielding his eyes from the glare.

"At least he's home," Callie said. The door, she discovered, was unlocked, and she waited for Oliver to join her before pushing it open. "Hello? Mr. Andover?" She had already taken a full step inside when she smelled the gas.

The next few seconds seemed to happen in slow motion.

Callie turned instinctively to the left, toward the smell and the propane-fueled stove positioned by the kitchen's open doorway. When she turned to the right, there was Henry Andover, the man they'd been searching for, lying on the sofa against the far wall, looking older and paunchier than he'd been in the photos. He was awake now, she saw, moving languidly, just rousing himself.

From behind her, Callie could feel a light draft entering the stuffy stillness of the mobile home, circulating the poisoned, flammable air. Another glance to the right and the man on the couch was raising his left hand from the carpeted floor, holding a lit cigar. "Henry!" she called out.

Henry looked up at her, seemingly puzzled by this strange woman standing at the edge of his living room. A second later, he noticed the smoldering cigar in his hand. The man smiled and then, out of a decades-long habit, began lifting it to his lips.

"Henry, don't. Put it down."

She was moving toward him, figuring how to make her way across the room full of old furniture and boxes of junk, only to feel someone behind her, pulling her away, pulling her back toward the door.

"What are you doing?" Those were the words she wanted to say as Oliver continued to pull her away. But she didn't have the chance. Henry's hand was already up to his mouth, drawing in a lungful of smoke and causing the end of the cigar to burn brightly for a moment.

But just for a moment.

CHAPTER 28

THE WORST PART, physically at least, wasn't the bruise and the soreness from where her back had hit the railing at the top of the metal stairs. It wasn't the fatigue or the bouts of dizziness that came and went. It wasn't the first-degree burns on her face and palms, which looked and felt no worse than a bad sunburn. She had also suffered two small bits of metal shrapnel, which had pierced her left thigh. They'd been removed in the ambulance, and the shallow wounds had not required stitches. No, the worst part was the ringing in her ears.

It had begun instantly, from the moment that Henry and his sofa and half of his trailer erupted in the fireball. Oliver had already dragged her back into the doorway. The force of the explosion did the rest, propelling them both across the landing and over the railing. Her body had protected his from the shrapnel and the worst of the burns. That was at it should be, she figured. He had probably saved her life. But there was still that damned ringing. Even when she couldn't hear any other sound.

It was day two, the day after. The ringing was no longer

as intense and she could finally hear again, although not well. The doctors had not wanted to release her, but after having been kept for a sleepless night of observation, without her alcohol and pills, Callie insisted on leaving, and legally they couldn't stop her.

She had just finished a bowl of chicken soup that Sarah had brought by and was lying on the couch, head propped up on pillows, trying to get the closed captioning to work on the TV. She had almost figured it out when there was a knock on the door. "Callie?" It was her brother's voice. "You up for some company? Can we come in?"

It was State, Oliver and Randal Greene, State's partner, all arriving together. She wondered, did they all come in the same car? Had they scheduled a meeting without letting her know? It had the feeling of a coordinated attack. "Hey, guys." She turned off the TV and momentarily thought about pulling back her wild hair to look a little more presentable, but the feeling passed.

She hadn't seen Oliver since they'd argued about the wisdom of running toward a man with a lit cigar in a gas-filled trailer. He was looking better than she felt, his permanent stubble almost disappearing in the glow of his artificial sunburn. He spoke louder than the others, an indication of his own aftereffects. She appreciated the volume.

"Are you using the Wepapua ointment?" he shouted, pointing to her face. "They say it's good for burns."

Callie bristled. "No," she shouted back. "I will never use that crap. Period. End of discussion."

"Me neither," he agreed, his shout turning a little sheepish. "I'll stick to the stuff the hospital gave us."

"Good." Her mouth tilted up in the smallest of smiles. "By the way, thank you. Again." She had thanked him before, at some point between the explosion and the ambulance.

"Yes, thank you," State chimed in. "My sister can be a little impulsive."

Oliver didn't appreciate State's tone. "Impulsive? This was the second time, you know. The second time she walked into a house and saw someone in a godawful situation and couldn't save them. I think we all might be a little impulsive." Callie was glad that someone else had thought about that. She'd been thinking about it a lot.

"You're right," State said. "I'm sorry, Sis. Are you going to be okay? We can always put this off."

"No, I'm fine," she answered. "Let's get it over with."

"We'll try to make it short." State settled into the armchair opposite the couch and opened his trusty notepad. They had spoken yesterday at the hospital, but neither Callie nor Oliver had been in a condition to officially answer questions. "Let's start with... Have you two spoken to each other since Henry Andover's death?"

Oliver answered first. "I asked her if she was okay, but I don't think she heard me. Then maybe, right before the ambulance came..."

Callie interrupted him. "That's not what he's asking. He's asking if the two of us compared notes on what happened or what we should say. No, we did not." Oliver nodded in agreement.

"Good," said Randal as he sat down in the other armchair. "So, what were you doing at Vista Verde Mobile World? Mr. Chesney, you start."

Oliver remained on his feet, shifting his weight from foot to foot, telling their story without embellishment or embarrassment – how Callie had seen the likeness no one else had seen, including the Austin PD, and how he himself had traced the man in the movie to the cemetery, which had led them to the diner and then to the mobile home.

All during the recitation, State scribbled in his pad, while Callie kept an eye on Randal Greene. The older officer was obviously impressed, despite his effort to hide it. Not much of a poker face, Callie thought, which was good to know for future reference.

Randal scratched at his hairline. "Is this how she operates?"

"I tried to tell you," State said then looked up from his pad. "Callie, in the hospital, you kept shouting that Beau Garrison killed Henry Andover. Do you still believe that?"

"I was shouting because I was deaf," Callie half-shouted. "But yes, he did. He came to visit the poor man and set it all up – the gas, maybe some meds to make him drowsy, the cigar, which burns slower and longer than a cigarette."

"And he killed Henry…" State referred to his notes. "… because Beau knew you had made the connection between the man in the jungle and the man in the movie."

"Yes," Callie said. "If all we have is two old photos, then Beau can lie his way around it. That's why he had to kill Henry. Not just kill him. Disfigure him, too."

"I get your logic," Randal said, his voice a low grumble that Callie could barely decipher. "But how did Beau Garrison know that you knew?" He gave the question a moment to sink in. "To kill someone is a big deal. A risky deal. Garrison would need to be reasonably sure that you'd pieced together those two video snippets. We didn't piece it together, God knows. No one did, other than you. Did you tell Garrison you had this evidence?"

"No, I didn't tell him. Why would I tell him?"

"Sorry," said Randal. "I'm not familiar with your investigative methods." The homicide officer leaned forward, elbows on his knees. "So, if you didn't tell him and Oliver didn't tell him, how did Garrison know he was in jeopardy?"

"I don't know how he knew." With her blood pressure suddenly up, the ringing was getting louder. "Are you trying to say this was an accident? It wasn't an accident."

State flipped back in his notepad then looked up and made eye contact with Callie. "Okay. A little background. Suzanne Pauling is Henry's sister, like you thought. She says that Henry moved here from Boston years ago with his wife, Georgia. After her death, Henry started having more and more trouble dealing with the world. At some point, Naomi moved out here. That's when she met up with Beau Garrison."

"Henry always smoked," Randal said, continuing the flow of information. Unlike State, he didn't need notes. "Usually cigarettes, but a cigar when he could get one. We had a long talk with his sister. According to Suzanne, Henry was becoming less able to care for himself. She was thinking about a group home, for his own safety. And then this."

"Do Suzanne and Naomi think it was an accident?" Oliver asked.

Randal answered. "We met Naomi only for a minute. It's hard to tell what she thinks. As for Suzanne, she does think it was accidental."

Callie scoffed at the idea. "That's what she would say, of course, especially if she knew about her daughter's fraud."

"Can you go after them for fraud?" Oliver was still on his feet, still speaking louder than necessary.

The detectives exchanged glances. "That's not us," State told them. "Austin does have a fraud division. You can take it up with them. They're mostly consumer fraud. They would have to establish that an individual or the public was defrauded in a material way."

"The public was defrauded," Callie said.

"In a material way," State repeated. "Yes, maybe Beau and Naomi created a fake backstory. From what you say, it's plausible. But there are a lot of fake backstories." He thought for a second. "For instance, the Keebler elves. I don't think they really make those cookies in a hollow tree."

"Keebler elves." Randal chuckled. "Good one." Even Oliver smiled.

Callie was having none of it. "This is not the Keebler elves. It would ruin their business. Their investors are being defrauded."

"Then go to the fraud division," Randal said. "But unless you have more than you've told us, or someone is willing to come forward as a witness – say Suzanne or Naomi – then the murder case seems pretty weak."

"So? You're not going to do anything?" She phrased it as both a question and a statement.

State avoided her gaze. "The arson squad is looking at the trailer, or what's left of it. But you guys are in a better position to do something. As journalists. If you want to expose Ka'Kala, you can. Just don't write anything that will get you sued."

"That's exactly what we're going to do," Oliver promised.

"I mean, not the getting sued part. The other part. It's going to be our next front page."

"Good." Callie was glad to hear him make this commitment, but it didn't seem enough. "And what about the murders? Beau killed two people."

Randal was about to say something, but State held out an arm, almost physically restraining him. "Callie, I know this is hard." He spoke so softly that she could barely hear. "You walked in on a suicide and then you saw a man die. I wish there was more we could do."

"Well…" State's partner slowly bobbled his head. "Maybe we can delay calling it an accident." His bobble turned into a nod. "The way we did with Birdsong's suicide."

Callie was surprised. "You would do that?"

"We can call it undetermined. Give you until next week to get your article out there." Randal flexed an eye into a conspiratorial wink. "Would that help your story?"

Oliver perked up. "Absolutely." He spread his hands, as if envisioning the copy. "'Austin homicide officers have yet to determine the actual cause of death.' That would say what we want to say, without giving Beau grounds to sue us. Thanks."

State turned to his partner. "You would do that for them?" he asked. "Why would you do that?"

Randal smiled. "I like your sister, McFee. Didn't think I would, but I do."

Those words Callie could definitely hear, loud and clear above the ringing. "Thank you."

The debriefing was almost over. As much as Callie wanted to stay outraged, she no longer had the energy. State could see this and made sure that the last few questions were quick, nonconfrontational and simple. He stayed for a minute or two after the others walked out, helping his sister get situated on the couch and covering her with a cable-knitted throw that Sarah had made for her a good twenty years ago.

CHAPTER 29

Callie didn't open her eyes again until late afternoon, when the light was angling its way through the front windows. Hobbling into the kitchen, she found the rest of the chicken soup still on the stove. When would she be able to look at a gas stove again, she wondered, without thinking of Henry and that trailer? She dished up the soup cold then wandered back to the couch and checked her phone. It had been on silent mode and she was surprised to see a voice message and three texts, all from Melissa, all asking if now would be a good time.

A vague memory tingled in the back of her brain. Had Melissa called her yesterday in the hospital? Had they shouted at each other and made some sort of plan for today? According to Melissa's texts, they had, probably in a moment of medication-induced euphoria when Callie thought today might be a good day. "Come by in the afternoon," she recalled having shouted over the whine in her ears.

Callie was still working on Sarah's soup when the doorbell rang. She was prepared to beg off, to tell Melissa that today was not a good day after all. But then she opened the door and saw not only Melissa but Diedre Westerman, standing by her side, looking so serious and concerned. Her mother's best friend. How could she turn them away?

"Your face," Melissa said then put her hand over her mouth. "Sorry."

"I know it looks bad, but part of that is the glow from the burn ointment. It's not really so bad."

"That's good to hear," said Diedre with a weak smile.

The nice thing about women guests, Callie knew, is that they're usually happy to take over your hostess duties. Melissa found the iced tea and the ice and the glasses and the sprigs of mint on her own, while Diedre rinsed the soup bowl and put it in the dishwasher. The older woman looked stronger than the last time Callie had seen her. Diedre said how upset they had been to hear of the explosion and promised they would stay only a few minutes. "We just had to come. Melissa was so worried."

As they sat with their tea, making small talk, Callie wracked her brain, trying to remember how much Melissa knew and didn't know about Beau. "So, did you ever find that zombie horror movie?" Melissa asked.

"Yes," Callie said, thankful for the cue. "I watched State's copy. But there was nothing in it, nothing that I could see."

"Really?" Melissa sounded dubious. "I assumed…" She used a straw to stir her ice cubes then took a sip. "So, what were you doing around a gas explosion in a trailer park? When I saw it on the news – one dead, you and your boss injured – I thought it must have something to do with Beau and Trevor. Some part of your investigation."

"No, no," Callie assured her. "Nothing like that."

"So, why were you there?" Melissa asked sweetly but firmly. "You can't blame me for being curious."

Could she blame Melissa for being curious? Probably not. "Oliver and I are working on a story," she improvised. "On mobile home parks. Some big companies are buying them up and squeezing the tenants with all sorts of bogus fees. It's a real problem." She had actually read an article in *the Wall Street Journal*, outlining just this situation. She hoped Melissa wasn't a *Journal* reader.

"Oh, that's horrid," Melissa said. "And you just happened to be there, interviewing this poor man? Just a chance thing?"

"Just a chance thing," Callie said. "Diedre, how's your tea? I know you like it a little sweeter."

Diedre had been staring vacantly into her glass. "Oh, no, dear. It's perfect. It's just that I…" She took a deep inhale and exhale, still staring into her glass. "I may not be the best company. But I'm so glad you're all right. We were worried sick."

"What's the matter?" Callie leaned forward, both to hear better and engage her better. "Are you not feeling well?"

"No, I'm okay." Then Diedre looked up. Her hazel eyes, more green than brown, seemed moist and sad.

"You don't have to say anything," Melissa said. "Callie will understand."

"No. It helps to talk about it. And she deserves to know. It's Stephen."

Callie knew immediately. "Your son Stephen?"

Diedre nodded. "Glenda Tilley, the private investigator, kept saying it was just a matter of time, and she was right. A DNA match finally popped up in her system."

"Are you sure you want to talk about this?" Melissa asked.

Diedre clutched the glass with both hands. "There's not much to say. Stephen is dead. It never really occurred to me that my son might die before me."

"Dead? Oh, Diedre," Callie said. "I'm so sorry."

"I suppose it was silly of me. I had all these fantasies, him growing into a healthy, loving man with a family of his own. My grandkids."

Callie sighed. One more tragedy in a life full of tragedy. "How did it happen?" she asked. "Was it a long time ago?"

Melissa's face clouded over. "Aunt Dee, you don't have to go into this. If it's too painful…"

"It is painful," Diedre agreed. The glass of iced tea trembled in her unsteady hands.

Melissa saw this and reached across to help. That's when it spilled, the entire glassful, ice and all, cascading into Diedre's lap. Almost instantly, her white blouse and black tweed skirt were soaked. Diedre cried out, "How clumsy of me," her voice filled with emotion.

The two younger women went immediately into rescue mode, grabbing towels and sponges from the kitchen. The damage would be insignificant, nothing a good dry cleaning couldn't cure. But Diedre was tired and Callie was tired, and the little mishap signaled the end of their brief visit.

Over the last few hours, the ringing had lost much of its intensity, but the muscle aches were coming back. After they left, Callie took two more extra strength Advil and decided on another nap. This time there would be no sleep, just lying on the couch with her eyes closed as her body tried to find a comfortable position. A pillow under her back alleviated some of the pain from the bruise.

She tried not to think at all, but her mind kept wandering back to her debriefing and what Randal had said. Would Beau really murder someone – Naomi's own uncle, a harmless man he probably knew – in order to protect a secret that had lain dormant for so long? He would if he felt threatened, she decided, no matter how ethical and morally centered he had supposedly become. Joey Gibson might have some better insight into the matter, she thought as she began to doze off.

When Callie slowly rolled herself off the couch, it was already after dark. She located her phone under her back pillow and texted her old school friend. He practically lived on his phone, so it was surprising not to get an instantaneous reply. She waited ten minutes then texted again then waited ten minutes more before going onto Instagram. Joey hadn't posted anything since this morning, she saw. That had been a snap of a blue Rolex Submariner and a caption vowing that he would buy matching Submariners for himself and Patrick, just for fun. Callie smiled at his overblown tastes then went to her Instagram settings and switched on a post notification.

At some point, she realized that she hadn't been outside all day, not since she'd come back from the hospital this morning.

When she opened the door, she found the night clammy and cool, a harbinger of the short Texas winter to come. Callie wrapped herself in Sarah's knitted throw and took a stroll down toward the big house. She would walk there and back and then think about something to eat.

"If you're considering joining us for dinner, you just missed it." It was Gil, coming toward her on the gravel drive. On the other end of a leash was Angus Two, busily sniffing under every tree. "How's the damage?" Undoubtedly, he had heard the whole story. "Let me look at your burns."

She waited until he was closer then tapped the flashlight on her phone and let him have a look. "Not bad," he said. "Couple of days and you'll be fine." Callie was grateful for his optimistic assessment. "Tomorrow you'll do something with your hair, put on some makeup and have a nice, long visit at the house. He's been asking after you."

"You didn't tell him?"

Gil snorted. "You didn't tell him either, which is fine. He doesn't need the excitement."

"I was busy getting blown up," she pointed out.

"Understood." Angus Two was starting to pull toward the next tree, but Gil held him in check. "I warned you to be careful, Calista. If Oliver hadn't been there, it could have been you."

Another warning to be careful. "Does this mean you think it was murder? If so, you and I are the only ones."

Gil shrugged. "We're a suspicious lot, you and me. I've seen witnesses die. I've seen accidental gas leaks. If someone explodes right before you interview him… That's trouble-some." Angus Two was pulling stronger now and making little yips, like a dog who had just smelled a squirrel. "Are you sure you don't want my help? It might be safer."

"I'm sure."

"Okay." Then he turned and let himself be dragged away. "Tomorrow," he called out over his shoulder. "Hair, makeup, long visit."

"Got it," Callie said as she reversed her path and headed back home.

She had just arrived within the glow of her own porch light when her phone emitted three short, muted tones, like the sound of a damaged xylophone. It was Joey's most recent post notification. Callie paused in her doorway and opened the Instagram link.

Joey and another young man – she assumed it was Patrick – were at a table in a decidedly upscale restaurant, taking a selfie with an open bottle of Dom Perignon snuggled between them. It was a typically Joey photo, but it was the caption that caught Callie's attention. "At the one and only Paicho's. CELEBRATION!!!"

Cute, she thought, then wondered what exactly the couple was celebrating. It wasn't Joey's birthday, she knew, and it wasn't their six-month anniversary; that had been a few days ago. Of course, it could be Patrick's birthday, but in that case, Joey would have led with the phrase "happy birthday" or some cliched reference to trips around the sun. No, this was something different.

She thought back to the other two oddities in Joey's recent behavior. One: he had not returned either of her texts. Not like him at all. And two: the last thing he had posted was the photo of a high-end Rolex and his plan to buy two of them.

"Damn it to hell," she muttered into the chilly night air. "Damn it, damn it, damn it."

CHAPTER 30

CALLIE HAD NEVER been to Paicho's. Since her return to Austin, she'd been out on only a handful of dates, none of them serious enough to warrant a visit to this extravagant Japanese fusion establishment, also lovingly referred to as Paycheck's.

She had raced to get there in time and, at the end, decided against the parking lot and in favor of the valet station. Her energy and focus were enough to get her past the hostess podium and around the three well-dressed couples waiting to be seated. She'd thought it might be hard to find them in the crowd, but Joey's voice could carry, especially after he'd had a few. His laugh was coming from a table in the far corner near the kitchen, not a prime spot, but then the event they were celebrating was not something they could have foreseen a month ago, even a week ago.

Joey was still chuckling when he looked up from his fruit parfait and saw her walking their way. "Callie," he said, his laugh stopping and his smile freezing. "Did you know the Japanese put cornflakes in their desserts. I'm not kidding. Want a taste?"

"Joey, Joey." Callie stood over her old friend. The ringing

in her ears had died down, but she still had to make a conscious effort not to shout. "According to Instagram, you're celebrating something big tonight. I'll bet I can guess what."

Joey's dinner partner was probably a year or two younger – slight and artificially blond, with a guileless openness in his smile. "We are celebrating," he said. "Joey's company got bought out. Newton, the big wellness brand. There's going to be an announcement tomorrow."

"Patrick." Joey said the name almost like a warning. "Patrick, this is Callie McFee. Callie, Patrick."

"Callie!" Patrick greeted her like a long-lost friend. Without getting up, he extended both arms in an air-hug. "At last. Joey's told me so much about you."

Callie could see his eyes wandering to her sunburned face. "Great to meet you, too. And congratulations. Did Joey already sell his shares?"

"Patrick." Another warning from Joey. "Can you go to the little boy's room, please? Callie and I have things to discuss. Sorry, Boo. Just a few minutes."

"Sure." Patrick took it well, as if being sent away for a few minutes was an everyday request. "Hope you can stick around. We'll get another bottle of Dom and you can tell me about the old Joey, in school with his gang of misfit toys."

"He was in a gang, yes, but they weren't misfit toys," Callie said and waved Patrick on his way to the men's room. She turned to her friend. "So, big announcement tomorrow."

"Callie, honey." Joey had pushed aside his parfait and was examining her face. She had pulled her unruly hair back into a clumpy ponytail but had not done anything to cover up her redness. "What in the world happened? You look like a beet."

"No," Callie said firmly. "You can't do that. You can't distract me by saying I look like a beet."

"Okay," he said slowly. "But really, girl, what happened to you?"

She had pondered how much to tell him about the explosion that he was at least partly responsible for. Out of consideration for their friendship, she'd decided to say as little as possible. "I'll be fine. Look, Joey, I know you told Beau. I just need you to confirm it."

His expression was all innocence. "Told Beau what? About your visit to the museum?"

"I asked you not to tell him. You promised."

"I didn't tell him."

"Then how did you get shares in Ka'Kala?" He didn't seem to have an answer. "When you brought me brunch last week, you said you'd turned down the stock participation. Now suddenly you have it."

"No, no, I had it all along," Joey stammered. "I just didn't read my contract right. You know me and numbers."

Callie scowled. "Joey, please don't lie. It's too important." She wasn't going to say this, but… "You told Beau what Oliver and I were up to. As a result, Beau murdered someone."

Joey's eyes widened. His voice lowered to a whisper. "Murdered? No, that's just one of your wild theories."

Callie framed her hands around her face, displaying the damage. "You asked what happened to me? Well, that was it. Beau engineered a gas explosion. One person died. Oliver and I almost died."

It was a lot to throw at Joey, she knew, especially when

he was drunk and celebrating. "Beau did that? Was it on the news? Was Beau arrested?"

"It was on the news," she said. "But they're treating it like an accident from a gas stove."

"And you're saying it wasn't an accident? Beau did it? You actually saw him do it? Was he there?"

"Beau did it," she insisted. "You spied on us at your office and you told Beau. And now someone's dead."

"No." Joey wagged his head, as if trying to dislodge the champagne bubbles. "I wasn't spying, not in any real way. All I said was that you two were looking at the big Ka'Kala painting. That's like fifty feet from my cubicle. You were talking about how the face was different in the painting. How do you get from there to murder?"

"When did you tell Beau?"

"When?" Joey had to think. "The next morning when I came into work."

"I knew it," she muttered. Here was the connection, the one State and Randal said didn't exist. From their innocent-sounding conversation about art, Beau had discovered his predicament. A few hours later and Henry was dead.

"You were looking at a painting," Joey said. "What's the harm in telling him that?"

"The harm is…" She sighed heavily then sat down in Patrick's vacated chair. "It's too complicated to explain. Why did you tell him anything?"

"Because…" Joey glanced over to the ice bucket and the dead bottle of Dom Perignon. "Because Beau and I had a deal, all right? I wasn't your spy; I was his. From the day we had the brunch in your office. I was honest with you. I said from the start I was spying. I just never stopped."

"Joey! I'm one of your oldest friends."

"I know, but…" Callie waited for his explanation. "Beau said you had some sort of vendetta and it would be good for the company if he knew what you were up to. He can be very persuasive."

"And that's when he offered you the shares? Your thirty pieces of silver?"

"Silver?" Joey asked, confused by the biblical reference. "The stock isn't in silver. Look, it wasn't just about money. This is a company I'm a part of." Joey lowered his eyes and toyed with his cornflake parfait. "As much as I bad-mouth Ka'Kala, I don't want some reporter coming along and ruining it. Face it, Callie, you do have a reputation for mayhem."

"I'm not trying to mayhem anything. I'm trying to hold this man responsible for a murder, maybe two."

"He really killed someone?"

"Yeah, he did. He killed Ka'Kala."

Joey was puzzled. "No, he sold Ka'Kala. Do you mean metaphorically?"

She waved her hands. "Again, too complicated. But a real person died, a couple hours after you told Beau. His name was Henry – a sweet, innocent man, whose only crime was doing a favor for Beau many years ago."

"You're serious? Oh, shit." Joey's forearms were on the table and now he planted his head on top of them. "Oh, shit – oh, shit, - oh, shit."

Immediately, she regretted her words. "I'm sorry, Joey. I shouldn't have put it that way. I feel responsible myself, for stirring the pot and putting this poor man at risk. But I'm not responsible and neither are you. Beau murdered him. No one else."

"You said maybe two murders. Are you talking about Trevor?"

Callie nodded. "If it was suicide, it was a very convenient one. Just like the explosion."

Joey sighed deeply. Finally, he lifted his head and his gaze turned sideways. "Damn." Patrick was standing not far from the service area. It must have been apparent, even to Patrick, that their celebration had turned into something else. Joey leaned across. "Please don't tell him. This thing of ours may go beyond six months, as strange as that is for me."

The six-month boyfriend was staring over their heads, pretending to ignore them as he patiently waited to be invited back. "He seems very nice, like he'd be good for you," Callie whispered.

"I think so." Joey, who had always been so casual about romance, looked uncharacteristically sincere. "He's different from the others, which isn't bad. I'm not sure how he would react if he knew any of this. I realize you don't owe me anything, especially now…"

"Right." Callie didn't want to let go of her anger. Joey's betrayal had nearly gotten her killed. But she had made plenty of mistakes herself and Joey was one of her few friends left. So, she raised her voice and adopted a cheery tone. "Patrick, I took your chair. I'm so sorry. Come join us."

Patrick switched his smile back on. It was only slightly less intense than before. "I can get another chair," he said then found one a few tables away and carried it over, being careful not to scrape it on the Japanese ash floor. "Did you guys get everything straightened out?"

Joey looked to Callie. She took a deep breath and tried to relax her shoulders. "We did. Everything back to normal. You have to tell me how you and Joey met."

Patrick settled in as Joey caught the waiter's eye and ordered a second bottle of Dom. They made sure that their guest got more than her fair share.

Callie found the evening strangely therapeutic, to be making small talk without any agenda, to ask all the usual questions and then to half-listen as Patrick's enthusiasm carried him from topic to topic – how he met Joey, what he did at the design firm where he worked, his life growing up as a gay kid in Corpus Christi. She made a point of changing the subject whenever the conversation started to veer in her direction.

They were the last three to leave the restaurant. Patrick, still fairly sober, brought the car around while the old schoolmates shared a hug. "I know you," Joey said. "You're not going to let this Beau thing go. But I don't want to know what you're up to next."

"I'm not sure what I'm up to next," Callie told him.

"Well, I don't want to know. Just be careful." Callie, who was in no shape to drive, asked the valet to move her truck to the parking lot, took the keys, gave him a generous tip then found an Uber floating just ten blocks away. She didn't want to feel guilty about calling Oliver so late, so she made a point of not checking the time before she called. He answered on the third ring. A TV or radio or computer was playing in the background, which made her feel better about the hour, whatever it was.

"How are you doing?" he asked.

"Probably the same as you." She groaned as she tried to find a comfortable spot for her lower back. "I cut out the painkillers, so I could drink. May not have been the best idea. By the way, Joey was the one who ratted us out to Beau. He heard us talking about the painting."

Oliver grunted. "I figured as much, but I didn't want to say. He's your friend."

"It was all my fault," she said. "I should have been more careful. What are you doing tomorrow?"

The sound from the TV or radio or computer ended. "I have to make an appearance at work, just to assure everyone that we're alive. And I want to try to track down the German tourists. That was a long time ago, but I'm hoping they'll have some details. Quotes like that always look good in a story." He paused, waiting for her reply. "And you?"

Callie thought. "Beau is holding a press conference, to announce the sale to the Newton Wellness Group."

"Yeah, I saw that on my feed. Please don't tell me you're going to show up and make a stink. Nothing says crazy like making a stink at a press conference." There was another pause. "Callie? Did you hear me? We'll get him with the article, when we can think through every word and not get sued."

"I won't make a stink," she promised. "I just want him to see my face, to remind him of what he did. I want him to know that I'm not giving up."

"You want me to come along?" asked Oliver. "Another burned face."

"No, you need to show up at work," Callie said. "I won't make a peep, not even raise my hand for a question."

"Do I have your word as a sixth-generation Texan?" It was a joke they shared, the highest level of promise in Callie's old-fashioned world of honor. "Otherwise, I'm coming with you."

"Okay. My word as a sixth-generation Texan."

"Good."

After the call, Callie stretched out sideways on the Uber's rear seat, taking some of the pressure off her back. Sitting for hours in a restaurant had not helped her recovery.

She had given Oliver her word. No craziness at the press conference. But afterwards? Afterwards was a different matter.

CHAPTER 31

THE PRESS CONFERENCE was in the same space as Trevor's memorial service, a venue that seemed either perfectly fitting or ironic or just creepy. Callie couldn't decide.

The open floor at the Ka'Kala offices was slightly more crowded this time, mostly with business and lifestyle reporters, plus senior members from both companies – Newton Wellness and its new subsidiary, Ka'Kala. Joey Gibson, graphic designer, had not been included.

As before, one side of Beau's ice cube was acting as a display wall, no longer featuring two portraits of Trevor Birdsong but the two corporate logos, perfectly lit on a black backdrop. The same videographer roamed the crowd, and the guests were all presented with flutes of the same champagne-like substance that Joey had described as having been made from rotting turnips.

The first person at the podium was Carl Benedetto, Newton's well-aged founder and CEO who had flown in from Denver and seemed enthusiastic, if a little uncomfortable. He read nearly his entire statement, speaking of synergy and mission and how important Ka'Kala would be in leading the industry into a new world of holistic health. Callie tuned out when he got to the part about Beau Garrison and what a brilliant, compassionate and innovative leader he was.

She had used her press credentials to gain entry and positioned herself directly under the oversized Ka'Kala painting, hoping that this would send Beau a not-so-subtle message. For the same reason, she had applied the burn ointment liberally this morning, so that her red glow might be a reminder. Ms. Callie McFee had skin in the game, quite literally.

She wasn't here for information. You rarely go to a press conference for the information. But she was hoping that her presence would unnerve Beau just enough to… She wasn't sure exactly what he would do. She had never seen Beau unnerved. But as the one-armed, man-bunned executive took to the podium and looked out over the audience, bathing in a healthy wave of applause, he did seem to lose a little of his luster.

Callie saw this and felt vindicated. It took a full minute for her to notice that his discomfort was not directed at her. Not at all. His body language – turning away from a certain segment of the crowd, eyes down, eyes back up, turning back and then away – might not be obvious to others, but it was to Callie who'd been hoping for just this reaction.

Stretching up on her tiptoes, she scanned the part of the room that seemed to be causing Beau's distress. There was a woman, she saw, positioned like Callie, her back to the wall, arms folded, staring brutally and expressionless at Beau. The woman seemed familiar: African American, large, in her sixties, her abundant hair held back by a wide, tie-back headband. It was Suzanne Pauling.

For a moment, Callie was jealous. She wanted to be the one to unnerve him. She had gone to the embarrassing length of emphasizing her burns in public, only to be upstaged. But this was better, she thought. The sister of the man he'd killed, showing up with folded arms and a withering glare.

Beau's speech was probably shorter than he'd planned. He did mention Trevor Birdsong, who had contributed so much to Ka'Kala and whose death had been such a tragedy. He also fondly reminisced about Naomi Pauling, his founding partner, the love of his life, who had been with him from the start but unfortunately couldn't be here today. He did not, however, mention Naomi's mother, who was right there, illuminated by the light from a wall sconce.

After the speech, Carl joined Beau at the podium and the two men shared the microphone, fielding questions about their new roles. Beau's title would be Ka'Kala Chief Executive and Carl promised that the new subsidiary would retain its autonomy, but with the power and expertise of Newton to back it up. Both continued to use the word *synergy*.

They were just finishing up, scanning the crowd for any last question, when Beau's face went ashen, turning a shade or two paler. He had just noticed what Callie would notice a second later, that Suzanne was no longer under the sconce. Callie got back on her tiptoes and glanced around. No longer under the sconce or in the room. And Beau was not happy.

Callie had been to her share of press conferences. According-ing to the unwritten rules, Beau should have stayed around for a few minutes of socializing. At the very least, he should have departed with Carl Benedetto, presenting a smiling, united front while the photographers got in their last shots. Instead,

Callie watched as Beau weaved through the milling throng, went into his ice cube and retrieved the car keys from his desk.

It was by sheer luck that Callie was able to follow him. On arriving here, she had toyed with trying to find a parking spot on the street but didn't want to be late. She had opted for the stupidly expensive underground garage in the Ka'Kala building. The garage's upper level, P1, was reserved for employees. P2 was open to the public. While Beau stood by the office elevators, doing his best to graciously escape, Callie edged along the wall and raced down the stairwell to P2.

As far as she knew, Beau was unfamiliar with her silver Yukon. She felt confident enough to pull up to the garage exit, raise her tinted windows and get in line for the visitors' pay station. By the time she got to the front, she saw a white BMW – license plate number KAK ALA1 – pull up next to her at the employee exit. Callie timed her payment, and their barrier arms rose almost simultaneously. She let KAK ALA1 exit the garage first.

The BMW turned right, speeding off in the direction of I-35. She had a good idea where it was going. When it took the ramp heading south onto the interstate, she knew for sure.

CHAPTER 32

Callie parked in the shade of the country windmill, hoping the scrub would hide her truck from the Pauling farmhouse. Suzanne's dusty gray pickup and the white BMW stood side by side in front of the white picket gate, informing her that Beau had already been allowed inside.

She didn't have much of a plan. In a perfect world, she would have a high-tech parabolic microphone and be able to overhear whatever was happening inside the Buda homestead. As for old-fashioned eavesdropping, it was doubtful that they would be seated next to an open, front window just to accommodate her curiosity. According to Suzanne, she and Naomi had not spoken to Beau in years, and it was frustrating for Callie to think that she would miss out on this confrontation.

The only alternative was to knock on the door herself, be as disruptive as possible and see what happened. It would be better than nothing, she thought. Why not? Callie had her hand on the gate post and was about to walk through the overgrown garden when a reedy voice, not much louder than a sparrow's song, spoke up. "You shouldn't go in there."

Naomi Pauling peered out from behind her mother's pickup. This time she wasn't dressed for gardening but wore jeans and a light sweater, her hair fastened in short braids. As before, there was a nervous and childlike energy to her. Callie couldn't help comparing this to the videos of the confident young woman who had stepped into the Indonesian rainforest.

"The devil's in there," said Naomi, emerging, but still several yards away.

"Hello, Naomi," Callie said. "Remember me?"

Naomi shook her head, quickly dismissing the question. "I ran out the back as soon as I saw him. You should run, too."

"You think Beau Garrison is the devil?" she asked. "Why?"

Naomi walked through the gate and into the garden. "You can't go in there," she said, pointing to the screen door. Turning back, she caught Callie's eyes and stared into them, the recognition finally dawning. "You're from *Zombie Blood*."

"Yes, *Zombie Blood*," Callie confessed. "I showed you on my phone. You don't like that movie, do you?"

"Why did you come here? You shouldn't be here."

"I came to help. To help make things right."

Naomi scowled. "It's a bad movie. Uncle Henry did a stupid, stupid thing."

"It wasn't his fault," Callie said.

"You have to know something." Naomi whispered it, like a secret. "We're not good people. The more they say and write about us, that we're good, the more horrible we are. All the lies. The devil's lies."

"What happened in the jungle, Naomi? Did it all start in the jungle?"

Naomi seemed about to explain but stopped herself. She had seen it first, beyond the garden, in the shadows of the porch, something moving behind the screen door. In an instant, she was gone, running past the parked vehicles and through the withering sunflower stalks. Callie didn't move.

The screen door opened and Beau Garrison stepped out onto the porch. He took a deep breath, looking smugly satisfied as he buttoned his jacket with his one hand and straightened the shoulder above his pinned-up sleeve. He was halfway down the crooked path when he noticed Callie. His face darkened. "I knew you were trouble, from the day I invited you to the memorial. I should have known. You and your damned paper."

Callie felt a tinge of pride. "So… Did you just buy Suzanne's silence? That was quick."

Beau shrugged and made his way out to the gate. "Suzanne wasn't happy, losing her brother like that. But it was an accident. You know. You were there."

"A very lucky accident."

Beau thought over his response. "I always liked Henry. There was a great simplicity to him. Do you know who he reminds me of?"

Callie didn't have to think. "Your old friend Ka'Kala."

"Totally right. They were very similar."

"Probably because they were the same person."

Beau allowed himself the smallest of smiles. Then he reached into his jacket pocket and pulled out his phone. "If we're going to talk… What's your number?"

Callie didn't ask why he wanted it. She recited the ten digits and a few seconds later heard the familiar ringtone, barely audible, wafting from the open window of her Yukon. "It's in my truck," she said.

"Good." He put away his own phone then glanced around to make sure they were alone. "It didn't start as any grand deception, I swear." He noted her skepticism. "At the beginning, the fans kept asking. 'How did you stay alive? What was Naomi mumbling about?' We tried to make the story as exciting as possible. For our fans. No fault in that."

"The truth wasn't exciting enough?"

"A couple of clueless, entitled brats getting lost and nearly dying? No. Being rescued by a lost tribe and finding redemption? Yes. Naomi came up with Ka'Kala, one of the nonsense words she'd been repeating."

"But then you needed a video."

Beau edged his way past her and was heading for his car. Something made him stop. "We never expected this to become a phenomenon. It was just a few seconds for the vlog. Like a prank. Henry was perfect. He didn't get out much. He didn't have friends. He didn't ask questions."

"And then Wepapua came. And the documentary. And everything else."

Beau nodded. "It's refreshing to talk about this. I never get the chance. Naomi…" There was real affection in his voice. "Naomi had dreamed about getting into wellness. No way we could remain these young, reckless travel vloggers – especially with…" He lifted his stump and wiggled it in the air. "You know."

Callie had to ask. "When did you find out about *Zombie Blood*?"

He turned back and joined her at the gate. "Henry was

quite the talker. It was hard to tell what was real and what was his imagination. When he told Suzanne that he'd been attacked by zombies in the cemetery…" Beau chuckled. "Eventually, we found out. I suppose we could have gotten an injunction against the film, for using his image without permission, but that would have brought unwanted attention. For the longest time, Naomi was freaked out. But nothing happened. We thought we were in the clear."

"Until you fired Trevor."

"Trevor." He said the name slowly. "Our horror movie geek. I don't know how long he'd been sitting on that little gem. Of course, it was in his own best interest not to blow up the company. His shares would have tanked, same as ours."

"And then you fired him. And he threatened you."

"He threatened me," Beau confirmed. "I told him we could work something out. I would have arranged for him to get his money. But the sorry bastard killed himself."

Callie pointed a finger into his chest. "He would never kill himself."

Beau brushed her finger away. "How do you know? You don't have a clue what was going on. He had a terrible relationship with his parents. He had legal problems, which your father was part of. For God's sake, he ran over someone while drunk. A convicted felon who'd just been fired."

She was thrown for a second, but only a second. "All I know is that the two people who could hurt you are dead. Very conveniently dead."

"Who is dead?" Naomi had returned, standing not far from her mother's rusted pickup. She was staring at Beau.

"Baby girl." He came toward her, extending his arm and a half. She winced and he pulled back. It's been quite a while."

"Who's dead?" Naomi repeated.

When Beau didn't answer, Callie did it for him. "Your Uncle Henry."

"Uncle Henry's dead?" She took the news with relative calm. "When?" She turned to Beau. "Did you kill him?"

"No." He seemed indignant at the very idea. "I would never."

Naomi shot him a knowing look. "You were thinking about it for years. I know. I know how your mind works. Poor old Henry."

"He was smoking," Beau insisted. "It was an accident."

Callie wanted to say something but was unnerved by Naomi's serene calm.

"It's a curse. And we gave our curse to Henry. It was supposed to be us, not him."

"It's not a curse." Beau spoke warmly, persuasively, his focus all on Naomi. "What happened to Henry is not our fault. You and I did great things. We made a company. We gave people hope, a connection to nature. The world is better because of what we did."

"We made him part of our lie," she said in a childlike whisper.

"No, no." Beau came closer, slowly, extending his arms and this time not lowering them. "It wasn't a lie." His voice was sweet, almost vulnerable. "We loved each other. We went through hell together. And then we made good things."

Naomi seemed mesmerized by his missing hand. She took a wary step back. "We should have died. But the jungle wouldn't let go. It sent zombies. The zombies came after us. After all these years."

Callie watched as Beau caught and held Naomi's gaze. He cooed and came closer. "Baby girl, there are no zombies. We're safe. I took care of everything." Then he pulled her in, wrapping his one arm around her waist and his half-arm resting on her shoulder. "I took care of everything." But, instead of relaxing, she stiffened. Her mouth shot open.

Naomi's scream was not as heartbreaking as the earlier one. This one was short, with more fear in it. Then she began pounding on Beau's chest, trying to free herself. "Let me go. Let me go." Wrenching herself out of his embrace was easy, with his half-arm barely able to hold onto anything. She pushed him away.

Seconds later, Callie heard the screen door slam. She looked behind her to see Naomi's mother racing off the porch and down the path. "Naomi! Naomi, stop."

By the time Suzanne got to the gate, the two ex-lovers were facing off, a dozen feet apart. Callie didn't exist. Suzanne existed only as a disembodied voice. "Beau, I'm sorry. I thought she went for a walk."

Beau had been about to say something but changed his mind. Naomi showed no expression at all as she turned and walked to the passenger side of her mother's pickup and opened the door. Before anyone could figure out what was happening, she was returning, holding the pink handgun. She raised her arm and pointed.

"Naomi, no." Suzanne spoke sternly. "Beau is your friend. He's helping us."

"I didn't want to go into that damn jungle. You have no

idea. The heat. The snakes and bugs. Everything we tried to eat made us sick. After we got out, it just got worse. All the lying and the stories. Making ourselves into heroes."

"But we got out," Beau said.

"You got out."

"Naomi." Suzanne took a step closer. "Beau is leaving. You and I can live here forever, just the two of us. We have nothing to worry about."

Her daughter disagreed. "He can't go." It was a simple statement of fact. "He's just going to hurt more people. Don't you see?"

Beau emitted a short, breathless, nervous laugh. He smiled, doing it purely from memory. "Naomi. Baby doll," he said. And that's when she shot him.

Beau stumbled back but kept on his feet. Instinctively, he reached for the source of the pain, his upper left arm. The motion was almost comical, a man reaching with a hand that no longer existed, trying to staunch the blood dripping from his one good arm onto his one remaining hand. Beau looked at his arm in disbelief then back up at his old girlfriend and partner.

Naomi kept the gun at arm's length, still pointed. She began to laugh, a small, closed-mouth giggle, but the pink pistol remained steady.

Callie's impulse was to run to Beau, to press something to the wound, an action he was not capable of performing himself. But she didn't move. Naomi was aiming again.

Suzanne gasped. "Naomi, no." It was no longer a command. "Please, no. Killing him won't end this."

"You're right," she said. But she didn't lower the gun.

Instead, she fired twice. The first shot went into Beau Garrison's stomach. He reacted in the shoulders as if wanting to grasp the fresh wound. Then he whimpered, bent over at the waist and collapsed.

Naomi fired the second shot into her own head and was dead before she hit the ground.

CHAPTER 33

KEITH SEEMED A little overwhelmed. The paper's media rep was on the move, pacing between Oliver's desk and the visitor's chair where Callie sat, patiently waiting. Keith's smile was genuine, but he was talking faster than Callie had ever heard him. "The phones, the emails, the texts, they just won't stop." This was only his second month at the *Free Press*, and he wasn't used to this kind of pressure. "Sunshine Cruise Line just offered us five times the banner rate for the home page. Five times. At two months guaranteed. And if they become a regular, which they're excited about doing, by the way…"

Oliver raised an index finger. "That's the Honey Plum banner space you're talking about?" Keith's head went up and down. Oliver's went side to side. "No. No way. I appreciate your work, but Honey Plum's been on our home page for years. We can't bump them every time we get a scoop."

The media rep smiled reassuringly. "I already talked to Kathy over at Honey Plum. She's fine with switching to the metro page. She's just happy to be onboard."

"Well, I'm not happy," Oliver said. "You call Kathy back

and apologize. Then you call Sunshine and tell them they can have the online classifieds spot."

"The classifieds?"

"The classifieds. For the same exorbitant price they offered, whatever that comes to. And if they're not happy, someone else will step up."

Keith wagged his head in disbelief. "You're seriously giving preference to a local health food store? This is national."

"I'm giving preference to a company that's been giving us preference for years." He smiled. "Plus, they offer ten percent off to all *Free Press* employees. Have you tried their homemade tofu?"

Keith stopped pacing and started sputtering. "This isn't a joke. If the paper can't take advantage of a moment like this…"

Callie checked the clock above the door. If they were going to make tomorrow's deadline, they had to get back to work. She let the two men keep arguing as she reviewed her notes.

The news had been huge, a lead story in almost every newsfeed. On the same day that a holistic health company announced a multimillion-dollar buyout, the company's two young founders, once a famously romantic couple, met at a farm in Texas, where the one founder shot the other with a pink handgun, then turned it on herself.

That was all the press knew, which made the speculators go wild. The couple had a fight over money, some said. Or the huge sale had rekindled the couple's rocky relationship. Or Naomi Pauling, who had been rumored to be unstable for years, was driven over the edge by the prospect of selling out to corporate America.

There had been two witnesses to all this, the police revealed, one of whom was Callie McFee, a reporter who had broken just this kind of sensational story before. Hours after the shooting, an alert popped up on the *Free Press*'s site, promising an exclusive story at six a.m. in the paper's online edition. The rest of the newsgathering world would be poised to reprint the headline and link themselves to the *Austin Free Press*.

Keith wasn't happy. But he knew when to stop, and it wasn't long before he headed back to his cubicle, closing the door behind him. "Good for you," Callie told her boss.

Oliver accepted the compliment with a half-smile. "It's part of our corporate culture, for lack of a better phrase." He jiggled his mouse, bringing his desktop Mac back to life. "I guess we should get back into it, right?"

"Right," Callie agreed. "So… what can we say about Trevor?"

Oliver thought it over. "As little as possible. Trevor's not our story."

"How is he not our story? He's the one who discovered the Ka'Kala fraud."

"Not now." Oliver was adamant. "Maybe when we do a follow-up. For now, the whole world is salivating over Beau and Naomi. That's a lot to digest, without us going into any wild speculation about Trevor's death."

"Wild speculation?" she asked. "Wild?"

"You know what I mean. Any speculation about his death will hurt the credibility of everything else – all the facts you worked so hard to unearth."

"Then how to we explain *Zombie Blood*? We got to the movie through Trevor. The whole reason I got involved was because of Trevor."

"That will be in our follow-up," Oliver promised. "As for now, we received the *Zombie Blood* footage from an anonymous source. That's our statement."

"Oh, you mean my six-year-old nephew."

Oliver grimaced. "We don't need to say that. But the footage proved that the Ka'Kala shaman, the heart of their business, had been Naomi Pauling's uncle. We can do five paragraphs on Uncle Henry alone. When Beau Garrison became aware of our interest in *Zombie Blood*..."

Callie interrupted. "We can't mention Joey's part in that."

"Of course not. Joey's indiscretion is not essential to the story."

"Plus, his father is the state attorney general."

"You make a good point." A substantial series of knocks interrupted their argumentative flow. "If the door's closed, we're busy, damn it."

"It's Detective Greene." The man's tone was unapologetic. "State told you we were dropping by."

"Sorry," Oliver said. "Perfect timing. Come in."

Detective Randal Greene entered alone, bulging in his slim-fit gray suit. Callie looked behind him, expecting to see her brother. "Your brother had some family business," Randal explained.

"Family business?" Callie asked. "I hope everything's okay. Is it Yolanda? The boys?"

"No, I think it's something with your father. A doctor's appointment."

"Really? I didn't know." For a second, Callie was unnerved. But it was actually a good thing. If anything had been seriously wrong with Buddy, Gil would have called her – no qualms

– despite her looming deadline. The fact that State was getting involved meant that he was finally stepping up. Good for him. And for her.

Oliver cleared off the second chair and insisted that Randal sit down. This was a small office and it was more comfortable for everyone to be on the same level. Randal sat. "You can identify me as a source within the department." He had become friendlier, Callie noted, less intimidating.

"Thanks," said Oliver. "We just want to be accurate." Then, as if to show his commitment, he brought out a pen and pad from his top drawer.

"No problem." The large detective squirmed in the small metal chair. "I just came from the hospital. Beau Garrison is still in intensive care, but no longer critical. It's like she magically missed the most vital organs."

"So, he'll survive." Callie wasn't sure how she felt about this.

"Probably. We've had one short interview, with his lawyer present. He admits to the fraud. How could he not? But he denies everything else."

"Has he been arrested?" Oliver asked.

"Thanks in large part to you guys. Murder one." Callie let out a little whoop, but Randal held out his stop sign of a hand. "It's heavily circumstantial. According to Suzanne Pauling, Garrison offered her money."

"A bribe for her to stay quiet about Henry," said Callie.

"Garrison said it was the right thing to do, considering the sale of the company. But he did not admit to killing anyone."

Oliver asked, "Does Suzanne think he did it?"

"She does," Randal said. "But that's a grief-stricken mother talking. I'm not sure what sway that will have."

"But there's other evidence," Callie said, her voice rising. "Tell us there is."

Randal nodded. Unlike State, he didn't need notes. "We have security footage from the parking lot of Debbie's Diner. Garrison in his BMW. When Henry drove off in his golf cart, Garrison followed. There's a security camera at the gates to Vista Verde, the mobile home park. It showed the golf cart coming in, followed by Garrison's BMW. The BMW drove away thirty-five minutes later. You guys, in the Prius and the truck, came through the gates nine minutes after that."

"Nine minutes." Callie recalled their time in the diner with Denise, as they toyed with their soggy breakfasts and plotted how to get in touch with Henry. "So close."

"You can't think of it that way," Randal said, sounding unexpectedly gentle. "You'll drive yourself nuts. As for the physical evidence…" He expelled the kind of sigh that typically preceded bad news. "Since we delayed calling it an accident, the scene was secured and relatively pristine. That's good. We lifted a few of Garrison's prints from the debris. No surprise. And we found traces of…" He took his time pronouncing the word. "…flunitrazepam. That's the generic term for Rohypnol. It would have incapacitated Henry fairly quickly."

Callie recognized the brand name. "The date-rape drug. A roofie."

"It's by far our best piece of evidence," Randal said. "Henry was on several different meds, but that one is illegal and hard to come by."

Oliver twitched uncomfortably. "How does a coroner test for drugs in a body that's… you know…"

"Burned in an explosion? They find some soft tissue that hasn't been burned." Randal paused.

"Go on," Callie prodded him. "What else have you got?"

"That's it," said Randal. "A good lawyer – and Garrison has one – will claim that he did indeed visit Henry's trailer. The two men spoke and, when Garrison left, the stove was off and Henry was fine."

"What about the roofie?" Oliver asked.

"A good lawyer will bring in his own expert and contest the toxicology." Detective Greene let this all sink in then did his best to put a good spin on it. "Look, the DA issued an indictment. Garrison had a strong motive. He had access. And don't forget the cigar. Henry didn't buy them. Too expensive. If some holistic type like Garrison recently bought cigars, that would be hard to explain. Not to mention buying roofies. We're tracking it down."

"So, there's a chance he'll get away with it." Callie angrily shook her head. "I can't believe that."

"It's not like he's getting away," Oliver pointed out. "He defrauded people. His life is in shambles. He's sustained massive injuries. And everyone will be suing him, including his new parent company. The courts will have a field day."

"And what about Trevor?"

For Callie, it all came back to this, the impetuous young man she'd barely gotten to know, the man-child who drank too much, loved bad horror flicks and had just been getting over a breakup. "Does Beau have an alibi for the time of Trevor's death? Did you even ask?"

"We asked." Randal was showing an admirable amount of patience. "He says he left work early that day. Like millions of people, he was at home, alone – which doesn't matter because we have nothing linking him to the crime, if there was a crime."

"There was a crime," she shouted at them both. "What does it take for you to see the connection?" Then she took a deep breath and forced herself to stop. "I'm sorry. It's been a long couple of days."

"I totally get it," said Randal.

After Detective Greene left, Callie retreated to her cubicle, staying annoyed with Oliver and the police and the world as she worked on the Ka'Kala article. Lunch was two bags of hummus chips from the vending machine plus, from the bottom of her bag, a beef jerky that was half a year past its expiration date. To her, it tasted exactly like the fresh stuff.

The article went slowly. As she described the two deaths, Naomi's and her uncle's, trying to engage the reader in the events of eight years ago and their tragic consequences, her mind kept wandering back to first death and how little sense it made as a suicide. Trevor had been in possession of a devastating secret, something Beau would pay handsomely for. Why would he kill himself at that exact moment?

She did less work than she'd intended and finally focused her energy on the confrontation at the farm. Oliver couldn't write this part. He hadn't been there. Before packing up her laptop and leaving for the day, Callie sent her section off. "I trust you to fill in the blanks," she typed. "You're a better writer, anyway. Be in late tomorrow, if at all. PS. I'm turning off my phone."

Callie was true to her word. She hadn't turned her phone completely off in years and it took her a few tries to manage it.

She got back to the gatehouse just before sunset and decided on a run through the woods behind the main house, something she hadn't done since the morning when she'd last seen Trevor, as he stood on the veranda, shouting at Buddy and Gil and threatening to get even.

CHAPTER 34

THE NEXT MORNING, Callie refused to turn on her phone or the TV or her laptop or even to check the time. It was well after six a.m., a few hours at least, and the chaos must have been in full swing. After a long, hot shower, she found herself suddenly, ravenously hungry. An inspection of the sad interior of her fridge led her to the decision to walk up to the main house and visit Sarah. She hadn't seen Sarah in days. It was time for a chat, to catch up the household gossip and perhaps, just perhaps, see what might be inside her father's fridge.

An unfamiliar car was in front of the house, a smallish, light brown SUV. She knew it didn't belong to the gardener or the handyman or someone from the cleaning service. They tended to park around to the side, anyway, near the garage. Callie didn't think about it again until she walked into the front hall and nearly collided with Sarah, who was just heading out. "Oh, good," Sarah said, looking relieved and a little frazzled. "I've been texting and calling. Why aren't you picking up?"

"I turned my phone off," Callie explained. "What's wrong?"

"Nothing's wrong. But you have visitors."

"Visitors for me? Here?"

Sarah lowered her voice. "Never met them before. And they obviously don't know you well enough to know you don't live here. I was just on my way to knock on your door."

"Did they give you a name?"

"Sounds like a made-up name, if you ask me. Songbird. The two of them look harmless enough, but…"

Callie smiled. "That's Birdsong. They're Trevor's parents. Trevor Birdsong was here several times."

"Why didn't they say that?" Sarah was miffed. "The guy who came shouting at Mr. Buddy then went off and killed himself. I do have eyes and ears. I just never knew his name."

"Okay, I can take it from here. Where are they?"

Sarah pointed to the room across the hall from the study. The door was closed. "I gotta get back. Mr. Gil is waiting on his usual eggs, ham and grits. He never eats it all. You want some? I can heat up a biscuit, too."

Callie's face lit up. "You are a lifesaver, Sarah. Thank you."

When Callie opened the door to the dayroom, she saw Gareth and Wendy Birdsong at the far bookshelf, standing tightly together, their backs to her, inspecting one of the many mementos that littered the shelves – dust gatherers, as her father always called them. They turned to face her, looking embarrassed, even mortified. Gareth returned a small, silver Revere bowl to its place on the middle shelf, centering it just so.

"Callie, how are you?" Wendy approached, arms extended. Callie accepted the hug.

"I'm fine," she answered. "Busy. And how are you? I'm so sorry I missed the funeral." At some point, an invitation had arrived at the main house, but Callie hadn't seen it until the date had already passed.

"I'm afraid we didn't give much notice," Wendy said. "Just family and a few friends." It was a statement meant to soothe but wound up making Callie feel even guiltier.

"Oh, we found your sunglasses," Wendy said brightly. She crossed to her bag on a side table and pulled out a pair of tortoiseshell frames with blue-tinted lenses and a slightly oversized, Audrey Hepburn vibe. "Probably one of the things you were looking for at Trevor's place."

Callie knew they weren't hers. They were much too nice, for one thing, given her propensity for losing just about everything. But she could see that Wendy wanted them to be hers and Callie wanted to please her so, for some reason... "Oh, thank you." She took them and smiled. "I thought they were gone for good."

"They were in his car," Wendy said. "When it came back from the repair shop, they were right there, in the center console."

Of course, they weren't Callie's. She and Trevor hadn't met until after his Tesla had been in the accident. The stylish pair must belong to the woman he'd been so hooked on, the one with the favorite restaurant Trevor had taken her to, the one people kept mistaking her for. What was her name? Reggie?

"I told you they were hers," Wendy said, turning back to her husband. "The McFees always have the best taste."

Gareth joined them in the middle of the room. "We saw your article this morning." It was the first thing he said to her and was obviously the real reason for their visit, not a pair of lost sunglasses.

"Yes," Wendy confirmed. "It was very disturbing, what those people did. I was surprised that the article didn't mention our son."

"That was on purpose," Callie explained. "We didn't want people drawing some stupid connection between Trevor's death…" She'd almost said suicide. "…and what happened a week or so later."

"Thank you for that," said Gareth.

"Trevor was not a part of what they did." Wendy was emphatic about this. "The Ka'Kala video was out there before he even started. It was one of the things that made him contact them in the first place."

"Did our son know?" Gareth asked. Callie wasn't sure how to answer. "Trevor loved cheesy horror movies. Just like me. Maybe the one thing we ever had in common. Ever since he was a kid."

Wendy spoke carefully. "The article said you received a copy of that horror movie from an anonymous source. That stood out when we read it, given Trevor and his collection. Was he your anonymous source?"

"In a way…" Callie sighed. "Yes." She might lie about sunglasses but not about this. "He owned a copy of *Zombie Blood*. That's how we found out about Henry Andover."

"So, he knew," Gareth said, looking stern and disappointed. "He knew about the fraud."

"Is that why he killed himself?" Wendy asked.

Callie wanted to tell them – that Beau Garrison found out about the copy, that she personally thought Trevor had been murdered but couldn't prove it and that the police stubbornly disagreed with her – but she decided on the simplest route. "I honestly don't know."

Wendy accepted this. "Trevor never confided in us about his work," she said. "I can't remember the last time we spoke."

"And who is this here?" came a low, cheery voice from directly behind them.

Buddy stood in the middle of the entryway, hands extended to the doorjambs, a smile on his face. He was dressed casually, in drawstring pants and a sweatshirt. Callie stiffened and began looking for the signs. Were his eyes focused or unfocused? Was his energy relaxed or manic?

"Mr. McFee." Gareth stepped forward, his hand outstretched. "An honor, sir. You don't remember us. We used to work at the country club."

Buddy shook his hand, then chuckled and entered the room. "Sure, I remember. I haven't seen you two in ages. How is everything with you? How's the family?"

"The family?" Wendy seemed thrown by this most ordinary of questions. "The family is fine."

Buddy nodded. "Good to hear, good to hear. Your name is... Don't tell me." He pointed to Gareth. "You worked security, right?"

"Gareth Birdsong. My wife Wendy. I'm not sure we ever really met."

Callie wondered. Was her father in one of his moods? Was he just bluffing an acquaintance in the harmless way that politicians often bluffed in social gatherings? Or was he somewhere in-between? "Daddy, the Birdsongs came to see me, not you." She affected a firm but teasing tone.

Buddy chuckled. "Pardon me, young missy. Sorry if I caught y'all in the middle of something."

Gareth said, "No, sir. We were just on our way out. Wendy?" He held out a hand to his wife. She didn't take it but followed quickly as he headed into the front hall. "We should leave the McFees alone. An honor to meet you."

"Nonsense," Buddy said, following them. "You should stay a while. My day's pretty free. Fill me in on this business you've got going with my little girl. Y'all in the mood for some sweet tea?"

"I'm sorry." Wendy seemed in agreement with her husband. "I wish we could stay. But we have other engagements. I'm sure you do, too." She turned to Callie, who was still in the dayroom, taking in whatever oddity was happening between the Birdsongs and her father. "Thank you for seeing us."

"Well, that's too, too bad," Buddy said. "Maybe another time." He clapped Gareth on the shoulder and the three of them headed for the door. "Let me walk you out, at least."

Callie stayed behind, standing in the middle of the entry hall, perplexed by this short, strange interaction between her father and these people whom he might or might not have ever met before.

CHAPTER 35

"C'mon, Callie. We've had so much interest." She could tell, even from his patient, controlled voice over the tinny speaker, that Oliver was getting annoyed. "They're all flying in. *The Today Show*, *60 Minutes*, *BBC*…"

She interrupted him before the list got longer. "You know I'm right. Any decent reporter is going to ask about my father or mention Trevor's death. Before you know it, I'll be spreading my wild speculations and getting everyone in trouble."

Oliver grunted. "You're still mad about that?"

She was. "You can do the interviews. They'll be happy to have you. Even *60 Minutes*."

"I always wanted to do *60 Minutes*," he confessed.

"Then it's settled. Gotta go. My grits are getting cold." And she hung up.

Callie was seated at the island in the big kitchen, scraping the bottom of the bowl and eating the edge of fat from the ham slice, which she'd promised herself not to do. After depositing the dishes in the dishwasher, she wandered out into the hallway, took two turns and found herself at a closed door. She knocked. "It's Callie. Can I come in?"

"Door's open."

It was a charming apartment at the rear of the house, cobbled together from the old laundry room, the butler's office and a few other rooms no longer needed in a modern house. They'd been turned into a spacious one-bedroom plus an office and a terrace with a view out to the pond.

Gil was on a barstool in his own mini-kitchen, finishing up his own portion of eggs, ham and grits, minus the biscuit that Sarah had added just for Callie. "And to what do I owe this honor?" Her father's aide had never seen the need for small talk.

"What do you know about the Birdsongs?" she asked.

Gil thought as he chewed. "They can be melodious."

Callie rolled her eyes, a move unseen by Gil. "I mean Trevor Birdsong. His parents, to be specific."

"I know nothing about them, to be specific. I've never met them."

"Do you think Daddy ever met them?"

Gil stopped chewing. "I wouldn't think so. Why?"

There was only one barstool, so Callie leaned back against the kitchen counter as she explained the events of half an hour ago. Pushing aside his plate, Gil got up and poured himself a second cup of coffee. "Your daddy was being polite," he theorized. "He's very sensitive about his memory. Or maybe he was in that zone where he thinks he remembers things but doesn't really."

"I get that," Callie said. "I'm more curious about their behavior. For people who seem to admire him so much, they couldn't wait to get away. That's how it looked to me."

"Yes, that is curious."

"I was hoping you could shed some light."

Gil shook his head. "Sorry. I could bring up their names with Lawrence, but I'm not sure what kind of answer I'd get." He looked at her for the first time since she'd walked in. "Oh, you found them. She'll be glad about that."

"Found what?"

He pointed. "The sunglasses." Callie looked down. She was still carrying the stylish pair with the tortoiseshell frames. "Melissa was looking all over for those."

"Melissa? No. These belong to a girl Trevor was dating last month. The Birdsongs found them in his car."

"Really? I could have sworn." Gil reached out and Callie handed them over. "They look like the ones Melissa lost. What a coincidence, huh?"

"Coincidence?" Callie asked.

"Yeah." Gil wiped his mouth. "Two young women, around the same place and time, losing their expensive sunglasses. They're just like Melissa's."

Callie was confused. "Mel said she'd left her sunglasses here?"

"She thought so," Gil said. "When she was filming Lawrence – early in the process – she would wander around with those perched on her head." Gil handed back the sunglasses. "She had us turning the place upside down."

"So, how did they wind up in Trevor's car?"

"I guess that's where she lost them. I didn't know she was dating Birdsong."

"She wasn't." Callie thought back to the moment when

she and Melissa broke into Trevor's house and found his body. "She said she didn't know him. I'm sure."

"Well, maybe I'm wrong about the sunglasses. I've been wrong before."

"Interesting," Callie said, understating her true reaction. Could Mel have been using a fake name in order to date Trevor? Why the hell would she pull a stunt like that? "Tell me about her documentary," Callie asked. "I've never seen any footage. Have you?"

"I have not. God knows we asked. We all asked."

"And this documentary…" She had to resist using air quotes. "How did it happen?"

Gil sighed. "Diedre Westerman called, saying this relative of hers really wanted this. Lawrence can be a pushover, especially when it comes to talking about himself. Melissa was here maybe four times in all."

"And she wandered around the house, you said. Looking for what?"

"What do you mean? She was filming background stuff and finding locations to interview Lawrence and me. You think she was looking for something?"

"I don't know what I think." Callie took back the sunglasses and waved them in the air. "I'll get these back to Mel. Thanks, Uncle Gil."

The late morning was blustery, not the best weather for a run, but Callie felt she needed to clear her head. Before heading out, she made a quick call. The man on the other end said he would be glad to help. Then she changed into her leggings and top and added a running belt for her phone, since she didn't want to miss his return call.

Callie stuck to the country roads. They were easier and took less focus. But instead of clearing her head, the run just made things worse. Were Melissa and Reggie really the same? According to Trevor's description of their brief relationship, he'd met Reggie at the same time that Melissa was working on her documentary. How were they connected, Callie wondered, their little affair and the documentary? Because they had to be connected.

She had just reached the end of Hacienda Road, the point where she normally turned around, when her phone rang. Stepping off the road and into the brush, she found a spot out of the wind. "Dr. Paget? Thanks for getting back so fast. What did you find out?"

Sam Paget was a UT professor of architecture. There were other people at the university she could have contacted. But these people would be doing her a favor, whereas she had already done a favor for Sam Paget – last spring, just after her move back to Austin. Her father had once compared an unreturned favor to a leftover sitting in the fridge. Favors. like leftovers, had expiration dates and it was a sin to waste them, even if a different choice might taste better.

"Melissa Miller is a UT student," Paget informed her. "She transferred from the El Paso campus this semester. A business major, not a film major."

"Is she taking any film class at all?" Callie asked.

"She is not registered in a film course. I checked with the two professors who regularly oversee these projects. She is not auditing their classes and neither one has ever heard of her." He paused. "Can I ask what this is about?"

Callie replied, "I'd rather not say. Sorry."

"That's all right. You have your way of doing things." Another pause. "I read your article this morning. Is this somehow related to that health company and that murder in Buda?"

"I'd rather not say," she repeated, this time without the sorry. "And if you could keep quiet about my questions…"

"Understood. I won't tell a soul. I appreciate your discretion, Callie, and I want you to know you can absolutely count on mine." He sounded even more indebted than he had last spring. This, Callie thought as she thanked the professor and hung up, was the strange power of favors owed and returned. She could see why her father liked the system.

*

On the drive over, Callie wore the sunglasses and repeatedly checked her reflection. The tortoiseshell frames complimented her red hair and the oversized lenses added some width to her naturally narrow face. It was a shame that she had to return them.

She parked in the circular drive, right behind a panel van from a company called At Home Designs. She still had the sunglasses on when Melissa answered the door. "Callie?" Melissa said, looking a tad perplexed. And then her hands flew to her mouth. "You found them. Oh, how wonderful. Where were they?"

"In the kitchen," Callie said. "Right by the blender."

"Ha," Melissa laughed. "That's the trouble with sunglasses. When you don't need them, you forget, until the next time the sun's out."

Callie took them off and handed them over. "Are you sure they're yours? If you're not absolutely sure, I can just keep them."

"I'm sure," Melissa said and put them on. "See?" The sunglasses, with their large, blue-tinted lenses, looked even better on her, accenting her short, dark hair and light complexion. She took them off and her expression turned serious. "You just have to tell me all about Beau and Naomi. This happened right in their beautiful garden?"

Callie had almost forgotten that Melissa had been so involved. "Well, you read the article this morning. That says it all."

"Yes, I read it." Melissa slapped her playfully on the arm. "And you lied to me. 'Oh, we're doing an article about trailer parks,'" she chirped, mocking Callie's voice. "Then it turns out to be murder."

"Sorry about that." Callie's grin was sheepish. "All of a sudden, it was getting very real, and I didn't want... You know."

"I get it," said Melissa. "I'm not a reporter. It was crazy enough for me to be there for Trevor's suicide and..." She titled her head and made a face. "Was it a suicide, by the way?"

"The police are looking into it again. But yeah, it seems so."

Melissa nodded. "I kinda thought. You know, we need to sit down with a drink sometime and go over everything."

"We absolutely must," agreed Callie. "I just came to return the glasses."

"Well, thanks. They're my absolute faves."

"Is it okay if I see Diedre for a minute?" Callie asked. The idea had just occurred to her. "As long as I'm here."

Melissa mulled it over. "Well, she's gotten worse, but she would love to see you. Just..." She raised a finger for emphasis.

"Just don't bring up Stephen. That's been very upsetting for her."

"Of course," Callie promised. "What happened exactly? How long ago did Stephen die? Was he married?"

"We can discuss this over drinks. It was very sad." And then Melissa led her friend into the Westerman house. As they passed through the living room, Callie noticed a man on one of the couches, glancing up from some architectural drawings laid out on a coffee table.

The sight of Diedre's bedroom was both unnerving and familiar. In the last months of her life, Anita McFee had had a similar setup, her antique sleigh bed replaced by a hospital bed with metal sides that lowered for easy access. Like Anita, Diedre had a wheelchair parked in the corner, an oxygen machine on standby and an end table devoted to her meds, all lined up in some sort of order. Callie approached the bed softly.

"Callie, dear." The voice was raspy and soft, but the hazel eyes still had a brightness to them. Diedre held out a hand and Callie took it, as if picking up an injured bird. "So good of you to come."

"I can only stay a minute. I had something to deliver to Melissa."

"Melissa." She said the name with real affection. "I don't know what I would do. I could hire help, of course. But there's no substitute for family."

"That's true," Melissa said. She had stopped in the bathroom to fill a plastic cup with water and push a straw through the lid.

As the ill woman took gentle sips through the straw, the two others sat down, both on the same side of the bed, and proceeded to chat about the most mundane things – Diedre's parents in El Paso, who missed their daughter and were threatening to come visit; the cool weather; the last of the fall flowers. When Melissa sensed that 'Aunt Dee' was tiring, she made eye contact with Callie who then made her excuses, kissed Diedre on the cheek and said her goodbyes.

As they passed through the living room, the man on the couch with the plans once again caught Callie's eye. "Some renovations?" she whispered.

"The place can do with an overhaul," Melissa whispered back. Once they were out on the circular drive, she raised her voice. "I don't want to seem ghoulish. You know how I love Aunt Dee. But the best designers, like Andrew, book up half a year in advance."

"I can imagine," said Callie.

When they got to the truck, Callie stopped. "Oh, whatever happened to your documentary?" She tried to make the question sound spontaneous.

"Oh, that." Her tone was dismissive. "I showed the outline and some footage to my professor. He absolutely hated it."

Callie furrowed her brow. "You told me your professor was a woman."

"Nope," Melissa said. "It's a guy, and kind of a jerky one. Anyway, I have to change projects. After all that work."

"What's your new project?" Callie knew there was no project, old or new. She just wanted to torture her.

"Um…" You could almost see the wheels turning. "It's something so boring. I'm embarrassed to even say." Then she glanced over Callie's shoulder toward the house. "Let's save it for our get-together. I need to get back to Andrew. I think he's charging me by the minute."

They air-kissed their farewells, and Callie watched the willowy young woman sprint her way up the front steps.

The drive back to the Ranch was just long enough for her to organize her confusion into a couple of key points. One: Melissa had wooed Trevor under a fake name and then cut it off. But why? And Two: Melissa had faked making a documentary. She had just wanted to bring in a camera, talk to Buddy about God-knows-what and wander around. What exactly had she been looking for? And had she found it?

Callie didn't stop at the gatehouse but drove straight up the gravel drive. There was no time like the present, she thought.

There was no one lurking on the main floor, so Callie started her search in the front study. This was the room least likely to contain anything of note. After the fire last spring, the file cabinets had been rebuilt, although the contents of the originals had gone up in flames. From other parts of the house, the study had been reappointed with a sampling of the family's collection of framed photos, awards and memorabilia. She inspected each photo and scrutinized every inscription. A decorative saddle horn from President Reagan. A winning chess piece from Boris Spassky, used in some world championship. What had Melissa been looking for? Had she found it? Callie guessed that she had, since her visits had suddenly stopped.

Callie went from the study into the main hall. Nearly all of the mementos were so familiar to her that it was hard to see them with fresh eyes. What would have been worth all this intrigue, the days of Melissa pretending to be filming while really looking for… For what?

Next came the dayroom, where she and her mother had spent time while the rest of the downstairs was being cleaned. Because of the floor-to-ceiling bookshelves, this room was more daunting than the others. Callie took a deep breath and thought about the most efficient approach. And that's when her eyes fell on the Revere bowl on the shelf across the room. Wendy and Gareth Birdsong had been examining the small silver bowl this morning when she'd walked in on them. Trevor's parents? Trevor's fake girlfriend? Certainly worth a look.

It was a six-inch bowl, modest in comparison with the other knickknacks. Callie remembered it as being there her entire life. Now, for the first time, she picked it up, examined the top and sides and turned it over. Like most everything else, it was engraved.

09 / 23 / 91

Forever Grateful

G. and W. Birdsong

Callie studied the names and the date. The names she knew, of course. And the date? That also seemed familiar. It took a minute of staring for her to remember where she'd seen it before. "Of course," she finally mumbled. "They're not anything like each other. Not at all."

CHAPTER 36

"Tilley and Associates. How can I help you?"

Callie recognized the warm Texas accent. It was after hours, but still… she hadn't expected Glenda Tilley to be answering her own phones. "Glenda? This is Callie McFee."

"Oh, Callie." The warmth stayed in her voice. "How are you, darlin'? From what I've heard, you have been a busy girl. Very impressive. I assume the majority of what was in your articles was true."

"The majority," Callie confirmed. She was growing to like Glenda Tilley.

"Well, very impressive. You know, if you ever want to quit your little paper and make some money, I can always use a smart, resourceful, attractive investigator who knows how to find things."

"Well, thank you. I'll keep it in mind," Callie said in the polite way that always means no.

"Please do. The door's always open. You know, I was expecting your call."

"You were?"

The private investigator chuckled. "About Diedre Westerman's son, am I right? You're a completionist, like me. You want all the answers."

"Some answers would be nice," Callie agreed.

Glenda chuckled. "Well, we wound up finding Stephen without involving your father, which was good for everyone. A DNA tracing. It was a lucky, odd little breakthrough."

"Diedre told me about the DNA," Callie said. "She was devastated to find out Stephen was dead. She had such hopes. But Melissa is helping a lot."

Well, that's good to hear."

This call was going better than Callie had anticipated and she felt emboldened. "Can you tell me exactly how you found Stephen Westerman?"

"I can," said Glenda. "But I need to ask you a question first. Tit for tat. And I need you to be honest with me."

"Oh." Maybe this wasn't going so well. "What's the question?"

"Did you ever find anything that implicated your father, like I asked you to? Did he leave any record?" There was a long pause. "This conversation is not being recorded."

"Oh, okay." Callie swallowed hard. "Yes, I found something just today. But I'm not going to share it."

"That's okay," Glenda said graciously. "That's all I need. Just wanted to know if the old man slipped up. We all slip up. Now, about Stephen Westerman. What do you need to know?"

*

Even when Melissa Miller tried to dress down, she looked dressed up. Callie thought this as her childhood friend walked through the door of Camille's, wearing a white linen jacket over a black T-shirt and the best-fitting pair of distressed jeans she'd ever seen. A nearby server, in his thirties, with a paunch beginning to push into his vest, gave Melissa a long glance then nodded in Callie's direction.

"Hey." Melissa waved as she swiped off her perfect pair of sunglasses. The women performed a single cheek-kiss and settled in at the same table where Callie and Trevor had had their only real date. "I'm so glad you set this up."

The server appeared almost instantly and took Melissa's order for an Aperol Spritz. Callie was already halfway through her glass of Sauvignon Blanc. "Cute," said Melissa as she looked around the dining room. "What made you pick this place?"

"You've never been here?"

"Never." Melissa's face brightened. "Now, please, I want to know everything."

Callie began by summarizing what she'd already written in the *Free Press* then adding a few details, including Joey's work as a double agent. Her monologue continued until the server, Josh, returned with the bubbly, orangey spritz. "Good to see you again," he said then hurried away.

"Huh." Melissa frowned. "Must have me mixed up with someone else."

"Really?" Callie asked. "Isn't this where you and Trevor used to come?" She downed the rest of her wine in one long swallow, judging that she would need it in her system very shortly. "He told me this was Reggie's favorite restaurant."

Melissa shook her short, loose helmet of hair. "You lost me. Who is Reggie? Is that a man or a woman?"

"It's you," Callie said, her voice hardening. "That's the name you used to get close to Trevor. I asked the waiter to see if he recognized you. He did. And those gorgeous sunglasses… They weren't found at the Ranch. I lied. You left them in Trevor's car."

Melissa shrugged and giggled. "Okay, you got me. They aren't mine." She lowered the sunglasses onto the white tablecloth. "They look a bit like the ones I lost, but they're much nicer, so I just claimed them. My bad."

"And you're not doing a film project. I checked with a connection of mine at UT."

"You checked?"

"I checked."

"Okay. It was a course I started at UT El Paso." Melissa kept her words clipped and precise. "When I transferred here, I switched to a business major, but I wanted the credit, so he's letting me complete the project." She folded her arms. "Callie, what the hell is this about?"

Callie was impressed. This woman could lie. "I'll tell you what I know." She scanned the room for the server, in sudden need of another white wine. "I'm sure you have some real affection for Aunt Dee. But the reason you moved to Austin was the inheritance. She has no close relatives, and you figured that a few months of attention and caregiving would pay off."

"I can't pretend not to be interested in money," Melissa admitted. "So what?"

"So, you had a problem. As Diedre got sicker, she began to fixate on her son, the one they told her had died. You went with her to the prison and met Kyle. You heard the whole story. Stephen might be out there. And then Diedre hired a private detective. That must have scared you. What if it was true? What if they found Stephen Westerman? Glenda Tilley said they would, sooner or later. Your one advantage was that Glenda didn't have access to Buddy McFee, the man who most likely brokered the deal. Buddy wouldn't talk to her. But he'd talk to you."

"And that's why I did all the filming? To get close to your father? That's so crazy."

Callie toasted with her nearly-empty glass. "Actually, it was brilliant. You could ask him leading questions, plus you had the freedom to search around for any records."

Melissa scowled. "Hey, if you want to talk to my film professor, I'll put you in touch."

"Yes, I'm sure you could arrange it. But let me go on. It's a damn good story." Melissa kept her arms folded on the table and leaned forward, glowering silently. She hadn't touched her spritz.

"There were no records," Callie said. "What you finally found was a little silver bowl with names and a date. The date was Stephen's birthday, the same date on Kyle's prison tattoo."

Melissa's eyes widened. "This is so fascinating. What was Stephen's birthday doing on a silver bowl?"

Callie stopped her. "This will go a lot faster if you don't play dumb. The bowl was a thank you from G. and W. Birdsong. Once you had their names, you just had to check the public records for any Birdsong boy born on that date. It turned out to be Trevor."

"You're saying that Trevor was Aunt Dee's son? He was adopted?"

"Not adopted. Just claimed as their own. Stolen at birth."

"How horrible." Melissa's feigned reaction was getting annoying.

"It took you a few romantic dates," Callie said. "But he confided in you. And the news was good. He didn't know. You were in the clear. All you had to do was wait for Diedre to die."

Melissa straightened her shoulders and took the first sip of her drink. Callie eked out the last drops from her glass then raised it up and signaled for a refill. "And then… And then disaster struck. Trevor got convicted of a felony. His DNA was now in the national database, along with his father's DNA and his mother's. You knew that. You knew that in just hours or days, the match would come through. Glenda's system would ping and Diedre would find her son. She could die happy."

"I don't know what's gotten into you." Melissa sipped again, this time taking several short swallows.

Callie kept going. "But you couldn't let that happen, could you? The long-lost son would get the house and most of the rest. It was inevitable."

"Are you saying I killed Trevor. Me? Is that what you're leading up to?" When Callie didn't answer, Melissa laughed. "Are you insane? I was with you."

Now it was Callie's turn to look uncomfortable. "You must have had an accomplice, someone who did the killing. And just to be safe, you set me up as your alibi."

"An accomplice? You mean, like a hitman or some murderous boyfriend?"

"I mean Trevor's actual killer. It's just a matter of tracking him down."

"A hitman?" Melissa's laugh was harsh. "Sweetie, I'm worried about you. First, it's a suicide. Then Beau Garrison did it. Then it's a suicide. Then I did it. Oh, and with a hitman, no less."

Callie bristled. "It's the only way the details fit."

"What details?" Melissa counted them off on her manicured fingers. "One: I am not this Reggie person. Two: I absolutely was making a film. Three: the fact that Aunt Dee's son is the same guy who committed suicide… Well, that's not my fault. I found out the same time as everyone else."

"Not quite true," Callie said. "When you and Diedre came over to see me, you knew. The private investigator told you Stephen's identity. You could have told me. Instead, you spilled the iced tea, just to make us change the subject."

"Now that's just silly." Melissa's expression turned softer. "Look, I know you don't want it to be suicide. You feel guilty that you weren't there. But you can't try to ruin my life just because you don't like the truth. You need to pull yourself together."

"Trevor had no reason to kill himself and you had every reason."

Melissa pushed back her chair and got to her feet. "That's it. You're crazy. Feel free to scour my life for this imaginary hitman. Oh, and thanks for the drink." She reached down for the tortoiseshell sunglasses, but Callie's hand was there first.

"And thank you for the sunglasses." Before Melissa could react, Callie had put them on. She smiled. "Since they're not yours, they must be mine."

Melissa seemed about to protest, but she didn't. She adjusted her linen jacket, pivoted on her heel and headed for the door. "I feel sorry for you," she said, without looking back over her shoulder.

Callie didn't let her smile fade until the other woman was out of sight, past the restaurant's front windows. Then she sighed, reached for her bag on the floor, pulled out her phone and turned off her voice memo app.

Nothing. She'd gotten absolutely nothing.

CHAPTER 37

CALLIE ARRIVED BACK at the Ranch just in time for dinner at the main house. She had missed cocktail hour, which was fine since she had already had two glasses of wine and was planning to drive again tonight.

Her father seemed clear-headed, in a good mood and with an appetite, a rare but welcome trifecta. It was Sarah's day off, leaving Buddy and Gil to fire up the Kalamazoo for some barbecued ribs and grilled asparagus. Callie hadn't been expected, but they always made too much and were happy to have her join them at one end of the long mahogany table.

She pretended not to be distracted by her disappointing meeting with Melissa and did her best to keep up with the table talk. The subject, quite often the subject at dinner, was Texas politics – who was up for reelection and who would appoint whom in return for what favor. It was the same conversation she'd heard a thousand times at this same table, just with different names filling in the blanks.

Buddy and Gil's idea of a cleanup was to leave everything on the table for Sarah to deal with tomorrow, but Callie forced them to fill the dishwasher, dispose of the garbage and wipe down the surfaces. Then she hugged her father, kissed him lightly on the cheek, and headed out through the main hall. She made sure that no one was in sight before detouring into the dayroom.

The Revere bowl was in its place, where it had been for as long as Callie could remember. She had just picked it up and was turning to leave, when she saw her father standing in the doorway behind her. "Have I got a little klepto here?" he asked with a grin, knowing full well what she was up to. "Do I need to lock up the silver?"

Buddy had been lucid all evening so, for once, she felt they could have an honest discussion. "I think you know what this is." She held out the bowl. He stepped into the room and took it, holding it gently with both hands. His brow lowered, throwing his eyes into the shadows.

"Sure, I know," he said almost in a whisper. "I used to stare at this all the time, every time I walked into the room. I should never have kept it on display. But the Birdsongs were so happy. And it acted as a kind of reminder."

"Reminder of what?"

"Hubris, I guess."

In the middle of the doorway behind her father, appeared the other member of the household. Buddy didn't turn but immediately sensed his presence. "Gil knows. I told him a few days ago."

"What do you mean by hubris?" Callie asked.

Buddy stared down into the empty curve of polished silver. "I was younger and full of myself. I had to be the man, the man people came to. Years after all this, when Diedre

Westerman and your mother became friends, they would sit here, just feet away from this thing." He said the word with disdain. "It wasn't easy, seeing her here, knowing I could tell her. I wanted to." His hands began to shake as he handed the bowl back to Callie. "But it wasn't my secret. The Birdsongs would have been in legal jeopardy. Sean and Pegeen, too. Their fourteen-year-old girl…"

"Fifteen."

"Fifteen. She was not giving up her baby. Her boyfriend turned out to be a woman beater, a druggie and a thief."

Didn't anyone notice?" Callie asked. "When the Birdsongs suddenly had a baby?"

"They had a few months to fake the pregnancy. Plus, they're private folk. It wasn't like today with gender reveals and everybody knowing everything. They took my word that this was the best way, the only way not to leave unwanted records." He noted his daughter's skepticism. "He wound up with a better life. They were good people who needed a child."

Callie thought of the unyielding, stoic couple and their quirky, selfish son. "I don't think we can guess how people will end up." That much felt true. Being raised by a teenage mother in the elite, judgmental world of Austin society… "Who knows which would have been better. But it should have been her choice."

"I get it," Buddy said begrudgingly.

She let his answer hang in the air. "Did you know who Trevor was when he came to see you?"

Buddy chuckled. "Gotta tell you, that was a shocker. The minute he said his name." He shrugged. "Okay, sometimes I forgot. You know me." He waddled a step backwards, a little off-balance. Feeling the soft edge of an armchair behind his knees, he eased down into the cushions.

Gil stepped in, always alert to safeguarding his boss. Buddy waved him away.

"I'm going to see Diedre," Callie said. She held up the bowl. "This is my visual aid."

"No," said Gil firmly. "Callie, that's not a good idea."

"Why not? Diedre already knows some of it."

Gil was adamant. "At this point it's just conjecture. Connecting the dots. You go there, you confirm this, and you could be opening us up to a shitload of trouble. Your father's license. His reputation."

"Diedre isn't going to tell," said Callie.

"You don't know what can happen." Gil stepped forward. For a second, it seemed as if he was going to physically stop her, or at least try.

Callie didn't back down. Instead, she reached out a hand to her father. "Why don't you come with me? It will do you good."

Buddy groaned. "I just sat down, dammit. Now you want me to get up?"

Callie kept her hand extended. "Come on. I could use the moral support."

"Lawrence, you are not going," Gil said. "Neither of you. This is ridiculous."

"Both of you, stop it," Buddy ordered. Turning away his head, he stared into the wall. "Sorry, sweetie," he mumbled. "I don't think I can." Then he looked over to his aide, now more of a guardian than an aide. "Gil, get out of the way. Let her go."

CHAPTER 38

Callie took her time, driving slowly and taking long pauses at stop signs. She had told Diedre that she would be there before nine and, thanks to the abbreviated cocktail hour at Camille's and the dinner that had already been on the table, she was well within the time frame. She had also said that this was important and that Diedre shouldn't say a word to Melissa.

"I don't know where Melissa is," Diedre had assured her. "Just ring the bell and I'll buzz you in. I'm not getting out much. Maybe you can help me into the wheelchair and we can go for a little walk, if that's not too much."

"That sounds lovely."

"Is this important?" Diedre had sounded alert and coherent, but a little short of breath. "Should I be worried?"

"No, not at all." There would be plenty of time for them both to worry once Callie got there and explained. "Just don't say anything to Melissa."

Callie had given this a lot of thought. She was still giving it thought. She hadn't gone to her brother for a good reason.

She had no proof. And State would be exasperated to hear her voicing yet another wild theory. But she had to do something. Melissa and her accomplice were responsible for the death of Diedre's son and Callie couldn't let them profit from it. Diedre would be devastated by the news, but she would believe.

While Callie was stopped at a flashing yellow light, she reconsidered. It was such a brutal thing to have to tell anyone, especially someone so vulnerable and dependent. But what was the alternative?

A pair of headlights pulled up behind her, and a light bump on the horn encouraged her to go. She inched through the light then pulled over to let the car pass. The Revere bowl was on the passenger seat, the one piece of evidence that backed up her story. Callie rolled down her window. The night air was cold and moist. She could feel that a shower was on its way, but she didn't mind. It had been a long day and she needed to stay alert.

The road turning off toward the Westerman property was at the top of a hill and easy to miss. Callie made the turn and started the winding descent through the woods full of native oaks and cedar elms. A vehicle behind her also made the turn and the glare from its brights made the going tougher than it should have been. Callie was sympathetic to drivers unfamiliar with these back roads. There was even a hairpin turn somewhere farther along.

She didn't get really annoyed until the car got too close for comfort. Callie slowed down and flashed her own brights, signaling the driver to back off.

For some reason, this signal did not agree with the person behind the wheel. The car quickly drew closer, coming within ten feet or so of her taillights. There were guardrails along this section, but a minute later, when the road straightened and the guardrails ended, Callie slowed down and edged over onto the grassy shoulder. There was plenty of room to pass now, even if someone happened to be coming from the other direction.

But the car did not pass. Instead, it slowed as well, matching Callie's speed and following her truck onto the shoulder. The bowl on the passenger seat bounced with the vibrations. What the hell was going on?

Callie didn't think of stopping. A woman driving alone on a country road doesn't stop unless absolutely required. She was still going – she checked her speedometer – about twenty-five miles an hour, over rocks and grass, when the guardrails appeared again, and she swerved back into the full lane.

The high beams from the other vehicle – a car, not a truck, judging from their height – were almost blinding. Callie turned her rearview mirror down. That made it better. And then it suddenly got worse.

An oncoming car appeared from around a turn perhaps a quarter of a mile away. The driver had switched from high beams to low. But then, faced with two sets of rude high beams getting closer and closer, he switched back. Now Callie was being blinded from two directions. Her hands clenched the wheel and she had to fight the crazy temptation to shut her eyes.

The horn from the approaching car blasted as it sped past and Callie used the distraction to step on the gas and try to gain some distance. Through her open windows, she could hear the soft roar of her pursuer also accelerating.

The headlights grew closer again, the glare taking up all her rear window. She couldn't see the hairpin turn, but she knew it was coming soon. A few seconds later and she felt the rear-end collision as it threw her body toward the steering wheel and her foot even harder into the gas pedal.

The galvanized steel guardrail was no match for an uncontrolled Yukon truck. It slammed through the curved barrier with some sideways thrust and began rolling down the rocky slope, plowing over saplings as it went. The front airbag deployed even before the truck started rolling. The sudden pain in Callie's chest was intense, but the airbag protected her from the shattering windshield. It could not protect her from the branches and rocks cascading through her open window. And it couldn't protect her from the Revere bowl.

The six-inch silver missile banged into her cheek then ricocheted off the truck's interior and connected with her forehead, where it sliced open a small gash just at her hairline. She counted four more assaults before the bowl landed, dented and bloodied, on the ceiling of the cab, right below her head.

Her world was now upside down, her torso held in place by her seatbelt. She had rolled one and a half rotations. With the airbag now deflating, she had a view through the passenger-side window, uphill to the gray, broken ribbon of guardrail and the dust-filled light from the car that had just attacked her, parked by the bend in the road, its engine rumbling in the otherwise empty night.

Callie watched a silhouette get out of the car, walk to the edge and peer down in her direction. She didn't move. She couldn't. From the wheels dangling above her head came the strong scent of burned rubber, but there was no smell of gas. Not yet. Thank God. And then the silhouette started to move, crawling carefully and slowly down the slope.

"Ms. McFee? This is OnStar." The blue light on the little device above the rearview mirror had turned red. "I've received a signal you've been in a crash. Is anyone hurt?"

She had forgotten that her old truck had come equipped with this feature and that the automatic payments had continued over the years. "Yes," Callie responded, keeping her voice as low as possible. "I'm hurt."

"Got it." It was a female voice, sounding professionally calm. "I'm contacting emergency services. Help is on the way."

Callie had to think fast. Should she tell the operator what was happening? How much information could she get across before... Before what? She didn't know.

"I'll stay on the line until they get there," the soothing voice said. "It shouldn't be that long."

"Yes, stay on the line," Callie said. "This is being recorded, right?"

"Yes, ma'am. All our calls are recorded, for safety and training purposes. And legal purposes," added the comforting voice. "Although that happens so rarely, that anything legal comes up. We have very strict guidelines here at OnStar and..."

"Okay, okay, okay," Callie interrupted. "Please shut up. I mean, please stay quiet. Don't say anything more. I'm in physical danger. The best thing you can do is just record this. No matter what happens, record this and don't say anything, not until I tell you. Can you do that? Please?"

There was silence on the other end, which she took to be a good sign, until... "Ma'am, what exactly is happening?"

Callie moaned. "You don't need to know. There's nothing you can do. Please do what I say. Don't say a word, not until I tell you."

"Are you being assaulted?" The voice had lost some of its professional calm.

"No, not yet. I'll tell you if and when I'm being assaulted."

"Well, that sounds like that'll be too late." This was turning into an unwelcome discussion. "I mean, you could be assaulted without being able to speak. Am I right? And if your assailant…"

"Please," Callie begged. "Not another word."

"Is this your husband that may be assaulting you? Or a boyfriend?"

"Not another word."

"Okay."

"Shhhhh," Callie whispered back, making the sound last as long as she could. "Thank you," she muttered at the end.

"You're welcome."

"Shhhhh."

The OnStar panel remained blissfully silent, although it was at least another minute before the silhouette had made its way down the slope. Callie felt bad for having been so abrupt.

Enough illumination spilled from her own headlights to let her see the person now approaching her window. Melissa Miller, her pal from the other side of town, the one she'd felt so sorry for, stared in curiously. Melissa gazed at the stones and the leafy debris and the upside-down driver with the gashes on her face. "I knew you would call her," she said, as if this were all Callie's fault. "Did you really think I wouldn't be on my guard?"

Callie watched as Melissa slowly put on a pair of black leather gloves then walked away. A few long seconds later, she returned, carrying a medium-size rock, as large and round as a mini soccer ball.

Callie eked out the words, "You never had an accomplice, did you?" It was a verbal ploy, to try to get Melissa talking and not acting. Melissa simply smiled and readjusted the weight of the rock. Her old friend, suspended from her seatbelt, wasn't going anywhere.

"I was right, wasn't I?" Callie said, trying again. "All except for the accomplice part."

"I had a friend also convicted of a felony," Melissa finally said. "Turned out he had two kids he never knew about. So, I knew the DNA stuff. I knew I had to get moving."

"You're the reason Trevor Birdsong got dressed up that night." Callie tried not to look up at the OnStar panel.

"Not me. Reggie," Melissa said. "When I called him, he was so excited, like a little boy. He told me all about Buddy and you and his situation with the law. I was understanding. I told him I would come over. Then when he answered the door wearing a tie…" She shrugged. "It just came to me."

"Faking a suicide by strangulation," Callie said, explaining it for the OnStar recording.

"M-hmm." Had Melissa said it loud enough to carry? "You'd be surprised how quickly men respond to the idea of kinky sex acts involving neckties. He even got on his knees. Very helpful."

Callie tried not to visualize the scene. "Were you already at Trevor's when you invited me for drinks?" It had always struck her as coincidental that the wine bar had only been two blocks from his house.

"I was in his bathroom," Melissa admitted, "looking up nearby bars."

Callie recalled all the hours she'd spent with Melissa,

puzzling over Trevor's death, treating it like a mystery game. "Why did you get me involved?" she had to ask. If Callie hadn't been there on the scene, if she'd just heard about the suicide the next day like everyone else, things might have been different.

"The keys," Melissa said simply. "To make it a convincing suicide, I had to lock up. Plus, there was always the chance my fingerprints would be around. Coming back with you gave me the chance to return his keys and return his phone and to touch things."

"Return his phone?" Callie hadn't even thought of that part. "All of his texts were from you. All of them."

Melissa beamed with a kind of sick pride. "They were. After he was dead, I used his face to open his phone. It worked."

"You opened it with a dead man's face?" Somehow that seemed as gruesome as the murder itself.

"We do what we have to," Melissa said. "Then I disabled his passcode."

Callie flashed back to that anxiety-filled moment at the wine bar. She had already received several desperate texts. The final one, the one that had sent them racing to Trevor's house, had come after Melissa had hurried down the block and joined her. Melissa had sat down. She was rummaging through her bag, offering the excuse that she was checking for her car keys. And then, voila… Callie got the final text.

"I'm kind of speechless," Callie said. It was the truth. She was growing dizzy from the blood flowing to her head. Her collarbone was aching, too, from where the seatbelt had caught her before the airbag hit.

"Good to know, because someone's going to drive by, and

I need to finish off your accident." Then with a grunt, she lifted the rock from the window's edge.

Callie recoiled as far as her seatbelt would let her. "OnStar," she shouted. "OnStar, can you hear me?"

Melissa was startled enough to ease the rock back down. "What?"

"OnStar. They've been listening the whole time. It's all recorded. OnStar?" But OnStar didn't respond. "You can talk now. I'm not kidding."

The two women listened intently. Then Melissa chuckled. "You had me scared for a minute." She hefted the rock again.

"Why?" Callie pleaded. She wasn't expecting an answer, but she had to ask. "You killed a man. You took away a sick woman's last chance at happiness. And now, you…" She didn't want to finish that sentence. "Mel, we were friends."

"We weren't friends," she answered bitterly. "I was the poor girl that you and your friends made fun of. I know the money doesn't seem much. That's something you can't understand. But to have it within reach and then have it snatched away by some drunk driver getting convicted…" The rock had grown heavy. She lifted it to her shoulder and balanced it, while her target squirmed in her seatbelt.

And then, echoing from a distance, came the sirens. Callie could almost see the thoughts swirling through Melissa's mind. How quickly could she do this and drive off? Should she stick around and pretend to be a Samaritan who arrived too late to help? The rock came off her shoulder and she aimed. The sirens were getting closer.

"Ms. McFee. This is OnStar. Can I talk now?"

"Yes, you can talk," Callie shouted. "Jeez. Didn't you hear me calling you?"

The voice sounded a little peeved. "Well, I wasn't sure, after all that." Callie watched as Melissa froze in place then let the stone fall to the ground. "The ambulance and police should be there now."

EPILOGUE

THE SNOW FELL in giant, translucent flakes that melted as soon
as they touched ground. It had been a good-size crowd, with
many of Austin's old guard showing up to say their farewells
to the last of the Westermans.

Callie stayed longer than most, standing by the columns
of the gray, Greek-style mausoleum and exchanging condolences. Buddy had given the eulogy that day, his second within
a year at this exact spot. On this occasion, he spoke from
a script – without mishap, Callie was glad to see. State, as
before, was one of the pallbearers.

It had been three weeks since Melissa Miller's arrest for
murder and nearly three weeks since her parents had taken a flight
from El Paso, to try to deal with the situation. Callie felt sorry
for them, perhaps even more than she had for Trevor's parents.

Gil had seen to it that bail was set high and that Melissa had
no means of contacting "Aunt Dee". Then it was up to Callie
and a few other stalwarts to keep Diedre away from the news,
maintaining the illusion that she had simply gone back home.

Melissa's abrupt departure set the groundwork for her

disinheritance. After some gentle, almost imperceptible guidance, Diedre made the suggestion herself. Why should Diedre leave her family home to a second cousin who had abandoned her without so much as a goodbye? Some more almost imperceptible guidance pointed her in the direction of the Birdsong Foundation, where Diedre's money, combined with her son's, could do some good.

Callie wasn't ready to leave, but she needed to sit. Generations ago, the Westermans had thoughtfully installed a stone bench beside their mausoleum. Snowflakes were beginning to stick to the cold granite and Callie brushed them aside before settling down. The doctor had said that she would get used to the clavicle brace that held her mending collarbone in place but, after three weeks, it still annoyed her, especially when she had to stand for long periods of time. Standing for a long period of time without a glass of wine in hand made her feel even worse.

Oliver had come to the service and was still there, bundled up and leaning against a tree. He had written the second article by himself, the one featuring Callie's attempted murder. They'd agreed that it would be better that way, both from a journalistic point of view and a legal one. As the intended victim, Callie didn't want to write anything that might affect the upcoming trial. Two upcoming trials, she reminded herself. Melissa's and Beau's.

"Mind if I join you?" Callie didn't answer but scooted over to give him room. "I talked to the DA. He says their case against Beau Garrison is firming up. That roofie drug he used…"

"I don't want to talk business." It was a sorry situation, she thought, when talking about murder became business talk.

"Right," Oliver apologized then sat down. "Do you think you'll get a new truck or something different?" Even without looking, he could sense her annoyance. "Sorry."

"You don't have to make conversation. That's okay." The silence lasted only a few seconds. "This morning, I watched some of her documentary footage. It wasn't bad, but it put me in a mood." She looked down to her hands. "He used to be my idol. Now…"

She glanced up just in time to see her father and Gil moving slowly toward the road and Gil's long, black sedan, the perfect vehicle to bring to a funeral. Buddy hadn't been in top form today, but his medication, the cholinesterase inhibitor, seemed to be helping. Many of his old friends, people who hadn't seen him in months or years, followed along, trying to get in a few words with the man who'd been at the center of everything for so long.

"*Now* doesn't change things," Oliver said. "The man has done a lot in his life."

"He has," she agreed. Oh, if Oliver only knew.

Sitting side by side, they watched as Buddy and Gil glad-handed and smiled and allotted just the right response to everyone who entered his sphere. That skill was second nature to him and would probably be one of the last things to go.

"Families are complicated," Oliver finally said.

"Words of wisdom," Callie replied. She edged a little closer to Oliver, for the warmth as much as anything. "I should put that on a tattoo."

He didn't laugh, but she could almost hear his smile.

THE END

ABOUT THE BOOK

In the world of moviemaking, there is a truism. What the audience really wants from a sequel is the first movie all over again, only different. It's a cynical assessment, but a valid one. If people loved the first one – and they did; otherwise, you wouldn't be making a sequel – then they'll want to repeat that emotional experience. Whether it's Bridget Jones or Indiana Jones, the sequel's hero needs to go through similar adventures that evoke similar emotions. When it comes to number three, then okay. Maybe you can branch out and let Indy travel with his dad and have a midlife crisis, but not in number two.

It was with that nugget of Hollywood wisdom in mind that I came up with the story for *Sins of the Family*. Callie is still dealing with Buddy, still feeling ambivalent about his work – and her research for a journalistic exposé still leads her into two puzzling mysteries that can't possibly be connected but are. I guess this is my way of saying that, yes, I am aware of the structural similarities between *The Fixer's Daughter* and *Sins of the Family*. I actually did it on purpose.

Another challenge in the world of sequels is how to deal with the past. Something momentous happened in book one or movie one. That's always the intent, at least. And the writer needs to somehow acknowledge this. But how much can you build on book one without either retelling the whole plot, or making a new reader feel left out by not telling enough? In this particular sequel, the most difficult choice I had to make was to not describe the event that destroyed a lifetime's worth of Buddy's records. This is not important to the current story. But if some new reader is miffed by not knowing the exact details of the fire in Buddy's office, I apologize. The good news is that *The Fixer's Daughter* is probably on sale somewhere. And it's pretty decent, if I have to say so myself.

ABOUT THE AUTHOR

HY CONRAD has made a career out of murder, earning a
Scribe Award for best novel and garnering three Edgar nomi-
nations from the Mystery Writers of America. Along the way,
he developed a horde of popular games and interactive films,
hundreds of short stories and a dozen books of solvable mysteries, published in over a dozen languages. Hy is best known
for his eight seasons as writer/co-executive producer for the
ground-breaking series, *Monk*. Other shows include *White
Collar* and *The Good Cop*.

In the world of theatre, his produced works consist of
Home Exchange (a mystery), *Ta-Dah!* (a musical), and *Quar-
antine for Two* (a socially distanced dark comedy about
the pandemic).

As a novelist, Hy authored the final four books in the
Monk series, the *Amy Travel Mysteries* and *The Fixer's Daugh-
ter*, a Barnes &Noble bestseller and the first of the *Callie
McFee Mysteries*.

When he looks up from his keyboard, Hy sees either the

hills of Vermont or the palm trees of Key West, depending on the time of year. He also sees Jeff Johnson, his partner of 42 years, now his husband, plus Nelson and Stella, the latest in a dynasty of mini schnauzers.

www.hyconrad.com
Facebook: hyconrad
Instagram: hyconrad1